Erin has just re their
family has lied 1 for
years, so Erin ...ics and Mermaids were
hallucinations. Not only are the supernatural creatures they
see daily real, but their grandmother is an Elf, meaning Erin
isn't fully human. On top of that, the dreams Erin thought
were nightmares are actually prophecies.

While dealing with the anger they have over all of the lies,
they are getting used to their new boyfriend, their
boyfriend's bullying ex, and the fact that they come from a
family of Demon Hunters. As Erin struggles through
everything weighing on them, they uncover a Demon plot to
take over the world.

Erin just wants some time to work through it all on their
own terms, but that's going to have to wait until after they
help save the world.

POWER SURGE

The Evanstar Chronicles, Book One

Sara Codair

For Skye

[signature]

A NineStar Press Publication

Published by NineStar Press
P.O. Box 91792,
Albuquerque, New Mexico, 87199 USA.
www.ninestarpress.com

Power Surge

Printed in the USA
First Edition
October, 2018

Print ISBN: 978-1-949340-92-1

Also available in eBook, ISBN: 978-1-949340-86-0

Warning: This book contains violence, discussion of off-page abuse, death of a parent, mentions of off-page sexual assault, brief on-page depictions of attempted sexual assault, self-harm, suicidal ideation, bullying.

For Grandparents: their stories, history, and love.

Chapter One

They don't like the sunlight, but that doesn't mean they won't venture out in it. Demons aren't like Stoker's vampires or anything else you read about in civilian novels. Even the Bible isn't accurate when describing the denizens of Heaven and Hell.

—A letter from Gertrude Bearclaw to Genevieve Evanstar, 21 Jan 1921, archived in the vault under St. Patrick's Church in South Portland, Maine

The cold March air burned my lungs and made my legs itch as I sprinted by boarded-up beach houses. Mel may have turned our warm-up into a race, but she was not going to win it. Grinning, I ran harder in an attempt to close the space between us. Despite my efforts, her footsteps grew softer and the ones behind me grew louder.

I glanced over my shoulder. The man behind me was closer. Steam rose from his pale nose as it peeked out from under the black hoodie. I shuddered. It wasn't unusual to see another runner follow us around two turns, but this one had followed me around five.

I sucked in the icy air as I crossed a bridge. The metal grates groaned under our feet. Water rushed below, blanketing brown muck with blue, breathing color and life into the field of dead marsh grass. Mel was so far down the winding road I could barely make out her short, muscular form.

I glanced at my phone. It was dead. Mel was too far ahead to hear me yell, and there was no one else around. I wasn't exactly defenseless, but I was tired and hadn't been in a real fight in almost two years.

Still, a small deplorable part of me hoped the man would catch up and he'd want to hurt me. I imagined myself ducking as he reached out to grab me. I'd jam my elbow up into his stomach and crush his face with my knee. I almost heard his jawbone crack, saw the shock in his eyes, and felt the pure bliss of adrenaline coursing through my body. I'd win. He'd end up hospitalized or worse, in the morgue. The last time I was forced to defend myself against someone who wanted to hurt me, Mel had to pull me off his unconscious body. The ghost of the rage, the rush and the guilt made my stomach churn.

I was a monster.

I couldn't let this man catch up to me. It was too dangerous for him.

My calves cramped. My side felt like a knife was jabbing into it. Mel vanished around a bend. I growled. She was shorter than me and worked out more, but she was my cousin—the daughter of my late father's twin sister—not some kind of professional athlete. If she could go that fast, then so could I. A few seconds later, I rounded the same bend. Our finish line, the gate for Foster Park, came into sight.

Picking up more speed, I closed the distance between me and the run-down guard shack. Mel got to it first and jogged in place, facing me until I arrived. I glanced over my shoulder and didn't see the man. Relieved, I nearly toppled over, gasping for air with my hands on my knees.

"Erin, you need to cool down before you stop." Mel wasn't even out of breath, and she had a smug smile on her perfect pink lips. I didn't see a drop of sweat on her face. Her gray spandex was dry; mine had soaked through my base layer to my baggy T-shirt.

I stood up straight, filling my aching lungs with big gulps of air as I looked around again. An iridescent blackbird leaped from a leafless maple with its wings slowly flapping as it flew across the path in front of us, but the man was nowhere in sight. "What was our time?"

"I didn't have my timer on." Mel walked down the dirt road.

"I really want to know how fast I went." Every part of my body throbbed as I moved. The bare birch branches around us were filled with warbling blackbirds; their screeches needled my eardrums.

"Not fast enough," snapped Mel. Her voice hurt more than the birds.

"Seriously?"

"You can do better. How is school going?"

"Mel, I don't think I have ever run that fast in my life."

"How is school going?"

I glared at her.

"How is school going?" she asked for the third time.

Shivering, I scratched my neck. "My teachers are determined to dispel the myth that senior year is easy by piling on hours and hours of homework. It takes forever without ADHD meds."

Mel frowned. "You thinking of going back on them?"

"We'll see how I do on my English test tomorrow. I don't want any of my college acceptances getting revoked."

"What does your mom think?" Mel's frown made deep crevices in her usually smooth forehead.

"Mom and the doctors want me to try a different kind. I think they forgot I took that in middle school and it made me equally sick."

"Both drugs stop your dreams," muttered Mel, staring at the gravel.

"And how is that a bad thing?"

Heavy silence hung between us as we approached our Jeeps. Hers was an orange Wrangler with a soft top, a spotless paint job, and a lift kit. My ancient Cherokee resembled the offspring of hers and a station wagon, pockmarked with battle scars from shopping carts and telephone poles. She opened her door, took out two water bottles, and handed one to me. "Are you still dreaming every night?"

"Yeah." I drank half my bottle in one long gulp.

"Did you try my suggestion?"

The Thursday before, Mel had told me to try focusing on one thing before I went to bed, so instead of dreaming of burning cities, gory battles, and apocalyptic storms, I would only dream about that one—hopefully more pleasant—thing.

"Did it work?"

"Sort of. Did you bring the sabers?" The whole purpose of the meeting wasn't so much the run but the subsequent sparring match. Since I hadn't found a good Kendo dojo in Portland, Mel was my only sparring partner.

"Of course." She pulled two bamboo practice swords out of her Jeep and handed one to me. "What does 'sort of' mean?"

"I focused on a person. The dreams stayed chaotic, but that person was in all of them."

Mel smirked as we walked across the grassy hill leading down to the pebble beach. "Which boy did you focus on?"

"I didn't say boy."

Mel arched her eyebrows. "I'm pretty confident we can rule out all the girls at St. Pat's. Who was it?"

"José." My cheeks burned.

Mel barked out a laugh that was simultaneously musical and abrupt as she stepped onto the beach. "And what did you dream about the boy who you won't admit you're in love with?"

"We're friends. I'm *not* in love with him." I stopped walking, leaned my sword against a rock, and stretched.

"Tell me what you dreamed."

I watched rippled waves roll onto the black and gray stones. Once wet, they glistened in the afternoon sun. Two cormorants floated around the jetty while seagulls perched on the rocks. Looking up, I stared toward the sun without blinking and imagined my eyes drinking in its warmth. It made them water, but my face relaxed.

When I couldn't take the light anymore, I turned my attention to a splashing at the end of the jetty. Minnows leaped out of the water followed by the stripers that were trying to eat them. Suddenly, a humanoid head covered in Irish moss burst from the surface, devouring a striper in one bite. I stumbled backward. A green tail flickered where the head had been, spraying water at the gulls. The head leaped back up and lunged toward the cormorant, sinking its fangs into black feathers and pulling the bird below the water.

"Holy Shit! Mel, did you see that?"

When she didn't answer, I turned my head and jumped a mile backward. She was completely engulfed in brilliant light that burned my eyes like the sun had. My feet landed on slippery seaweed, and this time, I did fall. I'd seen some weird things lately, but this surpassed them all.

"Erin, are you okay?" She reached out with a glowing hand, but I didn't touch it, afraid it would burn my skin right off.

"Why are you breathing so hard?" Mel's head tilted. Her eyes were maelstroms of grass green and sky blue.

I wanted to tell her that *she* was wrong, but I choked on every breath. I couldn't speak. This was weirder than the Pixies that perched in the trees near my house and pruned the bushes at school. It was more terrifying than the Mermaid I had just seen. Those had been straight out of Grandpa's stories and I vaguely remembered seeing them as a child. Mel had never been in Grandpa's stories, and I had never seen her glow.

"Erin, what are you staring at?" She crouched next to me. Her eyes seemed to see straight into my soul.

"I'm staring at you." The words were quick as quick as my racing heart, sharper than the rocks cutting into my hands.

"Why?" Her hair floated around her head, wriggling like a halo of eels.

"I don't know how your hair stays so neat while you work out." While part of me was desperate to confide in someone, I knew it couldn't be Mel. She had only ever kept one secret for me. Otherwise, she was a total snitch. Sophomore year of high school, I had discovered that cutting soothed me better than punching things. I told Mel and she told my mom. I doubt I would've broken the habit if Mel had stayed quiet, but this was different. Seeing Pixies didn't hurt me. Still, if she thought I was developing some new mental disorder, she'd tell. I'd recently stopped taking a bunch of medications because they made me sick to my stomach and dizzy. I wasn't ready to try something stronger. What if I was allergic? What if the side effects were worse?

I know you're not hallucinating whispered a quiet voice in my head. *The stories are all real. Your illness is real. There is a reason the side effects were so bad.* It sounded like Mel, but I didn't see her lips move. I shuddered. If I was hearing voices, then maybe I was getting sicker.

Mel sighed and plopped down next to me with enough force to scatter pebbles and send a plume of dust into the air. She cradled her head in her hands. "Are you going to tell me what you dreamed?"

I stared at the jetty. The surviving cormorant was on the rocks, with its oily wings spread out to dry in the wind. All that remained of its companion were a few floating feathers.

"Erin, I asked you a question." Mel's voice was painfully loud.

I took a deep breath. Perhaps talking about something else might make me feel more normal. "I watched José argue with his dad. It got physical; Dr. Estrella broke José's nose. I saw José dump Jenny via text message. Then things got weird. José fought this white thing that kind of looked like a skinny orc. First, it was in a parking garage then it was on a big dark field. I was fighting monsters too. José and I watched a city burn. We made out..."

The right half of Mel's lips curved up. "I see. And did anything from the dreams repeat night after night? Or happen in real life?"

"Nothing happened in real life, but the battle was in all of the dreams, and the parking garage part repeated until I figured out how to make José survive it. The kissy stuff was in a lot of the dreams too." My shoulders tensed and my hands balled into fists. I enjoyed the kissy parts, but sometimes, they were scarier than the monsters.

"Let me know if anything from the dreams does actually happen, even if it's not exactly the same as the dream." Mel put a hand on my shoulder and rubbed until the tightness drained from my muscles. She giggled. "You should totally ask José out after he breaks up with Jenny."

"Bad idea." Just because I dreamed the answers to my math quiz and predicted which colleges my friend Sam got accepted to didn't mean my dreams were premonitions. My subconscious was probably working through things my conscious mind couldn't focus on. My unconscious mind was very attracted to José and his secrets. Of course, I dreamed about doing stuff with him. Unfortunately, my conscious mind knew he never stayed with the same person for more than a couple months and that he liked to "hit a home run" before he dumped them. It wasn't worth risking our friendship.

Mel chuckled then said, "The color of your cheeks tells a different story."

"He was kind of flirting with me today." I glanced at her. The glowing was gone. Her hazel eyes were back to normal.

Her giggles turned to full-blown laughter. "What did he do?"

"Played with my hair in front of Jenny. She almost shoved us into a locker."

"Boys aren't the brightest creatures on the planet," said Mel.

"Humans, in general, aren't so bright," I muttered. José's gender had nothing to do with his stupidity. Boys, girls, and people like me, who didn't identify as a boy or a girl, could be equally stupid.

"Are you ready to spar?" Mel smiled, showing her perfectly white teeth. Without the blinding light, I saw muscles bulging under her spandex. She was barely five feet tall, but she could bench press me if she wanted to.

"Yes, please."

Mel touched her phone, making movie theme songs play. We stood, grabbed our swords, and bowed. We touched the tips together then stepped backward. I barely had time to block before her weapon swiped toward my neck. Shock waves traveled from the bamboo to my shoulder. Mel wasn't holding back; I wouldn't either. I smiled. My sword whipped toward her throat. She batted it aside like a cat would a fly and was on to her next attack.

The dance went on as more music played. Our feet moved in rhythm while we swung, parried, stabbed, and blocked. The longer we danced, the faster she got. Her sword was a blurred extension of her hand. I struggled to keep up, but I relished the challenge. The swift movements, burning muscles, and threat of blows made me feel more alive and focused than anything else.

After three tracks, she whacked my leg and thunked my shoulder. The sharp ache was like lighter fluid on a campfire. I growled, swinging faster and harder. She matched my pace. My Shinai didn't touch her. Pebbles shifted under my feet, making it harder to balance. I stepped on a slimy strip of kelp and wobbled. Mel never lost her footing. By the fifth song, my arms were burning. Her next jab was aimed at my heart. When I parried, my sword flew out of my hand.

"Dead," she said with the tip of hers touching my chest.

Panting, I dramatically fell to the pebbles and sand. I twitched a few times and lay still. Mel made choking laugh sounds that reminded me of bells in a storm. I opened one eye, saw hers were closed, swung my legs at her feet so she fell, grabbed a piece of seaweed, and stuffed it down her shirt. She squealed, rolling until she had me pinned, and smeared the seaweed in my face. We grappled until we were both on our backs in a fit of uncontrollable laughter, staring up at a sky full of towering cumulous clouds that morphed into angelic shapes whenever I went too long without blinking.

"You don't practice enough. I shouldn't be able to beat you so easily," said Mel.

I stood up and stretched. The sun was starting to get low, bathing everything in golden light. Behind us, muddy grass stretched back to the ruins of stone forts and the gravel lot where our Jeeps were. They were still the only cars, but there was another person in the park now. He leaned against a cracked concrete wall. Baggy black sweats hid most of his body, but they didn't hide his beaky nose. "I wonder how long that man has been watching us. He was behind me while we were running but disappeared when we got to the gate."

I glanced over at Mel when I didn't get a response. She was staring at the man with her eyes narrowed and her hands hovering over her hips. The cross hilt of a medieval sword faded in and out of my vision, just under her hand. Her shoulders were tense, and her teeth were bared. A halo of white flames surrounded her head but dissolved after I blinked a few times. "Mel? What's wrong?"

"Nothing. Let's get out of here. I'm starving." She exhaled slowly, gathered our practice swords, and walked over to me without taking her eyes off the man. She put her arm around my shoulders and pulled me close, placing herself between the creep and me. Her grip tightened as we passed him.

"Mel, my water is still on the beach."

"Forget it. Let's get to the Clam Hut." She practically pushed me into the car and didn't get into her own until my door was shut and my key was in the ignition.

Chapter Two

I tell Erin stories about their father. They think I'm as creative as J. R. R. Tolkien, but I'm merely telling the truth. I want them to know about their heritage, even if they don't believe it. They're safer if they don't believe.
  —The journal of Seamus Evanstar, 2006, still in his personal possession

My hands wouldn't stop shaking while I waited in line at the Clam Hut. The sweet scent of frying fish made my stomach growl, but I kept looking around the room to see if that man had followed us from the fort. Mel was doing the same thing but trying harder to hide it. Her head didn't move as much as mine, but I still saw her eyes twitch as she scanned the room.

"Why are you shaking?" Mel's head turned; she made eye contact.

"I'm hungry."

"Make sure you order what you want. Don't worry over fat or calories."

"I wasn't thinking that until you mentioned it." The words came out harsher than I intended. I had been too busy worrying about the creep to think of what the fried deliciousness did to my arteries and stomach. I'd put on ten pounds since I stopped the ADHD meds and my binders weren't hiding my breasts as well as they used to.

Then it was our turn to order. The growling interior of my stomach won over the part of me that was concerned with how feminine my body looked. I ordered fish and chips. Mel ordered a fisherman's platter, large fish chowder, and a side of crab cakes. She took the number, paid for both our meals, and walked toward the dining room, which was pretty empty since tourist season didn't start for a couple more months.

I sat down across from Mel. "Why did you practically shove me in the car?"

Frowning, she stared at an old harpoon hanging from the ceiling. "That man gave me the creeps, like he was something from one of Grandpa's campfire stories."

"The Demon hunter ones?" I asked, ripping my napkin apart.

She nodded. "Those were the only kind he told us."

I glanced down at my mess. The man's skin had been as white as my napkin.

"Grandpa did describe Demons as having skin the color of 'bleached bones'." I looked up. Mel was watching me with wide eyes and a half smile. "What?"

Her smile grew. "Are you saying you think the creep was actually a Demon?"

"Mel, there's no such thing as Demons." My foot tapped so fast the whole table shook.

She cocked her head. "The Bible references them."

"The Bible mentions Demons being cast out of people and tempting them to do things. Some of Grandpa's Demons possessed people, but most had their own bodies. The Bible doesn't mention the albino monsters Grandpa told us about. I've spent enough time reading it."

"The Bible was made by humans. It's not perfect. The Church only included a handful of texts in it."

"So are you saying the excluded ones have Grandpa's Demons?"

Mel shrugged. "They could. I haven't read all of them."

Unsure where Mel was taking this conversation, I waited for her to continue. She sighed, silently staring at me until our number was called. She went to get the food while I watched our stuff and resumed shredding my napkin. The movement helped me think. I almost got the impression she believed Grandpa's stories were true. If I was right, then she might also believe I was actually seeing Pixies and Mermaids. Jack McCormack, the main character in most of Grandpa's stories, had used a network of Pixie informants to help him locate and hunt Demons. His best friend, Antonio Azure, was always involved with Mermaids in one way or another.

"You look deep in thought," said Mel as she returned with our food.

I took my fish from the tray and tested the waters. "Do you remember Grandpa ever actually saying the stories were fiction?"

Mel's face lit up. "I don't, but I never asked. Did you?"

I watched her eyes. The colors stayed still and dull. "I asked him once, but he never gave me a straight answer."

"What did he say?" Mel shoved food in her mouth without breaking eye contact.

I pictured Grandpa toasting marshmallows on a campfire with mischief in his ocean eyes. "It was some nonsense about all stories being both true and false at the same time. Maybe there is truth in everything, but people are big liars, so they tell the truth in fiction and lie when they should be honest.

Mel was quiet for a few minutes while she inhaled her crab cakes. When they were gone, she asked, "What do you think he meant by that?"

I stared at my half-eaten fish. "There are real lessons I was supposed to take away, even though the stories were fictional."

Mel's smile faded to a quivering frown, giving me the impression that my interpretation of Grandpa's words wasn't correct. She didn't volunteer another explanation, but she did change the subject, so I didn't ask what she wanted me to say. I listened and ate while she fiddled with the diamond on her engagement ring and complained about her soon-to-be mother-in-law's involvement in wedding planning. It reminded me that Mel was almost an adult and I was her troubled seventeen-year-old cousin.

The conversations related to the Bible and Grandpa's stories were probably a convoluted way to get me to admit something was wrong. When she suspected I had started cutting, we had a similar conversation where she hinted that she cut too and I opened up to her. A few hours later, she told my mom. The same thing happened when I started sneaking out to parties. I had fallen for her tricks twice. I wouldn't a third time.

WHEN THE FOOD was gone, Mel gathered our trash and threw it out. I followed her to the parking lot, wondering if I'd ever be able to truly trust her again. She kept one secret for me, but I suspected that was because telling the truth would have gotten both of us in trouble and caused more harm than good.

Once we got to our Jeeps, she hugged me so tight I thought she was going to break my ribs. Confused, I backed away and saw glistening tears slide down her cheeks. "Mel, why are you crying?"

She sniffled and put her hands on my shoulder. "Erin, you can trust me with anything. You know that, right?"

"Of course," I said even though I didn't mean it. I couldn't answer any other way with her staring at me red faced and teary eyed. "Why are you even asking? You're my cousin, practically my sister. I love you."

She sucked in a deep breath. Her lips trembled. She wiped the tears away and brushed off her shirt. "I love you too. Drive safe. Please text me when you get home."

"You too. Bye, Mel."

Still bewildered, I walked over to my Jeep and climbed inside. Mel didn't watch me this time. She got in her own car and started it. I pulled out of the parking lot, and she followed me until we got to the highway, where she headed south toward Boston, Massachusetts, and I headed north toward Portland, Maine.

Mel and I grew up in the same neighborhood on the North Shore of Massachusetts, but I moved up to a town just south of Portland when my mom got a job at the University of Southern Maine. Mel moved out of her mom's house the summer before, a few weeks after her boyfriend, Mike, proposed. He worked in a lab at MIT, where he was studying for his PhD in Computer Science, so they had a small apartment near Boston. Sometimes I missed living near Mel, but after I endured an afternoon of her prying into my life, I generally appreciated the miles between us.

I kept music on for the whole ride home, but I wasn't really listening to it. I was thinking of Grandpa. Mel and I had spent a lot of time with him as kids, and he constantly told us stories about a group of Demon hunters called the Seven Stars. The Stars were made up of seven family-groups from around the world, each representing different faiths. Their goal was to protect humans from the Demons that preyed on them.

Some Demons literally ate people. Others fed off fear and hate, so they sought to sow those emotions among the human population. I'd believed in Demons when I believed in Santa Claus and the Easter Bunny. As I got older, the stories got scarier and scarier until Grandpa stopped telling them altogether. Though I supposed he had to. One of the main characters was dead and another was permanently in a wheelchair.

If I accepted the stories were real, I could assume the various ADHD medications and antidepressants I had taken throughout my life had somehow blocked what Grandpa called Sight, which was the ability to see through the illusions supernatural beings created to hide their true natures from humans. I vaguely remember seeing Pixies before I started school and medications, so seeing them now made sense. Having a Demonic stalker even made sense, since I had no shortage of negativity for it to feed off. The biggest problem with my theory was Mel's glowing.

The only thing that glowed in Grandpa's stories were Angels—winged, luminous creatures equally able to cause Old Testament–level destruction and heal serious injuries. They weren't five-foot-tall twenty-one-year-olds who ceaselessly meddled in their younger cousin's life.

I screamed curses at the dark exit ramp. I didn't want to be mentally ill or gifted with some kind of supernatural sight. I just wanted to get high school over with and figure out what I was supposed to do with my life. I blasted my rock music, hoping it would distract me, and checked my mirror a few times to make sure no cars followed me off the highway.

Grandpa was visiting over the weekend. It had been a while since he'd told me one of his stories, but if I asked him, maybe he'd tell me a new one. If I felt brave, I'd ask him if they were true.

Chapter Three

I slip out of time as soon as I close my eyes. Each flash tells a piece of a story. It takes days, sometimes weeks, to collect enough pieces to understand the entire prophecy.

　　　　—A letter from Liam Evanstar to his mother, Niben, in June 1985, archived in the vault under St. Patrick's Church in South Portland, Maine

My mind had two main states of operation: out of focus and hyperfocus. Out of focus was when I heard and thought too much, taking everything in at once while my mind flitted from one topic to the next. Hyperfocus was when I fixated on one thing, becoming so absorbed in it that everything else faded away.

Walking from my car to my house, I heard peepers welcoming spring with their rhythmic chorus, car engines growling along the highway, my engine clicking as it cooled off, my heart beating, Bessie barking, and squirrels chattering in the tree above me. I smelled thawing earth, wet dog, and my own sweat all while my mind skipped from analyzing my last conversation with José to the man who followed me on my morning run, to magical things I witnessed every day, and to the English paper I had to finish before bed.

For the past month, I'd been fighting a war against my unmedicated self, and I'd been winning. One of my biggest allies in the fight wasn't the therapist, Mom, or my friends but the shaggy mound of brown and gold fur that greeted me at the door whenever I returned home. The first thing I did when I walked into the house was kneel face to face with Bessie. I ran my hands through her soft fur, wincing as her massive paw landed on my shoulder.

"Erin, is that you?" yelled Mom from upstairs.

"Yeah, who else would it be?" Mom, Bessie, and I were the only ones who lived in the house. I barely remembered my dad. Mom and the few photos I had of him said he looked like me: short red hair, green eyes, and pale skin with lots of freckles. According to a newspaper article Mom showed me when I was five, a park ranger found his "mangled" corpse at the bottom of a gorge in Acadia National Park when I was three. I used to pretend he was one of the Demon hunters from Grandpa's stories and that he died saving the world—a slightly more meaningful death than a fluke encounter with a rabid black bear.

"I was just making sure. I'm up in my room, packing." Mom's voice brought me back to the present, standing in the middle of the living room with its plain white walls, discount store furniture, and Bessie leaning all of her 110 pounds on me.

I took a few deeps breaths to combat the rage rearing its heads like a hydra. It was unfair that my father had been taken away from me before I had a chance to know him, but there was nothing I could do about it. Anger would not make my life any better. I hugged Bessie tight, inhaling the musty smell of her fur, and didn't let go until my hands were able to remain open without curling into fists.

Feeling more in control, I plopped my bags down and took my phone out. I sent Mel a quick text: *I'm home. Are you?*

Maybe I was being paranoid, but I thought the man from the beach wanted to do something bad to one of us. I needed to make sure Mel got home safely, so I kept my phone out as I went upstairs. The old, fur-encrusted boards creaked beneath my feet. When I got to the top, my phone buzzed with a message from Mel, telling me she'd stopped at her mom's house.

I replied, asking if she had been followed before I stepped into my mom's room, which was as plain as the living room. The walls and carpet were both boring shades of beige. Her dresser was a step above a cardboard box. The only decorations were a school picture of me and the crucifix Grandpa had given her as a housewarming present when we'd moved in. Her room in our old house had pictures of my dad, a family portrait from when I was two, and some vintage superhero posters, but Mom had never unpacked those.

"How was your afternoon?" she asked. Her freshly dyed blonde hair fell in front of her eyes. She folded a shiny dress shirt into her carry-on bag. It was a far cry from the faded tee she had on.

"Good. Are you excited for the conference?"

Mom's brown eyes lit up as she laughed. "Am I looking forward to spending the weekend cooped up in a hotel full of PhDs who love to hear their own voices?"

"I wouldn't be, but you're one of them." She'd finished her PhD a little over two years before. While she worked on it, taking classes, teaching, and researching had consumed every minute of her life. I'd practically lived with Mel and Aunty Lucy.

"What an attitude." Mom attempted to return my glare, but it wasn't very effective since she couldn't stop smiling.

"Well, I should get started on my homework. It's almost eight." I had a long list of things to do, including the five-page paper that was due first period.

Mom hugged me. "Don't be up too late."

"All right." I squirmed away, went back downstairs, and continued my text conversation with Mel.

Eventually, I put my phone down and paced around the house, trying to figure out why I felt sick every time I pictured the creep's pale face and hooked nose. I got myself to sit still at the kitchen table long enough to begin my unmedicated homework ritual, which involved eating snacks, playing with Bessie, and checking Facebook between fifteen-minute long homework sessions. Whenever I took a break (my reward for finishing something), my focus snapped back to that man. It wasn't until I saw José come online and change his relationship status that I stopped worrying.

I sent José a message asking why he and Jenny broke up. He replied by asking me if we could Skype because his hands hurt too much to type. A whole new set of worries entered my mind, causing my foot to tap frantically while I waited for Skype to open. Those worries were confirmed when José's face finally appeared on my computer screen. His blackish-brown hair was rumpled, stopping shy of puffy, bloodshot eyes.

"Hey, Erin," his voice crackled through my speakers, slightly distorted by the ice pack he held against his nose.

"Hey," I replied half smiling, half cringing. "Did Jenny do that to you?"

He made a bitter choking sound and gave me a look that told me Jenny had not beaten him up. I stared into his eyes: two pools of melted chocolate surrounded a map of red veins. "You fought with your dad again."

He nodded. "I was talking to Will when Dad overheard me describe Jenny as a 'breathing sex doll.' He told me to be more respectful of woman. I laughed, told him to stop treating his girlfriends like toys if he didn't want me to do the same thing. We went back and forth until he smacked me."

"Did you hit back?"

José proceeded to describe, blow for blow, the fight I had dreamed earlier in the week. By the time he was done, my hands were tight fists. My shoulders and arms were cramping from the effort it took not punch the table or chuck my phone across the room. If José's dad walked into the kitchen right then, I wouldn't have been able to stop myself from kicking him where the sun doesn't shine.

"You won't tell anyone, right?" pleaded José.

I nodded, even though the knots in my stomach had become a hoard of monsters trying to claw their way out. I hated when José's dad hurt him. I could have told my mom, a teacher, the police or any adult with the power to get him away from his dad, but I never did. When I was thirteen, I promised to keep it a secret, and unlike my cousin, I wasn't a snitch.

"So, what happened with Jenny?" I needed to change the subject before I exploded.

"I just didn't care for her. It was like banging Barbie."

My cheeks burned. I snorted. "Some guys would kill to bang Barbie."

His face contorted as if he was trying not to puke. "Not me. I hate fake. Her bras are filled with more padding than boob."

"Why did you even go out with her in the first place? Her hair is a different color every week, and the only time she's ever honest is when she's trash-talking me."

"Guilt," said José. "I hooked up with her at a party and owed her a few dates."

I hated the idea of him sleeping with Jenny as much as thinking of him getting beat up by his Dad. Still, the idea of punching Jenny brought an evil grin to my face. José misunderstood my silent smile and told me way more than I wanted to know about what he did with her and how shitty he felt after.

"Then why'd you keep doing it?" I asked.

"She was persuasive...and it felt good while it was happening." He was staring intently, trying to read my expression. "Anyway, once I got word that the person I like actually might feel the same way, I dumped Jenny. I sent her a text saying it was over. I couldn't waste any more time."

"A text? Kind of harsh, isn't it?"

He shrugged.

"Who do you actually like?" A monster called jealousy gnawed on my insides even though I didn't have a right to be jealous. I'd done my best to hide how I felt for a good reason. Sometimes I was an okay friend, but I was a bad person, especially when something as messy as love tangled my emotions. José didn't need another bad person in his life.

"I've known them for a long time," said José, leaning into his ice pack.

"Where did you meet them?" My voice quivered. The monsters bit harder. Maybe it was his friend, Will. Maybe it was me.

"Down the Cape. We hung out a lot when we were thirteen."

"Do they have a name?" A swarm of butterflies attacked the monsters. At thirteen, José hadn't been a player yet. He'd just been the sweet, overly emotional person that now I only glimpsed when we were alone. I'd spent the summer on the cape at Mel's stepdad's beach house, which was right next door to the house José grew up in. We saw each other every day and had even kissed at the end of the summer.

I was a different person back then too. I was nicer, safer.

"How's your English paper coming?" he asked with rare awkwardness.

"What's their name?" It couldn't be me. We were both better off if it wasn't me. With a boyfriend I'd get emotional and distracted. My GPA would tank. Not knowing the truth would do all that twice as fast.

"Can we talk about something else? Are you doing okay with your paper? This is your first one without ADHD meds."

"Now you sound like Mel," I said with a nervous smile.

"That's because we both care." He leaned back and closed his eyes.

"Can you at least give me a hint?"

His lips curved up into a luminous smile. "They were my first kiss."

I stared at the screen, frozen as my mind raced back to the summer night when José kissed me in a rowboat. I could still smell the marsh at low tide, hear the waves lapping at the edge of the boat, and feel his lips gently brush against mine. He held his breath until I smiled and told him it was the best first kiss I could've asked for.

"Hey, I still have some homework to do, so I should go." José frowned.

"Right, bye." I wondered if should tell him my silence was me reliving a good memory, that it meant I liked him too and I had lied every time I told him I never wanted to be more than friends. His face disappeared, but I stared at the screen for a while after. How long had he liked me for? And more importantly, how long was he going to like me?

SLEEP WAS LIKE getting caught in a riptide during a northeaster. First, memory yanked me out to sea: I was five years old and chasing a little Pixie through a field of lupines. Its gossamer wings reflected rainbows while its spiky hair blended in with the flowers. I almost had it when Grandpa scooped me up in his big arms.

"What are you chasing?" he asked with a smile that made his blue eye twinkle.

"A Pixie," I said. "I want to play with it."

The sunny field darkened. Thunder rumbled and the clouds swirled into a vortex that scooped me out of the real memory and into my subconscious's twisted imagination.

Back at my current age, I stood beside a dented pickup truck in a parking garage. Every time I inhaled, I choked on rotten eggs and stale cigarette smoke. My ribs ached and my skin seared, but that didn't stop José from barreling into me and pressing my body against his.

"I love—

I kissed him in a way I had never kissed anyone before. It was fast, hard, and sweaty, but then the tide caught me again and swept me off to Spanish class where Mrs. Finn was droning on about conjugating IR verbs. After an eternity of boredom, the room faded.

I stood barefoot on a beach, facing a tall humanoid Demon clad in a black trench coat, his molten-coal eyes filled with hate. Adrenaline flooded my bloodstream as I swung a quarterstaff at its beaky nose. He stumbled and swung a purple staff at my head. I ducked, landing a blow to his gut. I stepped into a swarm of pins and needles, pulled them into me and pushed them out my foot. I stabbed my staff through the monster, leaving his impaled body pinned to the sand.

Chapter Four

The emeralds from the Elder Mines bestow True Sight upon any man strong enough to bear one on his brow. Only bequeath these treasures on mortals you deem worthy of such a gift.

— Excerpt from the Dwarf-Elf Treaty of 1345 AD. A copy of this document present in the archives

I woke feeling as if I was swaddled in pea-soup fog. I hid under my blankets, hoping it would dissipate. Alarms blared on my phone and stereo, but I didn't have the energy to shut them off. In the end, it was Bessie who pulled the blankets off me and licked my face until I got up, threw random clothes on, shuffled downstairs, and collected my books. I wanted to say bye to Mom, but she was already gone.

The mental haze muted the Jeep's growling engine, weighing me down so hard it was a struggle to keep my hands on the wheel. I shook my head and blasted music, but that didn't help. The potholes in the school parking lot jostled my Jeep and body, but the movement wasn't enough to break up the haze. I knew a few weeks back on antidepressants would thin it out, but those made me nauseated and dizzy, which wasn't much better than the depression. The doctor told me that with most people, the side effects went away after a few weeks, but I had the opposite reaction. I'd start out okay, but the longer I was on a drug, the worse the side effects got. I hoped that one day

I'd find something that actually worked the way it was supposed to.

Even though the morning was as gray as my mood, the parking lot glowed with fresh paint. Seeing all those shiny cars reminded me that most of the other kids were at St. Pat's because they were rich, not because their Grandpa was BFF's with the principal. I pulled into a spot next to a black pickup that was as new as the rest of the cars but distinguished with a handful of dents and scratches. As soon as my car was in park, my hands dropped to my lap like a guillotine's blade.

José's truck confused me. I wanted to leave a mysterious note on the window telling him how cute and funny he was, reminding him that he was worth more than his father wanted him to believe. However, I also wanted to slash his tires and smash his window for sleeping with Jenny Dunn when he actually liked me. Yes, I had rejected him last year, but messing around with other people was no way to win my heart, especially when it wasn't my heart that had driven me to say no, but a haze of depression and a dangerous temper.

My fist rose on a swell of anger. I punched my steering wheel. The horn beeped. I jumped in my seat, smacking my head on the roof. Cursing, I rolled out of the car, slung my backpack over my shoulder, and slammed the door. I needed to ignore José and his truck. I was almost through senior year. I had to finish without letting my grades slip or getting in any fights.

The sun broke through the gray clouds as I tottered across the parking lot. Beams of glaring light seared my sleepy eyes making it hard to see where I was going. After tripping in a pothole, I decided I'd be safer on the squishy lawn than the sidewalk. Parents often complained the buckled concrete was a tripping hazard, but Sister Marie insisted repairing it would damage the antique oak trees that lined all the walkways around campus.

I found myself inclined to agree with the old nun. The trees were beautiful with trunks too wide for me to get my arms around and gnarly branches that ended in buds waiting to burst into bright green leaves. Even though I was in a rush, I stopped to watch a blue jay leap from branch to branch. It nearly collided with another bluish creature that wasn't a bird at all, but a mini person with dragonfly wings and spiky blue hair. I blinked. The blue jay was alone on the branch. I shook my head hard and kept walking, this time at a faster pace. I had an exam first period. I couldn't afford to stand around wondering if Pixies were real.

As I got closer to the brick building that housed most senior classes, the noise became overwhelming. Laughter, shouts, and rapid-fire gossip drowned out the songs of newly returned birds. The way people segregated themselves by gender made me queasy. José stood near the door, surrounded by a group of guys from the soccer team. I knew the lanky blond was his friend Will, and the brown-haired twins were James and George.

José's band of cliché jocks was acting as a buffer zone between him and the girls clustered a few feet away. Normally, those girls and I did our best to ignore each other's existence. Today, they were staring at me, and their ringleader, the willowy Jenny Dunn, narrowed her eyes and bared her teeth like she was ready to rip my throat out. I decided it was safe to assume she believed I was the reason José broke up with her.

I glared right back, imagining one of the doves roosting on the windowsill pooping in her shiny hair. My eyes got watery from staring, so for a second, I saw double: two Jennys glaring daggers at me and two Pixies straddling the doves in doll-sized saddles.

A hand waved in front of my eyes. "Hello? Is anyone in there?"

I blinked until my vision returned to normal and focused on Sam. Her face was a few inches away from mine. Her smiling lips were the color of plums and her eyes were outlined with so much black pencil I got itchy just looking at them.

"Erin? What are you staring at? And what the hell are you wearing?" she asked.

"Good morning to you too. What's wrong with my clothes?"

Sam laughed. "Well, for starters, they don't match, and you're wearing a men's shirt with a skirt."

"It's comfy," I yawned, not wanting to admit I hadn't looked at what I put on. Sometimes I wore men's clothing to distance myself from my assigned gender, but long skirts made me feel like I was wearing a blanket. They were perfect for days I didn't want to get out bed and didn't care what my clothes made people assume.

Shaking her head, Sam put her arm around my back and guided me over to the oak her backpack was leaning against. She dropped her voice to a whisper. "People have been talking about you."

"Me?"

"Competing rumors. One says José broke up with her because he is hopelessly in love with you. The other is that she broke with him because he cheated on her with you."

"Great. That's just what I need." I leaned back, savoring the feeling of the rough bark scratching me through my cotton button-up.

"Yup. You can't expect to be 'just friends' with the boy everyone wants to date and think you'll stay out of the drama."

"People are stupid" was the most intelligent response I could muster.

José strutted toward us with his entourage not far behind, while Jenny's clique watched like a pride of feral cats, and Pixies flocked from all over the school with chocolate bars that were as tall as them. I couldn't picture how they could eat it all and not explode.

A clanging bell tried to shatter my eardrums. It was followed by a screeching voice telling people to get inside. Lateness meant detention, and according to Sister Marie, a malfunctioning bell system was no excuse. Sister Marie was standing on the steps to the school in black pants, a white button-up shirt, and a small habit that covered half of her head and the tips of her ears. She was a strange nun, clinging to tradition in some ways and throwing it away in others.

I covered my ears to shield them from the noise, walked toward school, and bumped straight into José.

"Hey Erin," he said with a hand on each of my arms.

I blinked, wondering if the green spot on his head was real or part of the hallucinations. It disappeared after a few seconds and my eyes became more focused on his swollen nose and bruised jaw.

"Your face looks like crap." My hands balled into fists until my nails stung my palms.

"And your shoulder looks like my face, but hotter."

"Sparring match with Mel." I smirked, thinking I'd enjoy bashing José's dad on the head with my practice sword.

"Erin! José! Keep your hands to yourself and get to homeroom." Sister Marie was only a few inches away from us, grinning as much as the Pixie sitting on her shoulder.

I muttered an apology, broke away from José, and sprinted to the doors. It was colder inside than outside. I charged past the rows of faded gray lockers and doors framed in ornate molding. José caught up as I slid into my homeroom desk a few seconds before the teacher called my name. Sinking in the desk next to me, José whispered, "You should wear padding when you spar with Mel."

"That's boring," I replied without looking. Daily Prayer played over the intercom, but our homeroom teacher was more focused on his phone than his students. Everyone else was talking, so I doubted José and I would get in trouble for our conversation.

"You should move out of your dad's house," I said.

"Don't talk about that here," hissed José. "I told everyone I fell because I tried to dribble a soccer ball up the stairs."

"That's stupid." I closed my eyes, hoping he'd leave me alone.

"Are you going to the dance tonight?"

"I hate dances and I hate dancing."

"You don't hate dancing."

"I hate dancing in front of people who aren't my cousin."

"Are you going?"

"Do you remember what happened last time I went to a dance?"

"You got into a fight."

"Exactly." The bell rang. I booked it out of homeroom before everyone had a chance to crowd the door.

"You still didn't answer me." José slid his arm around my waist as we walked through the crowded hall. He was grinning, but beads of sweat formed on his forehead and his hand quivered.

"Sam is making me go. Who are you taking?" My heart rate elevated and breaths caught in my throat. He hadn't asked me if he could touch me. Part of me enjoyed the way it felt having his hand glide over my stiff muscles, but I was afraid he would do more without my permission.

"Will doesn't have a date. I'm going with him, unless—"

He paused.

"Unless what?" I asked.

"Nothing." He let go of me as we turned the corner and went into English. I stumbled into the classroom not knowing what the "unless" meant and unsure if he and Will going together meant they were going "together" and if it mattered.

Like most of the other rooms in the original parts of St. Pats, it had scratched up hardwood floors, big windows, a crucifix, antique desks, a state-of-the-art smartboard, and an oversized-tablet pretending to be a computer monitor on top of the teacher's desk. I sat in the front row.

"Do you think you could save me a dance tonight?" José sat next to me.

The bell rang and Mr. Pearson reminded everyone of the consequences of cheating on an exam. I gawked at José for a few minutes before I realized my hands were still balled into fists and my nails were seconds away from breaking the skin of my palms. It took a lot of effort to unclench them, but I managed. I placed one hand on the edge of my desk, picked up my pen, and told myself I was not going to think of anything other than my exam.

I looked at the paper on my desk. The words blurred into a jumble of incoherent letters. My foot tapped faster than my heartbeat. I twirled my pen around my fingers and found myself looking up at José. Dark curls hung over his eyes as he read the questions on the page in front of him and chewed his lower lip. He was cute, even with his face messed up. Dancing with him would feel good and it didn't automatically make us more than friends.

Having made up my mind, I committed my attention to the test. It would have been easier to concentrate with noise canceling headphones blanketing the din with white noise. I heard the sucking whoosh of breathing, pens and pencils scratching on paper, and footsteps thumping as people completed their tests and handed them in. Someone behind me chomped on chewing gum. The ticking clock became louder and louder. A dozen hearts beat out of time with mine.

I jumped out of my seat when the bell rang. Standing at my desk, I scribbled a few more words into the open response section and dug my essay out of my notebook. My assignments were the last to join the stack on Mr. Pearson's desk.

I went back to get my bag and saw José waiting by the door, looking like a sad puppy. There was something green between his eyebrows, so I reached up and tried to brush it off. "One dance—and that's it."

The sad puppy looked like he just got a biscuit. "That's all I asked for. What are you doing to my face?"

"You have a leaf or something stuck to your head." As my fingers brushed over the object, I realized it was as hard and smooth as an emerald. His skin darkened in front of my eyes to the warm copper shade it would be at the end of summer.

"Erin, are you sure it's a leaf?" He put his fingers on mine and guided them around the edges of what was clearly some kind of gemstone.

"It wasn't there when we got into class," I said, trying to figure out when he had put it there and why he put that on his head to begin with. He guided my hand down to his cheek and held it there. It was warm and smooth, freshly shaven even though a little fuzz would have hidden some of the bruising around his jaw.

"It's always been there," he whispered. "You know what it is. Think."

All I was capable of thinking was how smooth his skin was and how intense his eyes were. I could've laid my whole self across him like he was sand warmed by the sun on a cool spring day, yet my hand remained glued to his face. My body and mind were playing tug of war. I'd lean a centimeter forward and pull back two until want and fear became tangible in the air between us. It heated up and sparked, a tractor beam drawing him toward me. I was a Star Destroyer and he was the Millennium Falcon. My lips tingled as they approached his.

"Hey, no kissing. Get to your next class."

My hands flew up to shield my ears from Mr. Pearson's voice and José shook his head the same way Bessie did when she got water in her ears. I hugged my books close to my chest and charged down the hall to history. I slid into a seat next to Sam seconds before the bell rang.

"Why are you breathing so fast?" she whispered as Mr. Whittle began his lecture.

"He tried to kiss me."

"Who?" Sam leaned forward. If she were a dog, her ears would have perked up.

I shared an abridged version in fast whispers.

"*You* tried to kiss José," said Sam when I paused to breathe.

"I guess." I dropped my head onto the desk and closed my eyes. I was not going to be able to focus on anything today.

History was a blur. I paid attention for the first few minutes of Spanish but stopped trying when I realized I knew every word Mrs. Fin was going to say before she droned it. The numbers and equations got jumbled on my math test. All I knew about biology were featherlight touches from José and whispered compliments.

Chapter Five

Winter Elves are calm, serene, and as patient as glaciers when it comes to vengeance. The children of summer are fiery, short-tempered Elves with little patience for anything. While Summer Elves are more violent than Winter, they are also more passionate, and that combination makes them excellent allies and lovers for Demon hunters (except for when we forget to make the bed).
　—The Demon Hunter Lexicon, a copy owned and annotated by Seamus Evanstar

The other students were a sea of noise that parted as José and I passed through them on our way to the cafeteria. He held my hand and thoughts captive. The monsters inside me wouldn't stop roaring because he hadn't asked to hold my hand. He'd just taken it, and he was all I could think about. Why now? Who had blabbed my feelings to him? Why didn't he ask to hold my hand before he took it?

His lips moved, but his voice was lost to the cacophony. His palm was sweaty, so I knew he was struggling to keep the roguish grin on his face, probably terrified I was going to reject his flirtations at any moment. I should've rejected them, but I didn't. I tried to laugh those monsters away, but they reminded me how it started with my last boyfriend: flirty touches, handholding, and hugging. He asked me out, I said yes, and he thought it meant he could use me however he wanted.

"Erin, if you squeeze any harder, you're going to break my hand," said José.

"Sorry." I let go and wrapped my arms around myself. "I don't know if I can do this."

"Do what?" He stopped walking to make eye contact.

"I don't know. You're distracting me. I don't know what to put in my lab report because I was hardly paying attention. Focusing was tough yesterday, but I remembered to take notes and to reel my mind in when it wandered. Today, it was impossible." The words were neither lies nor the actual reason I'd been strangling his hand.

José's smile vanished. His lips twitched as he struggled not to frown. "I'll help you with the lab report. I'll come over this weekend; we'll work on it together."

"Thanks." I wanted to tell him more and see how he reacted, but if I told him what my ex, Ricky, had tried to do to me, I'd also wind up telling him how I responded. I wasn't sure if José would even be my friend after hearing that.

Something hard whacked my shoulder, sending ripples of anger and pain through my body. I spun around, ready to lash out at the source of it.

"You shouldn't stand in the middle of the hall making bedroom eyes at your spic boyfriend," said Jenny, baring her teeth in a smirk.

"Bitch," I snarled through the haze of rage and lunged for her.

I didn't make it very far before a big hand grabbed my wrist and yanked me back. Jenny's shrill laugh battered my ears. Two big arms wrapped around my wriggling waist and pulled me up against a hard chest.

"Erin, calm down. Ignore her," said José.

"Let go of me." The more I wriggled, the tighter he held.

"Promise me you won't go fight her."

"Let me go." My wrist was aching where he had grabbed it. I felt trapped in his arms the same way I had felt trapped in Ricky's.

"Erin, one fight and you're done here. Sister Marie will expel you."

"Not your concern." His feet pounded on the pavement as he ran after me. I sped up, opening and closing my fists as I wove through the crowd honing in on Sam's spiky black hair.

"Hey. You and José a couple yet?" she asked as I fell into step beside her.

"No. And I don't think we will be."

"Uh-oh. What happened?"

While we waited in the pizza line, I told her about Jenny and his reaction. A glance over my shoulder revealed José a few people behind me, looking sullen while his friends laughed.

"He was just protecting you." Sam put two slices on her plate.

"I don't need protection," I said, taking three and ignoring the lunch lady's glare. José was the one who needed protection, but so far, he had rejected all my attempts to help him deal with or get away from his dad.

"Guys don't get it. That's why girls are better."

"That has nothing to do with it." I rolled my eyes and my upper lip twitched. José had heard me complain enough about Mel's misguided attempts to "protect me from myself" to know better than to try it himself.

"Erin, watch out!"

Sam's voice prompted me to pause less than an inch away from Jenny, who was balancing an open milk carton and salad bowl on the lunch tray that she held above her head. I looked into her icy blue eyes as she grinned and dumped the tray on me with a squeaky "oops."

I took a few deep breaths, trying to suppress the rage as cold milk, lettuce, and tomatoes dripped down my face. My pizza splattered on the floor. Jenny and her friends formed a half-round barricade in front of me, snickering. I was going to beat her to a bloody pulp as soon as I decided on the best way to start. She was still grinning that annoying, predatory smile. I cackled. She wouldn't smile so much if she were missing teeth. I shifted my weight and aimed a right hook at her mouth.

Before I felt her teeth crack beneath my knuckles, a hand yanked my arm. I pulled forward and swung with my left but was stopped short by a smaller pair of hands hauling me backward. Jenny and her friends were still laughing, grinning and talking in voices too shrill to understand. I needed to make them shut up, so I squirmed to get free.

"Erin, calm down," shouted Sam.

"Take a deep breath. Ignore the girls. They're not worth it," said José. He was in front of me now, looking into my eyes with his hands around my wrists. His warped nose and black eyes were the image of what I wanted to do to Jenny. I lowered my eyes and studied the way his fingers were wrapped around my wrist. I knew how to break his grip, but his knuckles were bruised and scraped. The night before, he told me his hands were too sore to type. I couldn't hurt him.

"I'm sorry. If I'd never fooled around, this wouldn't have happened." José loosened his grip so he was barely holding my wrist. Sam let go completely. Dozens of students were staring at us as Sister Marie pushed her way through the throng. The monsters were swarmed by hordes of buzzing hornets. Rage was swallowed by anxiety and shame.

The cafeteria spun. José's green gem glowed on his forehead. Pixies ate popcorn while they peered through the windows. My stomach churned, my eyes burned, and my skin crawled. I took a step back. José let go of my hands. I ran.

Sam and José called after me, but I ignored their voices and didn't look to see if they were following. I pushed past anyone who got in my way until I was through the black double doors and out in the sunlight. Mud squished under my feet. The song of birds and alien Pixie language drowned out the alarm I had tripped by opening the emergency exit. I heard feet chasing after me, but I kept my eyes on the parking lot where my Jeep was waiting with a knife stashed under my seat. Cutting would give the monsters a way out and make my skin stop crawling. If I were careful where I cut, no one would know I'd relapsed.

"Erin Lucile Evanstar! Where do you think you are going?" boomed Sister Marie's voice. I froze, turned around, and faced her.

"I have to leave," I said, struggling to control my breathing.

"Why?" said Sister in a surprisingly calm voice.

"I'm going to hurt someone if I don't leave." I ran my nails over my arms, tried to count to ten, tried breathing deep like I was attempting to inflate my stomach, not my lungs, struggling to picture rage leaving with my breath. It wasn't enough.

"You need your mother's permission to leave." Sister Marie moved a little closer to me.

I stifled a snarl. "My mother is on a plane."

She nodded. "Then I'll call your Grandfather. Your mother gave me permission to call him when I can't reach her."

She whipped her phone out of her pants pocket and called Grandpa. I paced around in circles while she explained why I was upset and wanted to leave. That was when I noticed Sam was watching from a few paces behind Sister Marie.

"He said you can leave, but he wants to hear all about what's going on when he sees you tomorrow. He also said you have to tell your mother."

"You're not making them go see the counselor?" Sam stepped forward, her head tilted in confusion. "When I tried to punch someone, you made me see the counselor."

"Erin is not you." Sister Marie laughed. "They need to get out of here and get some fresh air, maybe go for a run."

"A run?" Sam looked horrified.

"Yes, Samantha. You're eighteen and don't need parental permission to leave school grounds. Some exercise will do you good." Sister Marie walked away chuckling.

"Is this even legal?" asked Sam.

"I don't care." A nervous laugh escaped my lips. I couldn't cut in front of Sam, but some food and exercise might make the monsters shut up for a little bit. "A run and food will help. I could jump in the ocean. The shock of cold water will calm me down."

"You're insane," said Sam as she followed me to my car.

"You've no idea." I laughed more. It was a lullaby putting my monsters to sleep and letting a slightly more rational part of my brain take control.

Chapter Six

Never look a Demon in the eyes.
    —Common Hunter Proverb

Sam wanted no part of a run, and I couldn't persuade her that a dip in the frigid ocean would do anything but stop my heart. Afraid she was starting to think I was suicidal and not just having a bad day, I dropped the subject and suggested we walk around downtown Portland, which was only a ten-minute drive from school. She agreed to that, and after a brief stop at my house to change and wash the salad dressing out of my hair, we were on a mission to find new clothes for the dance.

"Do you think Sister Marie will even let you in?" asked Sam as we walked out of one store empty-handed. Everything inside had been way too expensive.

"She never said I was in trouble." I closed my eyes, soaking up the sun and briny air.

"Do you still plan to dance with José?"

"Yeah. He sent enough apology texts. It was kind of pathetic, but in a cute José way." I couldn't stop smiling as I walked across the old cobblestones. "I think there is a consignment store around the corner. Things will be cheaper there."

"Pathetic is not a word I generally use to describe José," said Sam. "And he didn't do anything he needed to apologize for."

"You don't know him how I do. He did need to apologize. He was being controlling."

"He stopped you from doing something stupid," she muttered as we rounded a corner to a more modern street with blacktop and sidewalks. It was lined with multi-story brick buildings. The first floor of each had larger windows than the top, indicating stores on the bottom and apartments or offices above. I ignored everything with the word artisan or boutique on it and headed to Renew Revolution.

"You seem to know a different José than everyone else," said Sam.

"It's a long story." I stepped through the glass door into a room filled with faded jeans, floral dresses, and dark sweaters.

"Tell me." Sam picked up a sparkly purple and black tunic while I eyed a steampunk vest.

While we shopped, I told Sam how neither José nor I were originally from Maine. He grew up on Cape Cod where Mel's family owned a seasonal cottage. When Mom was too busy to deal with me being out of school, I'd spend the entire summer with Mel and Aunty Lucy, which meant that for three months out of the year, José and I were neighbors. Every spring I'd count down the days until school ended. My summers were epic until he moved to Maine and Mel stopped vacationing on the Cape so she could spend time with Mike, her boyfriend-turned-fiancé.

"I'm guessing you kept in touch," said Sam as we paid for our finds. Her tunic and leggings fit into a small bag, but my vest, button-up shirt, and corduroy pants barely fit in a paper grocery bag.

"Yeah. Facebook and Skype. I think that's when we got closer because we never saw each other in person. It's easier to be honest with someone you don't have to face in real life."

"Was it weird when you started going to school together?"

I shrugged. I'd already shared enough with Sam for the moment. She didn't need to know I'd been too depressed to care, despite José's ceaseless efforts to make me smile.

BY THE TIME we left the thrift store, people were out and about, enjoying the early spring weather. Gulls squawked in the distance while smaller birds sang in the trees. Car engines growled and a dozen different songs blared out of open windows. A few storefronts behind us was a man wearing a black trench coat and fedora, with the same pale skin and beaky nose as the man who followed Mel and I the day before. The sight of him made my skin feel tingly and my stomach churn.

"Let's look in here," I said, pulling Sam into the next store we walked by.

"I thought you wanted to eat," she said, stumbling along beside me.

"I do, but this place looked neat." I grinned at the hemp jewelry, leather jackets, and display case full of switchblades and pocketknives, thankful the store actually was the kind of shop I'd want to browse. It would've been awkward if it had been a fine jewelry store or a tobacco shop.

"I've never been in here before." Sam walked over to a wall filled with ornate swords and quarterstaffs.

"Me neither." I ran my fingers along the blade of an orange-hilted katana, tracing the Old English runes carved onto its side. When my fingers reached the tip, I was pleasantly surprised to find that it cut my skin at the lightest touch.

"Can I help you?"

I jumped away from the sword and turned to find a man with black dreadlocks, a tie-dye shirt, and round sunglasses straight out of the sixties. His walking stick was more ornate than any staff on display.

"The sword is beautiful," I said, closing my fist so Sam didn't see the blood pooling on the tip of my index finger.

He grinned. "That the orange one?"

"Yes."

"I carved those myself. An Anglo-Saxon battle prayer on a Japanese sword. You won't find one like it anywhere else."

"I don't doubt it."

"Are you looking to purchase one?" he asked.

I shook my head. "We were passing by and I thought the shop looked interesting. I wasn't expecting so many weapons."

"I see. Let me know if you have any questions."

The man made his way to a chair next to the counter, where he sat below a picture of himself leaning his shoulder on a man who reminded me of an ad for a lumberjack show.

"I've always wanted to learn how to use one of these," said Sam, running her hands over a black staff with purple lines whirling across its surface.

"I can teach you. I'm a little out of practice, but I doubt I've forgotten much."

Sam picked up the staff and awkwardly swung it. "Do you have one?"

"I used to have a training one, but I might've broken it."

"Might have?"

I grinned. "Well, either I broke it or Mel's thick skull did."

The man at the counter chuckled. "Those are the real thing. You hit someone hard enough, their skull is going to snap, not the stick."

"That's why Mel and I switched to Shinai; they're more durable and less painful."

"Smart choice," said the man. "My name is Andre."

Sam was busy playing with the staff, so I went over and shook his hand. "I'm Erin."

"Evanstar?" he asked.

"Yeah. How'd you know?"

"Your Grandpa comes in here a lot. So does your boyfriend."

"I don't have a boyfriend," I said, realizing this must have been where José got the swords he bought me for my birthday the year before.

"How much are the staffs?" asked Sam.

"That one there is fifty dollars, but they're on sale, two for one. It's twenty-five dollars apiece if Erin buys one too. There should be a green one at the left end of the wall with flaming orange vines. I bet it's perfect for them."

STEPPING OUT OF the shop, I was overcome by a wave of sunlight and heat. Once my eyes adjusted, I realized the man in the trench coat was sitting on a bench across the street from the shop, looking like a modern-day Sith lord. I grinned at the weight of the ornate staff in my hands. Sure, it was painted green and decorated with sharp runes, flaming vines, and dragons, but there was no mistaking it for anything but a weapon designed to break bones. I glared at Darth Trench Coat, using my eyes and snarling lips to tell him I wasn't afraid. I hoped the combination of an attitude and a weapon would deter him.

He returned my glare. His lips pulled back in a parody of a smile, revealing six rows of pointy teeth.

"Erin, what are you staring at?"

The weight of Sam's hand made me jump. "Some creepy dude's following us."

"Where? Is he hot?"

"How do you get *hot* out of *creepy*? See the guy on the bench?"

"The goth one? He is cute. A little pale, but that's kinda the point."

"Do you see his teeth?"

"No. Are they crooked or something?"

I shook my head, realizing she wasn't seeing what I was. "Let's just get food. Burrito Bar sound good?"

"Sure."

I kept glancing over my shoulder as we walked. Darth Trench Coat got up off his bench and followed us. Sam rambled about something, but I couldn't spare any attention for the conversation. I picked up my pace. Sam complained but kept up. Unfortunately, Darth Trench Coat did too. When we got to Burrito Bar, he followed us inside.

"I wonder which one of us he is interested in?" Sam alternated between reading the menu on the wall in front us and looking at the man.

I cringed. "What happened to preferring girls?"

"I was thinking of potentially serious relationships, but that doesn't mean I can't be attracted to boys as well, and this guy's eyes are amazing, like staring at a meadow."

To me, his eyes were two pools of motor oil: shiny and black with no whites. When I looked at them for too long, my head spun and my legs wobbled. I tried to stay focused on the line of people in front of me and kept repeating what I was going to order—a veggie quesadilla, no sour cream, extra peppers. It wasn't enough to stop my legs from shaking, my hands from fidgeting, or my head from turning around every five seconds.

I knew for certain he was following us. What I didn't know was why, and which version of him was real: the one I was seeing or the one Sam saw. If I truly was sick, my fear of repeating what happened with Ricky could be manifesting itself in the form of a hallucination. My mind could be taking the imagined monsters from Grandpa's stories and superimposing them over some college guy who was working up the courage to introduce himself. However, I couldn't fully rule out the possibility that Demons were real, Darth Trench Coat actually was one, and I had the ability to see through its glamour while Sam couldn't.

"Erin, it's our turn to order."

I frowned at Sam, told the cashier that we wanted our food to go, paid, got a number, and before Sam had a chance to argue, I was pacing by the restaurant's emergency exit. "We should eat outside in the sun."

"I agree. Want to go to the picnic tables near the ferry terminal?"

DARTH TRENCH COAT followed us there too. He sat a few benches away from our table, staring at us while we ate. "Should call the police?"

"What's your problem? The poor guy is probably too shy to talk to us. He'll get brave if we stick around long enough."

I didn't want him to get brave or come any closer to us. I wanted to go home or go back to the weapons shop he didn't follow us into. Sam had other ideas.

"Maybe we should go talk to him." She squished her taco wrapper into a ball.

I shook my head. Even if the eyes and teeth were hallucinations, the guy gave off a stalker vibe.

"Stop being lame," she said.

I looked around. Darth Trench Coat wasn't the only weird thing in sight. Gray Pixies rode seagulls while Mermaids floated around the harbor, watching me as intently as our stalker was.

"I have to pee," I told Sam quietly. This terminal didn't have neutral bathrooms, but I could handle feeling alien for a few minutes if it got me away from Darth Trench Coat. "It can be a test. If he follows us to the women's bathroom, then we know he's bad news and we'll call the police. If he waits out here, then you can go introduce yourself."

"Whatever." She rolled her eyes but got up and walked into the ferry terminal with me.

Darth Trench Coat studied us, but he didn't get up when we stepped into the glass atrium. I lost sight of him when we turned into the waiting area and went behind a concrete wall to the bathrooms.

"See, he's not a creep," said Sam when we got inside.

I ignored her, headed to a stall, and did my business. When I exited, Sam's feet were still visible below a gray partition.

"I'll meet you outside," I told her and stepped out into the hallway.

Darth Trench Coat was waiting for me.

"Finally, we are alone," he said in a deep, croaking voice.

"Who are you?" I made eye contact and held my head high, hoping I looked confident, not terrified.

"I have many names. None of them will mean anything to you." He lifted his spindly fingers to my cheek. I tried to back away, but my legs wouldn't move. Claws caked in dried blood brushed my cheek and neck and then traced the outline of my collarbone. "First, know that you are not hallucinating. The Mermaids, Pixies, and I are as real as you. The people closest to you have been lying to you, trying to protect you, but they are actually killing you slowly. You are a great warrior, and I can show you how to unlock your potential and take control of your life."

My heart should have been racing, but it was sluggish. My hands should have been clinging to my new staff, but they were barely holding it up enough to prevent it from clattering to the floor. I opened my mouth to yell. No sound came out.

He grinned. "By trying to protect you from the truth, they have left you defenseless. I can show you real power that will let you get revenge against anyone who has ever hurt or neglected you. Power that will put you not only in charge of your own life but in control of those who seek to govern you."

Even though my body was paralyzed, my mind was still working, searching through my memories for an explanation for what was happening. In Grandpa's stories, the hunters all knew to never look Demons in the eyes. If you made eye contact, they saw into your soul and controlled you—or manipulate your neurons—depending on whether or not Mel had been there to correct Grandpa. Either I had gotten sicker, or I was facing a real Demon that had watched a few too many weight loss infomercials.

A forked tongue licked my cheek, burning like liquid nitrogen. The pain made me angry and more aware of how Darth Trench Coat's hands were slowly slipping below my shirt. I growled.

The spell broke.

I didn't fight the impulse to kick. My foot hit a cold hard stomach and made him stagger just enough to break eye contact.

"I am not defenseless," I snarled. Heat flooded my body and my muscles tensed up. My head cleared. Darth Trench Coat hissed, a snake ready to strike, so I kicked him again. This time, I balanced my weight right, and he flew backward into the wall with a satisfying thud. I didn't wait for him to respond before spinning the staff around and smacking him in the ribs. Whether his Demonic appearance was real or not, the man had tried to sexually assault me. He deserved broken ribs.

The echo of pounding feet caught my attention. I spun around, raising my staff into a defensive position in case the man had an accomplice and found myself facing another person I wanted to hit: José's dad, Dr. Pedro Estrella.

"Erin, are you okay?"

Suppressing the urge to break his jaw, I glanced back at the wall Darth Trench Coat had just hit. He was gone. As much as I hated Dr. Estrella, I was curious if he had seen Darth Trench Coat. "Did you see a man by the wall? He was super pale."

Dr. Estrella shook his head. "No. I heard a bang and ran out to see what it was. Was someone bothering you?"

I looked down the hall and back at the wall. There was no sign of Darth Trench Coat. The only evidence of his existence was a circle of frost on the bricks and a chip in the mortar. "He was staring into the women's room when I was trying to leave. What are you doing here?"

Dr. Estrella stared at the chip with his brows furrowed. He bit his cheek and smiled. "I took the ferry over to Peaks Island to collect some data. The wireless transmitter keeps breaking on my water thermometers. Are you here alone?"

"I'm with Sam." I stared at his eyes. They were the same dark brown as José's with tiny pricks of black in the middle, just how eyes were supposed to be. He had the same green gem above his nose and a piece of kelp in his wet hair. As if that wasn't strange enough, his shirt was damp and wrinkled. It made me wonder what he was actually doing here.

"Erin? Are you okay?"

"You have a piece of seaweed on your head." I had been hoping to see his nose as broken as José's, but his face didn't even have a bruise. Alone in this hallway, I could change that. I could teach him not to hit his son using his own methods. There was a thick wall between the waiting area and us. I could get a few blows in before anyone heard us, but they'd hear us, and Mom would be furious when the police called her down to get me. José might hate me if he found out.

"Thank you for letting me know." Dr. Estrella brushed off his forehead, running his hand over the green gem.

"The seaweed is in your hair, not on your forehead." I forced a smile, trying to think more about Grandpa's stories than what I wanted to do to Dr. Estrella's nose. Antonio, the hunter with a thing for Mermaids, always had a green Elf Stone on his head. It had been mined in the Faerie realms, so its magic allowed him to see around illusions even though he didn't have Sight like Liam. Without it, Antonio wouldn't have been able to see his precious Mermaids.

"Right, thank you. Have a good afternoon," he said with a charming smile capable of fooling anyone else. I saw right through to the asshole behind it.

"Tell José I said hi and to make sure he keeps icing his nose."

Dr. Estrella turned and walked away as I heard Sam's feet and voice coming up behind me. "Sorry I took so long. The fish taco didn't agree with me. I guess mystery boy didn't follow us. I hope he's still outside."

"We're going home," I snarled. "I feel sick and need a shower."

Chapter Seven

The Sacred Sisters of St. Patrick, also known as the Sisters of the Seven Stars, are an order of hybrid nuns dedicated to hunting Demons. Most are Elf-human hybrids, but a few are part Demon. An even smaller number are part angel. They spend their days among the normal population as educators, charity workers, and police officers. One of their most distinguished members, currently known as Sister Marie, has been running a small Catholic school in Maine under different names for the past two centuries.
—Added to the Demon Hunter Lexicon on 12 Feb 2015 by M.M. in his attempt to digitize hunter archives

With a freshly ironed suit and reinforced denial, Sam and I got in the Jeep. The engine growled to life. Rock music blasted out of the stereo. For a few glorious seconds, I thought the fifteen-minute drive to St. Pat's was going to be normal.

I was wrong. As soon as I took the first turn off my street, a boxy Camry pulled up behind me. I took another turn, but it followed. The windshield's glass was tinted, but I still recognized the driver's Demonic face. I took the next two lefts I came across so I was heading toward town, not school.

"Erin, you're going the wrong way," said Sam.

"We're being followed. Look at the car behind us."

She looked out the back window. "Shoot, isn't that the guy from Portland?"

"Yup." I took an abrupt left. The boxy Camry did too.

"I guess he is kind of stalker-ish."

"You guess?" I took another random turn and so did Darth Trench Coat. He sped up so he was riding my tail, close enough for me to see triple-jointed fingers and filthy claws clutching his steering wheel.

"Just drive to school. Officer Karen is usually at the dances, and if she's not there, another cop will be."

I attempted to memorize his plate number while I took the most erratic route I could think of, running stop signs, red lights, and waiting until the last minute to make every turn. Darth Trench Coat matched each move, staying right on my tail until we passed St. Patrick's Church. Sam and I both blessed ourselves as we sped by, then I yanked the wheel right. My tires screeched as I pulled into the senior parking lot. Books, candy bar wrappers, and empty water bottles went flying, but the Camry didn't follow us.

Some of my muscles relaxed, but my heart was racing as I circled through the sea of sleek BMWs and Mazdas I assumed were borrowed from parents for the night. I found a spot in the middle of the lot, pulled in, and jumped out of the Jeep. I didn't see José's truck anywhere, but I already heard the bass pounding in the gym. The gray Camry was parked at the top of the street, a few feet away from the entrance to the school property. No one got out of the car.

My shirt felt too tight and I worried the strained buttons might pop and expose my binder tank to whoever lurked in that car. I locked my doors as soon as Sam was out, and power-walked toward the gym, wishing my boots had smaller heals. The rapid *thump thump* of the bass got louder. I flew through black double doors as fast as I could and ran straight into Sister Marie, knocking the half habit off her steel gray hair.

"Watch where you're going," she scolded.

"I'm sorry," I muttered, trying to get control of my lungs. I kept taking big breaths, but none of them seemed to have enough oxygen. My heart felt as if metal clamps were squeezing it.

"Erin? What's wrong?" Sister Marie straightened out her shamrock vest.

"A car followed Sam and me here," I blurted, hoping if she realized I had a genuine reason to be running, she might not punish me.

"Are you sure?" She leaned toward me.

"Yes." I forced my sweaty palms open, keeping my fingers spread out.

"Can you describe it for me?"

"It was a gray Camry from the 90s, Maine plate starting 66 but I didn't catch the whole thing. The driver followed me all the way from my house. I kept taking weird turns and he followed me until I got here. He parked a few feet away from the gate."

She put a bony hand on my shoulder. "Erin, take a deep breath with me."

I did. After the third one, my chest relaxed and my lungs stopped hurting.

"Have you ever seen the driver before?"

I stared into the old nun's gray eyes. For a second, I could have sworn they turned feline oval.

"Erin, have you seen him?"

"Yes. He's been following me around for two days. He was behind Mel and me while we were running. He watched us spar. Then he was following Sam and me around Portland."

"Why didn't you call the police?" Sister Marie looked over her shoulder and waved at Officer Karen, who had been standing by the gym entrance, occasionally searching bags and inspecting water bottles. She nodded to Sister Marie, returned a Coach purse to a student and joined us near the gym entrance. Apparently, she had heard our whole conversation because she jumped right in with: "Erin, can you describe the man for me?"

"He was really tall and super pale. He had dark eyes and a hooked nose. He wore all black. Yesterday it was sweats. Today it was a trench coat."

"You said he had dark eyes. Can you remember what color they were?" asked Officer Karen.

"Sam thought they were green, but they looked black to me. She might give you a better description." I glanced over my shoulder to see if Sam was still around. She wasn't.

"I sent her into the dance. It is easier to talk to witnesses one at a time. Now, tell me exactly where you were when you saw this man and what you were doing."

I launched into a very detailed account, only leaving out the parts where Darth Trench Coat looked more monster than man. When I was done, Officer Karen and Sister Marie went outside to see if the car was still there.

I walked toward the ticket table but turned around to think before the noise muddled my thoughts. One of the characters in Grandpa's stories was a nun who ran a school by day and hunted Demons at night. He described her as having gray hair, cold eyes, a thin upper lip and a small frame that made her seem frail. Despite her outward appearance, she was a fierce fighter in possession of superhuman speed, strength, and magic that she inherited from her Elven father. I suspected that Sister Marie might be the inspiration for the character, if it wasn't actually her. Grandpa had always just referred to her as "Sister."

"Erin, are you all right?" José waved a bruised hand in front of my face. I blinked a few times and stopped moving. He had white medical tape on his nose. "I saw Sam. She told me you were out here with Sister Marie and Officer Karen."

I nodded and forced my lips into a smile. "Some creep followed me here, so they went to check it out. I think he's been stalking me. How come I didn't see your truck?"

"I came with Will. Why didn't you tell me about the stalker?"

"I had other things on my mind, and..." I hesitated, afraid the truth might ruin the night.

"And what?"

"Well, it wasn't obvious that he was actually stalking me until this afternoon."

"Right." He stared down at our feet. "Are you still mad at me for holding you back from Jenny?"

"I'm thankful you didn't let me hit her." I reached out and squeezed his hand. "I was being irrational. I probably would've hurt her bad if you hadn't grabbed me."

He smiled. "So how about that dance?"

"I need to get a ticket first." I walked toward the ticket table, reached for my wallet, and realized it wasn't in any of my pockets. I closed my eyes and tried to picture getting out of my car. I didn't recall having it with me. Knots reformed in my stomach. "I left my wallet in the Jeep."

He pulled out his wallet and paid for my ticket.

"Thanks." I was relieved I didn't have to venture out to the parking lot yet.

"You're welcome." He took my hand and led me into the dance.

My senses were overloaded. Hip Hop, shouting voices, and stomping feet blended into a hellish cacophony. The nose-burning blend of designer perfume and drug store cologne made me sneeze. Hundreds of students were packed into the gym, dancing under an array of colored lights. Clusters of girls bounced while others tapped their feet and moved their lips.

After a few minutes of gawking and blinking, I finally forced my eyes to stay focused on one thing: Sam. She was trying to dance with a few of her friends, which meant she looked like a dying octopus. I lost my focus when José's hands slid around my waist and his lips brushed my ear. "Sam's busy; let's go dance by ourselves."

I nodded, wondering if Sister Karen had forgotten to talk to her.

José's hand closed around mine. He led me right to the center of the dance floor, where most of the couples were grinding, shielded from the chaperone's eyes by the bodies of other students. He pulled me close, but I held him at arm's length, shouting, "There are rules. I can't break them!"

José grinned. "Look around. The sisters are gone. Two teachers and one parent can't watch everyone."

I scanned the room and realized he was right. There wasn't a nun in sight. The music slowed down, and I let him pull my body right against his. I hadn't noticed the hollow space in my chest until it filled with the soft heat that poured out of him. Every one of my body's cells was vibrating faster than normal, making me feel as if I was becoming liquid. I rested my head on his shoulder and he kissed my forehead. Then I closed my eyes and let everything else fade away.

I told myself I was only going to dance with him once, but he didn't let go of me when the music sped up. I should have pushed him away when his body moved quicker and pressed harder against mine. His hands roamed all over my back and traced curves that my suit hid from his eyes but not his hands. I didn't stop my hands from exploring his shoulders and back, and I didn't stop my body from moving in rhythm with his.

We weren't supposed to be dancing this way, but currents of electric pleasure erupted everywhere he touched me. I wanted to be as close as I could with no space between us. Other people tried to get his attention, but he ignored them, refusing to take his hands or eyes away from me. The song changed to some pop/R&B blend, and the DJ announced it was dedicated to me from José.

I was impressed, for a minute, until I recognized that it was a song about two friends becoming lovers by getting drunk and having sex. Somewhere, deep down inside, part of me was hurt and offended. However, that part of me was losing a war against a more animalistic part that wanted to do exactly what the song said. "You know, you could have picked a much more romantic song to try to seduce me with. Something that tells me how I'm your world, how much you care."

He grinned and massaged my back as we continued to dance. "True, but I show you that every day. I've never told you how bad I want to sleep with you or to have your face be the first thing I see when I wake up in the morning. Sometimes I feel like we're standing on opposite sides of a raging river, and until last night, I thought that river was always going to be un-crossable. I want to swim in it with you, not stand stranded on different banks."

"What changed?"

The song ended and the music slowed down. José cupped his hand around my cheek. "A little bird told me you'd had a crush on me for years. I realized I had been an idiot to try to get over you. I decided not to waste any more time."

I could've left. I could've answered with words that would push him away and keep him safe from me but caught up in a blissful moment, the thought fled as quickly as it came.

I leaned in so my forehead was touching his. "Aren't you supposed to ask me out first, before you tell me you want to sleep with me, then work your way up from kissing?"

He smiled. "You're my best friend. You know me better than anyone else. Will you go out with me?"

Giggles gushed out of me. "That sounds like a marriage proposal. Are you always this dramatic when you want to get in someone's pants?"

He pulled away and stared with a deadpan expression. "Erin, I'm being serious. I want to be more than friends. I've wanted to for a long time."

"All right. We'll try 'more than friends,' but without the sex part."

A smile bloomed on his face, and before the song ended, our bodies were pressed together. I silenced the little voices telling me to reject him, and for the next five songs, all I was aware of was us blending together in a river of sound.

His phone buzzed. He tensed, let go of me, looked at the screen, muttered an apology, and raced out of the building, leaving me stunned and alone in a too-loud gym.

Without his touches keeping me distracted, I was cold and shaky. Green, white, blue, purple, and yellow lights flashed in time with a dubstep remix of a song I half recognized. I ducked just in time to avoid getting smacked by a dancer's flailing arm. Screeching giggles wounded my ears. A sneaker stomped on my foot. The moving bodies were a gauntlet between the bathroom and me. I darted under hands and ducked under arms until I froze in front of two doors: the girls and boys bathrooms.

I took a deep breath. A pack of beefy jocks from the freshmen lacrosse team trampled into the boys' room. I ducked into the girls' room and prayed it was empty.

I froze when I saw a blond girl in a neon pink dress that was missing most of its back section. I snuck behind Jenny and her friend, stealthily slipping into a faded pink stall. I listened to her while I peed.

"Did you see how José was dancing with that ugly bitch? I'm shocked the chaperones didn't kick them out."

Jenny's voice sent chills down my spine. My monsters roared. *She* was the ugly bitch, not me.

Her friend giggled. "I'm shocked he didn't notice you dancing with Will."

"I might sleep with him at the after party, but first, I want José to see me all over him. Maybe if he gets jealous enough, he'll ditch Erin."

"It's a good plan," said the friend. "You can sweeten the deal by showing him how you do things most girls are afraid of. Give it to him so good he never wants anyone else."

There was silence. I fidgeted with a piece of toilet paper, shredding it so I wouldn't shred skin: Jenny's or mine.

"Take a picture of me," said Jenny. "I'll show him what he's missing."

I dropped my pile of shredded toilet paper, took a step toward the door, and halted. I wanted to stomp on her phone and flush it down the toilet, but I couldn't. I focused on my breathing and dug my nails into my arms just enough to hurt but not hard enough to break skin, holding myself in check until the clicking of their heels grew quiet and vanished.

Once I knew they were gone, I left my stall, washed my shaking hands, and leaned on the sink, breathing and taking a much-needed break from the dance's chaos. Sweat made the make-up Sam had put on me run down my face—a muddy stream filled with fool's gold. Shadow and mascara burned my eyes. Makeup and freckles blended, darkening my skin until it matched José's. My green irises brightened to the color of an over-fertilized lawn and my ears grew pointed.

Fed up with the hallucinations, I closed my eyes, vowing to ask Grandpa about the stories in the morning. If he said they were false, I'd start researching withdrawal symptoms of the meds I had been on and disorders that caused hallucinations.

Satisfied with my plan, I tossed myself back out into the storm. The music was still blaring, but the crowds had thinned. The doors to the lobby were open, presenting a table full of snacks. I zigzagged to the table, hungry and dehydrated. My dance with José had been as strenuous as a sparring match with Mel, but more sexual than anything I had willingly done before.

The air was cooler in the lobby, and the white LEDs were stark in comparison to the dance floor's rainbow strobes. The music was dulled, but more people were talking.

"Hey, you okay?" Sam's voice effortlessly sliced through the babble.

"Yeah, I'm just tired and it's too crowded in here." I buried my hands in my pants pockets, wishing I had money stashed in them.

"It was crowded on the dance floor too."

"I was a little distracted out there." I looked around but couldn't spot José.

"Where is he now?"

I shrugged, hoping he wasn't in trouble or jerking off to the picture Jenny sent him. "On the phone or something. Can I borrow a few dollars? My wallet is in the car."

Sam handed me a pile of crumpled ones that I used to buy a sports drink and a couple of candy bars. I shoved scrumptious bites of chocolate covered caramel and wafer in my mouth while we walked outside, where the lack of noise was pure bliss.

I looked up the road, relieved to see the Camry was nowhere in sight. Clumps of chattering students were spread out across the lawn, but José was alone in the parking lot. His furrowed eyebrows, frowning mouth, and lack of words indicated that he was on the phone with his dad, probably getting yelled at for something stupid. I waved. He cracked a smile at me. Jenny didn't stand a chance of getting him back.

"So how was dancing?" Sam plopped down on the grass with her back against a tree.

"Nice." I sank to the ground across from her letting the memories warm my chest.

"Nice? That's all?"

I winked then told her about the inappropriate dancing and the way José asked me out. She looked like she wanted to puke by the time I finished.

"Romance is overrated. Promise me you won't get to attached him, all right?"

"We're friends." I watched José hang up the phone and jog toward us. "I'm already attached. The only thing that will change is the way we touch each other."

"Whatever you say," muttered Sam.

Every group José passed waved to him, but he didn't stop until he was sitting beside me.

"Mind if I join you two?"

"Not at all," I said at the same time Sam said, "You kind of already did."

"Sorry I ran out. It was my dad." José slid his arm around me.

"I figured. You looked miserable." I snuggled closer, listening to the air rushing in and out of his lungs.

"I have an idea," said Sam. A wicked grin spread across her face. "You owe me a staff lesson, and I'm getting bored with this dance. We should ditch and go to the beach so you can give me my first lesson in a dark, empty place where no one can watch me mess up."

I looked at Sam, José, and all the people hanging around outside the school. Normally, I preferred an empty beach to a crowded dance, but I felt safer here. José wouldn't try anything more risqué than dancing or a quick kiss, and Darth Trench Coat had been unwilling to follow us onto school property.

"I was going to invite you two to Will's party," said José. "His parents are away, and his brother got us a few cases of beer and some vodka. It's not the beach, but he lives on the bay."

"I am not going to that party." I glared while Sam laughed.

"You used to go to parties all the time, and if you weren't exaggerating, they were way wilder than anything going down at Will's."

"I was definitely exaggerating. You should come to the beach with us." The party was way more risky than chancing an encounter with Darth Trench Coat. Both potentially led to violence, but I'd feel a lot less guilty roughing up a sexual predator than Jenny Dunn. "I can either drive you home later tonight or early tomorrow."

José's face exploded with a smile. "I'd rather spend the night with you."

Sam mimed vomiting then stood up. "First one to the Jeep rides shotgun."

Chapter Eight

INCUBUS: A highly intelligent mid-level Demon that feeds off pain, rage, guilt, and other negative emotions. The Incubus requires intimate contact with females to properly absorb these emotions and the accompanying energy. Defensive strategies include speed, strength, excellent swordsmanship, and the ability to distract enemies by fueling their most lustful desires. It also uses its ability to induce lust as a method of seducing women so it can impregnate them with its hellish spawn. They are most effectively banished with the Latin phrase "Recesserimus ab hac terra. Totiens iam amplius mulieres cum lumbis tuis glaciem. Recedemus. Recedemus. Recedemus. In nomine Dei, et vade.
 —The Demon Hunter Lexicon, 1886

Crescent Beach's gravel parking lot was empty. I pulled in next to the weathered boardwalk, took off my shoes, and got out of the car. Sam grabbed the staffs out of the back while I ran down to the water, feet pounding through chilled, grainy heaven. The ocean was a mirror, reflecting a strip of silver moonlight. Only the smallest ripples rolled toward shore, breaking just shy of where I'd stopped. I took a step forward so the waves kissed my toes. A green Mermaid tail flickered then disappeared below the shimmering water.

"So how about that lesson?" Sam tossed the green staff toward me. Thankful for my quick reflexes, I snatched it out of the air.

I started by showing her how to hold it and had her mimic me as I ran through a few basic moves. José watched from a safe distance with a relaxed grin on his face. He looked ready to fall asleep, lying there on the sand, using his sweatshirt as a pillow, so I decided to get him involved.

"I think Sam needs to watch us go a few rounds so she can picture the moves in action," I said, walking over to him.

"I'd rather watch," yawned José.

I offered him a hand. "I did your kind of dancing at school. You'll do mine here."

He let me pull him up.

I turned my attention to Sam and her staff. "Can he use that for a few minutes?"

She reluctantly handed it over.

"Maybe you should stick to showing her moves. I'm not very good at this."

"José, I promise Sam won't say anything at school. Your secret is safe." I twirled my big stick in the air.

"My secret?"

"That you're as big a geek as me." I swung at his chest. He blocked without breaking eye contact.

Grinning, I tried to sweep him off his feet. He parried, and this time, he retaliated. I batted his attack away as easy as Mel had deflected mine the previous day and then went on the offense again.

"Now this is what I call dancing," I said, pounding him to the edge of the waves.

"The other kind hurts less."

"Stop being a baby." I swung toward his head, high enough to miss if he didn't block in time. My staff thunked against his as he blocked successfully.

We twisted, swung, jabbed, and jumped, dancing to the music of sparring. The clanging of wood on wood was a percussion; our lungs were trumpets. I saw a dozen ways to disarm him and knock him down, but his bruises and determination made me hesitate. José acted confident around his friends, but I knew he felt hardly a fraction of the arrogance he showed.

I could've blocked the swing he aimed at my thigh, but I let him hit me. Pain blossomed where oak collided with flesh. I dropped my staff as I went down, grabbed a big arm full of bladderwort, rolled inside his guard, and swung my legs so he fell. Before he even hit the sand, I stuffed the seaweed up his shirt. With a roaring laugh, he pulled it out and tried to dump it down mine. I ran out of his reach but didn't try too hard to stay ahead of him. He tackled me, but I twisted and flipped him so I was on top.

"You two are disgusting. Just bang and get it out of your systems," said Sam, snatching my keys out of my pocket and replacing them with a condom. I jumped up and glared. I would have chewed her out for putting that in my pocket, but I didn't want José to get ideas. "Bring me chocolate when you come back. My stash is in the center console."

She laughed and gave me a look hinting she knew things I didn't, which was true. She had a lot more experience with both boys and girls. It made me nervous because José did too. The closer he got, the shakier I became. Mel and I had sparred much longer and harder; I knew I had plenty of energy to defend myself if I needed to. José was my friend, so hopefully, that wouldn't be necessary. I could tell him I wasn't ready, and he'd stop without a fight. We could both keep our impulses under control.

His hands slid from my waist to my stomach as he drew me close enough for my back and shoulders to touch his chest. He rested his chin on my shoulder and whispered, "Thank you."

"For what?" I took a few slow breaths to calm my confused body, which was quivering with fear and excitement. José's chest was a hot brick oven transforming my icy body into weightless goop. His hands ignited a fire in my stomach that spread to my toes and all the way up to my throat. The flames kissed my protests so they evaporated before they reached my mouth. It was terrifying bliss; for all intents and purposes, we were alone. Sam thought she was doing me a favor.

"For the dances—both of them. The second—the 'dance' with the quarterstaffs— was good; I did well, even if you did let me win. For a minute, I was actually good at something that mattered. I needed to feel that."

"José, you're good at a lot of things." I turned around. "You were MVP on the soccer team. You have a high GPA. Heck, you're the only reason I'm passing Spanish and Biology."

"You'd do fine on your own in Bio if I wasn't distracting you." His hand slid up my spine, making my whole body shiver. It glided over my neck and stopped on my cheek. "Still, those things don't matter. Not really."

"What are you talking about? School matters. We can't get anywhere without it."

He shook his head, closed his eyes, and pressed his forehead against mine. He hugged me tight. I expected him to start kissing me, to start trying to do what Sam left us alone to "get out of our system." He didn't. He let go and sank down in the sand with his knees up and his fingers digging through his hair.

I sat down next to him and rubbed his back. "What's going on?"

He looked up at me with his jaw clenched and his lips frowning. "I need to tell you something."

"Then tell me."

"I'm afraid to. You might not like me anymore. You might hate me."

"José, you tell me everything. *Everything*: People you hook up with, parties, and problems with your dad."

He shook his head. "Not everything. There are some things I've kept from you, and they're big."

"There are things you don't know about me too," I said, tilting his chin up so I was looking in his eyes, "but I suppose if we are serious about this more than friends thing, we'll have to spill all our secrets, sooner or later."

He shook his head. "This is different. It will change things."

I waited, afraid his words were going to make me regret my decision to say yes to that dance. I watched without blinking, even when my eyes burned and my vision blurred. The green gem was back on his head again, and suddenly, I realized that I should tell him about the hallucinations. I opened my mouth, struggling to find words, when he spoke again.

"I know you tried to kill yourself two summers ago. Mel told me."

I backed away as betrayal and anger snaked through my gut. "Mel? Were you talking about her last night, the person you really liked? Did you sleep with my cousin?"

"No. God no!" José screwed up his face and then he burst into laughter. It took him a while to catch his breath. "Erin, I've been in love you with since I was thirteen years old. I messed around with a lot of people trying to get over you, but never your cousin. Never anyone you were close to."

"Then why did she tell you?"

He took my hand. "We talk. She's a mentor, the big sister I never had, and she was worried when you moved up here and you still weren't talking to her, so she called me to check on you."

"Is that all you wanted to tell me?"

He watched me for a few seconds, brushing my cheek with his hands. The air between us was charged like it had been in the hallway. I moved closer, so our faces were merely inches apart, and ran my fingertips across the gem on his head. "José, today in the hall, did we actually talk about that gem? Did you tell me I knew what it was?"

He nodded. The tips of our noses brushed together. My face tingled and his hands were back on me, one on my thigh, and the other on my back. "Can you see it now?"

I nodded, and this time, when our noses touched, so did our lips. He pulled away. "That's what I need to tell you, but I don't know where to start."

We just looked into each other's eyes. The air around us was freezing, but between us, it was burning hot. I couldn't wait for him to talk. I didn't care what he was going to say. All that mattered was right now, getting as physically close as we could. We collided as our lips pressed together and he rolled onto me. He was heavy. Too much of him pressed down on too much of me. His hands ran up my sides and inched toward my chest. Chills short-circuited my brain.

Cold fear flooded my body. The last time I had kissed someone, it had been at night, on a deserted beach similar to this one. That boy had plunged his hand through the tux I wore to prom, searching for boobs hidden beneath layered fabric. Before saying no out loud, I had punched him in the face, breaking his nose. I absolutely could not let myself do that to José.

"Stop! Stop! Stop!" I sat up wriggling away from José, but it was too late. My stomach cramped up and my throat tightened as a wave of remembered emotion washed over me: an instance of feeling powerless crushed by a wave of pure rage leaving me stranded with sickening guilt.

"Erin? What's wrong?" José's voice was distant.

"Mel didn't tell you everything." I shivered and turned my eyes back to him. Shadowy vines surrounded us, retreating like the emotions José's hands had evoked. Their appearance after the small panic attack supported the "developing an additional mental illness" theory more than the "all the stories are true" theory.

"What secret is she keeping for you?" José's voice was quiet and gentle.

"I'd rather not talk about it." I didn't want to talk or think of what happened that night, and I certainly did not want a repeat of it to happen with him, tonight, on this beach. "We should go find Sam."

"We should talk first. I—"

"We can talk another time. I want to find Sam." I dug my phone out of my pocket and picked up the staff I had left lying on the sand. My phone was off. I hit the power button on the side. Nothing happened. "José, can I use your phone? Mine is dead."

"Mine too," he said, staring at his iPhone with wide eyes. He scanned the beach, as if he expected to be attacked by some psychopath because his phone was dead. "We should get back to your car. Hopefully Sam didn't go too far."

It only took a couple minutes to get back to the boardwalk. Sam was at the end of it, leaning against a sign informing beachgoers of the fragile nature of the sand dunes. Shadows surrounded her as she smiled and twirled her hair, apparently enjoying a conversation with Darth Trench Coat.

"Oh crap." José grabbed my hand. "Tell me that isn't your stalker."

"It is. You know him?"

"Yes."

"Describe him." I squeezed José's sweaty hand.

"His skin is as white as death. His eyes are black holes. His teeth look like a shark's," growled José.

"Then why isn't Sam freaking out?"

"Do you know what the man is?"

I stared at José. He might look different and he might know things most people didn't, but he was still the same person. In school, when I first saw this new version of him, a teacher had seen the regular José and scolded the both of us. If he could mask his appearance from some people, then Darth Trench Coat could too. The Demonic version of Darth Trench Coat we both saw was real. My heart raced, but my chest was light because I knew I wasn't hallucinating. I didn't need to add a new symptom to my list of existing psychological problems. There was more truth to Grandpa's stories than some obscure lesson or moral.

"Erin, do you know?" he asked a little louder.

I looked right into José's eyes. "It's some kind of Demon, isn't it?"

He let out a slow sigh and somehow seemed lighter. "Yeah, an Incubus. It has a glamour on so Sam can't see how it looks." His voice was calm and relaxed, free from shock. He'd seen this stuff before.

"You can see through the glamour because of the stone thing on your head, but why can I see it? I don't have a magic gem on my brow." In Grandpa's stories, glamour was something most supernatural creatures used to hide their true nature from humans. Hunters who were fully human needed a gem called an Elf Stone to see through glamour. The ones who were part Elf usually had True Sight and didn't need an Elf Stone.

However, Grandpa had never told me a story about an Incubus. I'd read a fantasy novel in which one had the ability to steal energy from women by touching them. Generally, fantasy novels had more tame versions of creatures than Grandpa's stories, so I doubted this Incubus was conflicted about its nature like the one in the book. If it had anything in common with Grandpa's Demons, it was going to either eat Sam alive, feed off her emotions, or some combination of the two.

José didn't answer me. I lost patience. Worry for Sam's well-being overcame the more logical data-gathering response, and I took off toward Sam and the Demon.

"Erin, wait!" José was right behind me, and I wasn't sure if he wanted me to slow down or stop. I ran until I was a few feet away from the Incubus.

"Hey, Darth Trench Coat, why the hell are you stalking us?"

"Erin, chill," said Sam. "This is Vincent. He wanted to introduce himself to me earlier. He was too shy, so he followed us. Isn't that sweet?"

Vincent the Demon creep responded by opening his toothy maw and letting out a laugh that sounded more like a dying frog than a noise that would come out of a human's mouth.

Sam continued talking, twirling her staff through the air with more grace than I had ever seen her move. "He invited us to go back to his house to check out his library. He has a whole bunch of cats."

"Sam, we're leaving. Now."

She grinned. "Seeing as I have your keys, I don't think that's going to happen."

"Samantha Willow, give Erin their keys back," commanded José.

"Do not listen to them," said the Demon, twining skeletal fingers through Sam's hair. "Now, Erin and José, I advise you two to do exactly as I say and come back to my lair."

"What did you do to her?" I shouted.

The Incubus bared its teeth.

"Erin, watch out." José pushed me to the ground as Sam's purple staff swung where my head had been seconds before.

I cringed at the thud of wood whacking muscle. José doubled over. I rolled to my feet, raising my staff into a defensive position just in time to block Sam's next attack.

"What did you do to her?" I asked again.

In the stories, if a hunter asked a Demon or Faerie a question three times in a row, it was compelled to answer. I snuck a glance at the Incubus. "What did you do to her?"

Sam swept the staff at my knees. I blocked.

"I seduced her and bound her to the Puppet Master, exactly what I will do to you and your pathetic boyfriend," said the Incubus.

"The Puppet Master?" I parried a blow meant to crack my skull.

"It's controlling her. I have to banish it." José spun around a few times then ran toward the parking lot.

Pain exploded at the base of my neck. I stumbled, growled, and whipped my staff around toward Sam's ribs. She blocked and continued swinging at me with a skill I didn't expect from someone who had never held a quarterstaff before today. But then again, Sam wasn't the one in control. Grandpa had told me stories about Puppet Masters. They were Demons capable of twining dark energy around people's limbs and controlling them like a marionette. They were skilled fighters but seldom ventured to earth unless another Demon commanded them.

Sam's eyes were unfocused and her head hung limp as her arms and feet wove attack after attack. In spite of the Puppet Master's ability, Sam's limbs were weak from lack of exercise, and her body could only move so fast. The next time she tried to break my legs, I leaped over the staff, kicking her stomach before I landed. We both stumbled, but I recovered quicker and disarmed her. As soon as the staff clattered to the wood planks, I lunged forward, hit her in the head with the palm of my hand, and caught her unconscious body before it hit the ground, hoping she'd agree that a concussion was better than being a Demon's puppet.

I lowered Sam to the sand. I looked for José and found him grappling with a shadow on the other end of the boardwalk. I moved toward them, but a chill ran up my legs. A glance over my shoulder revealed the Incubus swinging Sam's staff just in time for me to jump and avoid a bone-breaking blow to the back of my knees.

As soon as I landed, I swung at his skull. He blocked with a speed Sam couldn't muster and tried to break my ribs. The impact of his staff on mine shook my whole body, but I was used to that kind of force from my sparring matches with Mel.

It took all my effort and concentration to fend off his attacks, leaving me little space for a proper offense. I hadn't been wrong in my assessment of him when I first saw him following me. I tired before he did and soon, he knocked the wind out of me with a blow to my abdomen.

"Submit," he hissed.

"My cousin hits harder than you," I snarled, already planning my next move.

He did his dying frog laugh, and while he was distracted, I swung my staff high and smacked him in the head. The blow would have cracked any human's skull. He hissed and attacked with more speed and strength than he had shown before. Each time I blocked, my whole body shook from the impact. Friction was burning the skin off my hands where I held the staff. I miscalculated. His staff struck my hip, evoking a sharp pain that shot down to my heels.

"How do you feel now? Yield and I will not cause you any more pain."

This time, I laughed. Pain didn't make me weak; it reawakened a blaze that had been mere embers for the past two years. Rage surged through every inch of me, fortifying my muscles and focusing my attention. I matched the speed of his attacks. I dented his perfectly round skull. I made his knee cave in. I hit his ribs so hard they popped out of his skin. He had more ribs than a human, and they were thinner and rounder than the ones from the fake skeleton displayed in the biology lab. I hoped that meant I had done a lot of damage.

"That rage is delicious," he hissed. "I need you."

Apparently, broken ribs didn't stop Demons from breathing.

I lunged forward, whipping the staff at his throat, but found myself slowed by a cloud of invisible pins and needles. The more I resisted, the harder they poked me. At first, I wasn't sure if the needles were magic or panic. They made my skin itch so bad I almost stopped fighting to claw it open with my nails and let the buzzing out. I tightened my grip on my staff so my nails reached around to the other part of my hand, but déjà vu kicked in and saved me from cutting mid-fight. I had dreamed this last night. With a deep breath, I mimicked my actions from the dream and pulled the pins and needles into me, willed them to travel downward and burst out of my leg as I aimed a flying kick at the Incubus. My foot collided with the Incubus' iceberg abdomen.

He turned translucent. I whacked his temple with my staff, and his flickering body crumpled. I stabbed down. The staff sunk into his semi-corporeal gut, pinning him to the sand.

"Take that, bitch," I snarled.

The shadow José had been grappling now resembled a bleached Gumby. It was pressing a knife down to José's throat. He had a hand wrapped around the Puppet Master's wrist, but it was only slowing the creature, not stopping it.

I lunged forward and tackled the Demon off him. Its body was frigid, freezing my skin as we rolled on the gravel. It came out on top, but with a twist of my hips, I rolled again until I had it pinned beneath my knees. I pummeled the Puppet Master with punch after punch. I let two years of pent-up frustration, fear, and rage fuel each blow as I pulverized the Demon's face into a slushy blob. I kept punching long after it stopped moving, vaguely aware of José shouting the same Latin phrase over and over again: "Recesserimus ab hac terra. Totiens iam amplius mulieres cum lumbis tuis glaciem. Recedemus. Recedemus. Recedemus. In nomine Dei, et vade."

The Demon vanished, and my fist hit gravel with enough force to shred the skin of my knuckles. I watched blood bloom around bluish-purple skin and form tiny pools in the dirt beneath me. José and Sam spoke in the background. Apparently, the last thing she remembered was declining "Vincent's" invitation to go for a walk. She asked José what happened. He lied, telling her he saw the man punch her. He claimed I chased after them and fought the man, but he got away. Sam asked if I was okay.

José laughed. "Are you kidding? Erin *loves* punching people. This is probably the happiest they've been since before they moved up here."

"That's not true," I said, finally finding my voice. Sam was sitting up, and José was grinning until he took a good look at me. He ran toward me and hugged me. "You are okay, right?"

"My hands look like I was using an icicle as a punching bag."

"I take it this was your first time punching a Demon?" he whispered, warming my hands with his.

"Yeah. Also, the first time I don't feel guilty about a fight. I'm calm, but I don't think I should be calm. I fought and killed two Demons. Yesterday, I didn't believe Demons were real."

José pressed my hands against his chest. "You're strong. You're calm because you're finally doing what you're supposed to be doing."

"Maybe." I squeezed José's hands, wondering if he was right. I was focused during the fight. I had felt alive and powerful, but I'd also been angry and out of control. If I'd been in such a rampage from the start, Sam could have gotten hurt bad. "How is Sam?"

"She's confused but okay. Do you have a first aid kit?" José let go of one hand but clung to the other as he led me over to my car.

"Two, actually. One from Mom and one from Grandpa. No clue where in the Jeep they are."

José unlocked the door and began searching while I stumbled over to Sam. My head was wobbly and my legs were shaking, but I hadn't felt this relaxed in a long time

"Thanks, Erin." Sam's voice was faint and breathy.

I put my hand on her shoulder, more to steady myself than comfort her. "We should get you to a hospital. You probably have a concussion."

"No way!" She blinked. Her eyes focused. Her voice got stronger. "Mom will flip if she finds out I was at the beach and not just at your house. I'm still technically grounded for skipping school a few weeks ago. She only let me out because you're such a goody-two-shoes. Plus, José checked me for a concussion. They train soccer jocks to do that stuff because they're always getting hit in the head with balls."

"He's not a doctor, and you took a bad hit to head. What if your brain is bleeding?" I said.

Sam rolled her eyes. Her lips moved, but all I heard was myself screeching as alcohol wipes stung on my scraped knuckles.

"You could've warned me," I hissed.

"Let's get back to your house." José grinned and started walking toward the Jeep's driver side door.

"What do you think you're doing?" I asked as he climbed into the front seat.

"Driving. You're still kind of wobbly."

"I'm fine."

"Erin—"

"Nobody drives the Jeep but me!" I stared at him with my arms crossed until he crawled over the passenger seat. I turned the key and hummed along with the bear-song of the Jeep's engine.

Chapter Nine

Elves are among the most wondrous creatures on the planet. Their magic allows them to look through time, move faster than sound, and manipulate raw energy. They can bend light to change what you see, make water freeze, and melt ice, all with the power of their minds. They can harness the raw power of a lightning storm, but when it comes to love, they are just as vulnerable as any human.

—An excerpt from Seamus Evanstar's personal journal, written in 1972 and confined to archives after his son's death

I hit the light switch. Bessie was there, wagging her tail and licking dried blood off my hands. I scratched her neck and let her outside, watching the shadows to make sure none of them morphed into dog-eating Demons. She did her business promptly and returned to the house without incident. Once we were all inside, I locked the deadbolt, wondering if doors stopped Demons. The hunters in Grandpa's stories put protective fields of magic around their homes to keep Demons out. I looked at José, wishing he saw the question in my eyes. Had he already put some kind of ward around the house? Were we safe? I needed to get away from Sam so I could bombard José with questions.

"Hello? Erin? Anyone in there?" Sam waved her hand in front of my face.

"Yeah." I shook my head.

I was home, behind thick walls, with Bessie, who'd hear anything approach the house. I was safe. I took a mental inventory of what weapons were nearby. The two swords in my room were dull, but there was a rifle in the basement. There was a pocketknife under my mattress and steak knives in the kitchen.

"Are you just going to stand there and stare off into space all night?" asked Sam.

"No. I'm going to get a snack." Snacks made everything better. Food would stop the growling in my stomach and steady my spinning head. Then I could find an excuse to get José alone and have him answer my questions.

"Good. Get me one too," said Sam.

Bessie, who was currently getting a belly rub from José, barked her agreement.

We went to the kitchen, where Sam and I devoured cookies, chips, and ice cream. José watched from the doorway. Bessie did her best to steal bites when we weren't looking.

"Do you want something?" I asked José.

"Fruit? Or salad?" He stepped into the room.

"There are both in the fridge. Help yourself."

I returned my attention to shoving cookies in my mouth until he placed two glasses of water in front of Sam and me. "You both should have something to drink in case you're dehydrated."

I looked at him funny but didn't reject the water. Sam sipped hers while I gulped mine. José refilled my glass, absent-mindedly rubbing my back.

"I'm exhausted." Sam looked down at an empty bowl of ice cream. "You're still okay with me sleeping over, right?"

"Of course. Do you want me to get the guest room ready for you?"

"Sure." She yawned her way to the living room, plopped down on the couch and turned on the TV.

"I'm going to go find some blankets upstairs. I'll be right back," I said, holding eye contact with José for a good minute after I stopped talking. I jerked my head at the stairs and walked toward them without looking back.

No feet made the stairs creak behind mine. Disappointed he didn't get my hint, I continued into my mom's room, picked up the house phone, and tried calling both Mel and Grandpa. No one answered, so I emptied blankets out of Mom's closet.

"How are you feeling?" asked José as I emerged with my arms full.

I jumped, dropping them all. "I didn't hear you come up."

He shrugged. "We need to talk."

"We do," I said, even though conversations beginning with that phrase never ended well. "Are we safe here?"

"Of course. Mel has so many wards around this house that it could survive a nuclear attack."

"What does she have to do with wards?"

"You really are clueless." José barked out a nervous laugh. "And I thought she was the one who taught you how to fight Demons."

"Mel taught me how to fight Mel." I stifled a snarl. "She never said Demons were real. Grandpa told us stories about them, but I assumed they were fictional. I asked Mel if she thought they were real, but she never gave me a straight answer."

"They weren't fiction, at least, not all of them. I'm guessing that's how you knew the Rule of Three?"

I nodded, struggling to focus on the stories and not how Mel had been so oblique on Thursday. "The hunters used that trick often."

"Okay. And is that also where you learned to slow your perception of time?"

"My what?" I asked.

"Never mind."

"What? You have to tell me now."

He shook his head and smiled. "Some hunters can slow down how they perceive time, so they can move super fast. It generally isn't something people do by accident. I suppose you also turned its power against it by accident?"

"I dreamed that part last night." All the things José was telling me made sense in the world of Grandpa's stories, even if some of his terms were different. I knew the pins and needles feeling had been the Demon's magic. Most of the hunters in Grandpa's stories could've turned that power against the Demon if they felt it in time.

"What do you mean you dreamed it?" José edged closer to me until he put his hands on my shoulders.

"I don't know. I have weird dreams. Sometimes they happen. Mel thinks I'm some kind of prophet." And if she knew about Demons and how to put wards on houses, then maybe she was right.

I shook like a cartoon egg ready to hatch. "If Demons are real, does that mean other things are too?"

"What kinds of things?"

My breath caught in my throat, but I still forced the words out. "I've been seeing Pixies and Mermaids since I stopped taking ADHD meds last month. I thought they were hallucinations...some kind of withdrawal symptom."

"Those definitely aren't hallucinations." José picked up the blankets I'd dropped and piled them on the bed. He was smiling when he turned around. "I see them too. Pixies help us watch for Demons. The Mermaids try not to get involved with Demon hunting, but my dad likes to get involved with them."

"Who is us, and what do you mean by 'involved'?"

"By us, I mean the Demon hunters. When it comes to Dad, 'involved' can be anything from researching their biology to 'researching their biology'." José put his hands on my hips. The contact and the look on his face hinted that he wanted to "research my biology."

"Have you seen anything else?"

"Mel," I said as my heart fluttered. "She glowed."

"She does that." José laughed. He was close enough now that I felt his chest brush up against mine every time it filled with air. Part of me wanted to pull him closer so his body would fill me with warmth as it had at the dance. Part of me wanted to push him away because we were alone in a bedroom.

"Why does she glow?" I froze, torn between what my body wanted and my brain feared.

"I think you need to ask her that." He closed the small space between us.

Before I told him she was ignoring my calls, his lips were on mine. His hands roamed up and down my back. It felt good, so I tried not to think about where else they might go if he kept kissing me. I used his hips to steady my hands and tried to focus on how soft his lips were and how solid his body was. It worked until his hands slipped below my belt. The muscles in my chest seized up. My arms moved before my mouth did and he flew halfway across the room and crashed into my mom's bed.

What did I do?

"Erin, what the hell?" he shouted, clambering to his feet. His hands were clutching the area above his hip where I pushed him.

I was breathing too fast to say anything. Yes, I panicked. Yes, I pushed him off of me. I didn't want to push him across the room. I had simply needed space, a few inches of space, so I could talk. But I was panicking and my arms and brain didn't communicate. I acted like a monster. Again.

"What's going on?" He walked toward me.

I wrapped my arms around myself and backed away, half hoping he'd run away and never talk to me again, but also wishing for him to stay.

He paused. "Why did you push me?"

"I...I...wanted you to stop," I said between gasps. How do I explain that?

His shoulders sagged.

"You could have just told me. I promise I would've stopped."

"But words...they don't always work right." I leaned my head against the wall, squeezed my eyes shut and tugged my spiked hair. I wanted to rake my nails down my cheeks until they bled to punish myself for what I'd done and for trying to make excuses. I resisted. I took deep breaths until the anxiety was replaced with an embarrassment so deep it made me want to puke. I wanted José to leave so I wouldn't have to face him.

I listened to him take big, deliberate breaths. His feet made the floor creak as he walked around the room. The sheets and blankets swished gently. By the time I worked up the courage to turn around, he was sitting on my mom's bed with everything I had dropped neatly folded and stacked. His head was bent over and his fingers were digging through his curly back hair. When he looked up at me, he had the same fear in his eyes that he got when his dad was angry. "Are you going to tell me why you freak out whenever I kiss you?"

"Not tonight. Are you going to break up with me for hurting you?"

"Do you want me too?"

"No. But you should." Agreeing to be more than friends might not have been my best decision, but I was pretty sure it would be the end of our friendship if we broke up. I liked him, and I was attracted to him, but I was also afraid for him.

The silence grew heavy and painful. Eventually, he walked toward me until he was at arm's length, slowly reached out, picked up my hand and pressed his lips to my fingers. "I'm not going to break up with you, but please don't hurt me again. Enough people do that already."

A glance at his broken nose made my insides reel. This morning, I had been so protective of him, but it didn't stop me from becoming the type of person he needed protection from.

"I'm sorry." I squeezed his hand. "Please try not to do things to me without my permission. Just because we're a couple doesn't mean we have to have sex. Ask before you do anything. Always."

He nodded, but before he spoke, the house phone rang. Curious who was calling so late, I walked over to the phone and saw it was Mel. I picked it up right away and launched into a rant:

"Mel? Seriously? You knew the whole time we were talking yesterday—you knew what I was seeing, and you didn't tell me. Seriously. You were freaking glowing, like you walked through a nuclear reactor or something. I thought I was—"

"Erin!" she screamed into the phone. I nearly dropped it because it hurt my ears so much. "Will you please calm down a minute?"

"How come I haven't been able to reach you all day?"

"I didn't have access to a phone. I just saw all of your gazillions of missed calls and texts. I have a whole bunch from Mom and Mike too. I called you first."

"Good. Why did you lie to me all my life?"

"Not telling you isn't a lie."

"Debatable. Why didn't you tell me?"

"Because I couldn't. I made a vow not to, and I couldn't break it. Did José explain everything?"

"Sort of. He told me a few things, but we kind of got distracted." I glanced over and saw him watching with a bemused half smile, and then I walked out of the room. When I was out of earshot, I told Mel what happened the two times I tried to kiss him. As mad as I was, Mel was the only one I could truly vent to when it came to the ghosts from sophomore year.

"You should just tell José. If you don't, it'll drive a wedge between the two of you."

When I didn't respond, Mel kept talking. "What did he tell you about the supernatural world?"

"Only that Demons, Pixies, and Mermaids are real. Of course, that was after I impaled an Incubus with a quarterstaff and broke a Puppet Master's face with my fists," I said, relieved that she chose to change the subject instead of forcing relationship advice on me.

Mel laughed so hard she hyperventilated. "I guess it was worth kicking your ass every week."

"I thought I was losing my mind. I-I don't even know what I am anymore. Demons are real. I'm good at fighting them. You glow for God's sake!"

"We'll talk tomorrow, all right? Grandpa and I will explain everything. I promise, but I have to go now. I've got a lot of stuff to do."

"Like what?"

"I can't tell you. Bye, Erin. I love you."

"Mel, you can't just go," I said, but she had already ended the call.

I chucked my phone at my pillow then collapsed onto my mattress, punching it a few dozen times before I flopped over. Tears leaked out the sides of my eyes, but I refused to outright cry. I stared at the two katanas that hung above my bookcase. Their emerald sheaths were ornately adorned with mysterious symbols. I recalled José explaining what they meant, but I hadn't been focused enough to remember. What I did know was that the blades they housed were dull. However, I suspected they'd be sharp soon enough.

Chapter Ten

It is advisable to keep a firm hand when training young hunters. Demons feed off pain and fear, so we must train our next generation to be as immune to such feelings as any human can be. However, a man must be cautious that he does not cross the fine line between discipline and abuse. A boy who fears his father and teacher will become the game, not the hunter.

> —A Master Hunter's Handbook, secretly published in 1887

Bubbling laughter filled my ears as I walked down the stairs. The couch was pulled out and covered with blankets. Sam was curled up under a quilt, looking toward the kitchen where José was pouring chocolate pancake batter into a frying pan.

"Erin, did you actually eat pancakes that had clams in them?" asked Sam.

"They were quahogs," said José and I simultaneously.

"It's Mel's fault," I continued. "I was twelve, and she was sixteen, so everything she suggested sounded awesome." At twelve, I still thought Mel, and everything she did, was perfect. I trusted her with every secret. She was the first to know I wasn't a girl, the one I whispered to about my first kiss too, and the one who listened to me rant on how much I hated myself. All the while, I never realized she was hiding the true nature of reality itself.

I ambled into the kitchen. Dropping onto the chair and sipping the water I'd left on the table, I stared at grains in the table's wood, listened to the pancakes sizzle, and wondered what else Mel had hidden from me. José's fingertips brushed my shoulders. I leaned into his touch. Before he returned his focus to cooking, he placed a tiny kiss on my cheek. I hadn't ruined things quite yet.

We spent the next couple of hours eating pancakes and watching ninja-challenge game shows since they were the only decent things on TV at 1 a.m. Sam fell asleep buried under blankets on the pullout couch while José and I shared the armchair, sitting so our legs and hands were barely touching. No one spoke. Eventually, I lost interest in the program and my mind wandered to the day's less pleasant events.

"José," I whispered, squeezing his fingers. "Are you still awake?"

His head twitched. "Yeah. We should probably make the guest bed if you want me to sleep there."

I stood and helped him out of the chair. Once we were in the hall upstairs, I asked, "Is the Incubus dead?"

José shook his head. "You can't kill things that aren't alive. Were there banishing spells in your Grandpa's stories?"

Dozens of stories played in my head. "Hunters said them once the Demons were incapacitated. It made the remains disappear."

"That's what the Latin words I said at the beach were. I got all the words right, but my attention was split between too many things. They'll both be back soon."

"How soon?" I opened the door to the over-glorified closet we called a guest bedroom. It was barely big enough to fit the desk and twin bed that inhabited it, leaving very little room for José and me to maneuver as we made the bed.

"A week at best, a day at the worst." José unfolded the fitted sheet and began stretching the purple fabric over the mattress. "We're safe here, even if they come back sooner. Nothing will get past Mel's wards."

I questioned him as we made the bed, but his answers confirmed things I knew from Grandpa's stories. Most Demons were as cold as ice, not hot and fiery like they're portrayed in popular myths. European Elves were as fair-skinned as the ones in *Lord of the Rings*, but American Elves were as diverse as the continent's population. Winter Elves could be as serene as feathery snow falling from the sky, or as angry as a blizzard. Summer Elves were passionate, hot like the summer sun, and when enraged, they carried the power of a hurricane.

Pixies spied for Demon hunters as long as they were paid with ample chocolate. Mermaids had no official alliance, but that didn't prevent individuals from aiding hunters or Demons.

It was real, and I wasn't surprised.

Grandpa's stories had taught me so much about the supernatural word that it seemed pointless to keep asking José questions, but I kept on asking because those questions were easier than ones that really needed answering: who else in my family knew this? How involved were they? *Why* did they hide it from me?

When we were done making the bed, José perched on the edge and stared at me with a terrifying intensity.

"Well, goodnight," I mumbled, slowly backing away. "I'll see you in the morning."

"Please, Erin, wait." He snatched my hand. "I don't want to be alone."

I stared into his eyes.

"Please just sit with me for a few minutes," he continued. "I promise I won't kiss you or anything. I won't even touch you at all if you don't want me to."

"Okay." I sat down on the bed with my back to the wall. He sat beside me, a few inches away. I squeezed his hand. "Was there something specific you wanted to tell me?"

"Lots of things, but I don't want to talk about them right now. I don't want to be lonely."

"Lonely?" I stared at him with my head tilted, suddenly more curious about how the boy who was friends with everyone at school ever felt alone.

He leaned his head against the wall and closed his eyes. "I can be with Will or at a party with twenty other kids, and I still feel alone. They haven't seen the things I've seen. They don't know what I know, and if I told them, they'd think I was crazy or on drugs."

I leaned over and pressed my lips into his smooth, curly hair. It smelled like beach sand peppered with cinnamon.

"It's not that way with you." He yawned. "Never has been, even when you didn't know. It was hard not to tell you the past few weeks. I kept seeing you stare at things no one else saw."

"Why didn't you tell me?" A sense of betrayal returned. I understood him keeping it a secret if he thought I wouldn't believe him, but if he knew I was seeing things, telling me the truth was the right thing to do.

"I promised your Grandpa I wouldn't. I told him I saw you staring at Pixies, but he didn't believe me. He said you were probably just spacing out."

"And you listened to him?" I sat up so I was looking down on José, and what he was telling me sunk in. It hadn't clicked when Mel and I were talking, but it did now. And I was pissed. "Wait a minute. *You* know my Grandpa through Demon hunting."

"Yes." José buried his face in his hands.

I stood up and paced around. "You, Grandpa, and Mel are all up to your eyes in this crap and thought letting me think I was hallucinating was better than telling me the truth?"

"Well, you never actually told anyone what you were seeing." He stood up and faced me. "What if he had been right? What if it had been a coincidence there was a Pixie on the bush you were staring at? Maybe I was so sick of having to keep it secret from you I was imagining you seeing things, so I'd have an excuse to tell you? If I was wrong, I would've driven you away, not pulled you closer. I couldn't risk it. I need you in my life; just friends is better than nothing."

There was nothing to say to make him feel better, so I hugged him. His body was tense, but I didn't let go. I hugged him tighter until his hands were on my back and his muscles relaxed. I tucked him into bed like he was little kid, not a bulky, Demon-hunting-soccer jock. Then I sat on the edge and ran my hands through his hair. "I'm only one room over. You're not alone."

"Goodnight, Erin," he said with a sad smile.

"Goodnight," I whispered and then walked down the dark hall to my room.

I changed into pajamas and climbed into bed. My sheets were cold. I found myself missing the steady sound of José's heart beating and his stomach's deep rumbling. I wanted his body to be my personal space heater and his breath to tickle my neck.

I rolled onto my stomach, cocooning myself in blankets. I whispered Hail Marys, Our Fathers, and pleas for guidance. The previous night, my mind and dreams had been chaos. I needed tonight to be different. I wanted to know what was going to happen with José and me, but I also wanted to know more about the Demons that seemed to be hunting me. I needed to pick one focus; otherwise, my dreams weren't going to make sense. I fell asleep before I decided.

THE SUN BEAT down on my scrawny thirteen-year-old shoulders. I threw a small white pill into still water.

"I hope that wasn't important." José plopped down next to me.

I shook my head. "I need it to sit still and pay attention, but it upsets my stomach. You can have my sandwich if you don't tell anyone I didn't take the pill."

He scooted closer; his leg touched mine. "Eat. I promise I won't tell."

The pleasant memory was ripped away as my shoulders filled out and my stomach inflated. The beach faded to a sterile hospital room where I was squeezing José's hand. My body throbbed inside and out, inflamed with the worst pain I'd ever felt.

The room faded to black and the dreams became rapid flashes:

A brick wall knocked the air out of my lungs. I rolled to the left, gasping as a fist flew toward my face.

I sat on a thin carpet, eating chocolate bars with Sam as older people lined up to look in a casket.

Grandpa sped down the highway in his wood-paneled Wagoneer. Rain poured from the dark sky. Lightning flashed. A wet woman in a long raincoat stumbled in front of his car and burst into flames. Grandpa swerved. Smoke rose from the car when it finally came to a stop upside down in a gully.

Dr. Estrella sunk to his knees while the ocean roiled

behind him.

Cold and darkness swallowed me whole. Clammy hands grabbed my legs, trying to pull me toward the sea. I flailed and kicked, trying to break free. I was freezing. More hands grabbed me, restraining me so I could only twitch. I had no control. I couldn't fight. I couldn't feel. I was too cold. I screamed even as my ribs strained against the hands.

"ERIN!"

Hot hands touched my forehead and cheeks. Someone shook me, said my name, and begged me to wake up. I stopped screaming and took a slow breath. Warm air filled my lungs. I opened my eyes. The light was on, so I squinted, forcing my room into focus. José was kneeling on my bed with his hands on my shoulders. "Erin, what were you seeing?"

My throat was tight, my stomach was burning, and tears were leaking out of my eyes. Squeezing them shut invoked the image of hundreds of moldy hands reaching for me. I yelped. José scooped me up and pulled me close. I threw my arms around him, clinging to his rock-solid body so it would ground me in the present. The dam restraining my tears burst. They came in a flood, washing away the fear while José held me, occasionally stroking my back and my hair.

"It's okay," he whispered. "Whatever it was, it hasn't happened yet."

When the crying finally stopped, I was too embarrassed to speak. José laid me back down on the bed and tucked me in. "Do you have a notebook or a file you record the visions in?"

I shook my head and forced words out. "I thought half of them couldn't happen, because of the monsters."

"Did tonight's dream have monsters?"

"Demons," I whispered. "Lots of them."

He nodded, looking around the piles of junk blanketing my floor until he somehow found my history notebook. "Tell me what you saw. I'll write it all down and help you understand."

My front teeth sank into my lower lip. Normally, Mel was the only person I shared my dreams with because she was convinced they were premonitions. I'd been skeptical, but if Demons were real, then dreams could be prophecies. One of the hunters in Grandpa's stories dreamed true, meaning he saw the past, things that were happening elsewhere while he was sleeping and things that might happen in the future.

"Erin, please tell me before you forget. You might be able to stop whatever made you scream."

"All right," I told him. He stopped after I described each segment and asked me for as many specific details as I remembered. He said the Demon I saw attack Grandpa's car was a Pyrollusion, but I hadn't seen enough for him to identify what made up the horde that had been restraining me.

When I was done, we hugged. The embrace turned into cuddling. I hadn't planned to go back to sleep. I usually didn't when I woke up from nightmares, but José's heartbeat was a lullaby, so I drifted off into the land of dreams where I saw my future in a tiny cottage. In it was a green bedroom where José and I did all of the things I was too afraid to do in the waking world.

Chapter Eleven

The veins in his head appeared to have burst from the effort he exuded in the telepathic battle against the Puppet Master.

—Autopsy report of Julian Gorgon, 1947, archived under St. Patrick's Church

I woke to the rhythm of rain ricocheting off the rooftop. Gray light trickled through the shades. I was still cocooned in my blankets, with something warm and heavy on my back. Memories from the night before seeped into my consciousness as I struggled to discern what was dream and what wasn't. The weight on my back was José's arm. I picked up my head and watched him roll away. Thankfully, he was fully clothed and on top of the blankets.

My phone was dead, but my clock told me it was 10:04 a.m. Grandpa had never shown up. I jumped, that is, if one can jump while lying down. It was more like I flailed my way upright, tripped over my blankets, and landed on my math textbook's spine.

"Erin?" José sat up, alert with eyes wide.

"Grandpa should have been here two hours ago," I spat, wobbling to my feet. I should've been woken by the growl of his wagoner's engine, followed by his stomping feet, and the slink of his sword cane unsheathing at the sight of a boy in his grandchild's bed. Grandpa was never late for anything.

"Check your phone," said José.

I hunted for my charger, plugged the phone in and saw one voicemail. It was Mom checking in. I called Grandpa. He didn't pick up. If something had come up or his car had crapped out, Grandpa would have called. My thoughts flashed to the dream of his Wagoneer flipped in a ditch. I prayed that had been an ordinary dream, but my fledgling instincts said otherwise.

"Dad, have you heard from Seamus? Erin said he was supposed to get here by eight," whispered José.

I spun around. José was frowning with his phone to his ear.

"And you didn't think to tell me?" José raised his voice. "Right. We'll see you there. Bye." He pounded the End button with his thumb.

"What's going on?" I asked.

"Your Grandpa has my dad listed as an emergency contact—they hunt together. Anyway, Dad just got back to a place with phone service. He had a message from Mercy Hospital."

"Is Grandpa okay?"

José bit his lip. "He wasn't conscious when the EMTs brought him in."

Switching into auto-pilot, I yanked my pj's off and then threw on the first pants and shirt I found, barely aware enough to be impressed by the fact that José kept his back to me while I changed. I dashed downstairs, grabbed my wallet and keys, only pausing long enough to yell, "Sam wake up. My grandpa is in the hospital! Please let Bessie out before you leave!"

"Shouldn't you make sure she heard you?" he asked as he climbed into my car.

"No time." I put the Jeep into drive.

I SHIFTED MY weight from foot to foot while the frogish woman at the nurse's station looked up Grandpa's room number. José was standing next to me, looking a lot calmer than I felt. Papers shuffled and keys clicked. As soon as the woman informed me he was in room 226, I was on the move. I skipped the elevators and took the stairs three at a time, charging out the door at floor two and barreling down the hall. I only paid attention to the numbers, so I nearly knocked three people over. José hung back to apologize, so I beat him to Grandpa's room.

I froze a few feet away from the bed. Grandpa had tubes pumping oxygen into his nose and liquid into his blue-gray veins. There was a bruise on his head, and his left arm was in a sling. A woman with frazzled gray hair and a dirty flannel shirt sat beside him with his hand in hers. For a moment, I thought I was in the wrong room.

"Erin, thank God you're here." The woman turned around and winked at me.

"Sister Marie, is he okay?" I asked. I almost hadn't recognized her out of her usual clothing, but I couldn't say I was surprised. It seemed everyone around me was a Demon hunter, and Grandpa had told me so many stories featuring the hunter nun.

"Why don't you ask him?" She winked again, whispered goodbye to him, and gave me a stiff hug. "I need to get back to St. Pat's. I'll check in later."

"Thanks," I said and took her place beside Grandpa.

His eyes were closed. His chest quivered as it rose and fell. He looked too fragile to be my grandpa. He had always walked upright with loads of energy. The broken man in the bed hardly looked the same as the man who skied black diamond trails in February and wanted to hike Tuckerman's Ravine one last time before he got "too old." I didn't believe it was actually him until he opened his ocean blue eyes.

"How's my sunshine?" he asked in a hoarse voice.

"How am I?" I walked closer to the bed, too relieved by the sound of his voice to bristle at the pet name. "How are *you*?"

He attempted to chuckle, but it came out as a dry cough. "I've been better."

"What happened to you?" I handed him the glass of water that was on his tray.

"Doctor says I had a stroke while driving." He paused, took another wheezing breath, and raised a hand to his ribs. "Anyway, I lost control of the car and flipped it into a ditch."

"How bad are you hurt?" I eyed the nasty purple bruise on the left side of his face and listened to the slow but steady beep of the heart monitor. I was pretty sure if I were hooked up to it, the beep would be going twice as fast.

"My arm is broken. I cracked a rib, got a concussion and a little nerve damage from the stroke. They say I'm going to have a twitch in my left hand. When'd José get here?"

"He came with me." Hyper-focused on Grandpa, I'd forgotten José. Oddly, he wasn't looking at Grandpa but at the empty chair beside Grandpa's bed.

"Please wait in the hall. I need to speak with Erin alone." Grandpa furrowed his bushy eyebrows and glared at José.

"Yes, sir." José's voice was formal; he silently left the room. It reminded me that they had a separate relationship I didn't know about.

"Erin, there are things I need to tell you before I go." Grandpa closed his eyes and took in a deep breath. The wrinkles around his eyes and jaw looked deeper than normal.

"Before you go? What do you mean?" He looked weak, but people recovered from strokes all the time.

"The stroke wasn't natural. Something tried to kill me," he whispered.

"A Demon." I pictured my dreams while emotions battled inside me. I was terrified I was going to lose the closest thing I had to a father, but I was furious at him for lying to me. "Was it the Pyrollusion that made a flaming girl appear in front of your car?"

"How did you know that?" Grandpa jolted upright with his eyes narrowed.

"I saw it in a dream last night."

"Sometimes you're so much like your father." He slowly lowered his upper body back to his pillows, holding his rib as he did it.

"My father?" Mom had never mentioned my dad having strange dreams, and Grandpa hardly ever spoke of him because it made him sad and angry.

"Your father never had dreams. When he slept, he'd see things that happened, were happening in other places, or were going to happen. One time he described it as watching endless movie trailers stuck on fast forward. Sound familiar?" His bushy gray eyebrows twitched.

"Oh yeah." The left side of my lip curved up, but the right turned down.

"I should have known your nightmares weren't normal," he paused, shaking his head. "I was foolish to think you weren't able, and that I could protect you."

"You were," I snapped. "You've no idea what I'm capable of."

"Did José tell you?" Grandpa looked past me toward the hall.

"After we were attacked by an Incubus, he told me enough for me to realize I wasn't hallucinating, but all I really know is that Demons, Pixies, and Mermaids exist."

"You know so much more than that," said Grandpa. "The only fictitious aspect of the stories was that they were fiction at all. Of course, I did give everyone pseudonyms. Jack McCormack was Liam Evanstar. Liza is your Aunty Lucy. Tulip was Amelia."

"So I was Ray and I'm guessing Antonio Azure is Pedro Estrella?" As I spoke, my mind raced through dozens of memories until it found one of the saddest stories Grandpa had ever told: the story of my father's death.

He and Grandpa had gone off into the woods in Acadia National Park, investigating reports hikers posted online about a white yeti. They got separated on the trail. The next time Grandpa saw my dad, there wasn't much left of him. His chest had been ripped open by giant teeth and most of his insides had been devoured. His spine and shattered ribs were all that remained of his midsection. Grandpa never found the Demon that murdered his son. At the end of the story, I yelled at Grandpa for being so graphic and killing off my favorite character. If I had known what he was really telling me...

"Yes," said Grandpa with a sad smile. "You haven't forgotten much."

"I loved those stories," I said, distracting myself from thoughts of my father by trying to figure out how José fit into all of this. His dad and my dad had been friends. The fictional version of Dr. Estrella had been a goofy scientist who helped my dad puzzle stuff out when he wasn't fraternizing with Mermaids. It was hard to reconcile him with my boyfriend's jerk of a father. "But José was never in them."

"Like you, he was a baby when Liam was alive. There was no need to include him. You were only in the stories because I needed to tell you how much your father loved you. He knew he wouldn't see you grow up and wanted me to protect you when he died. His dreams told him that much, but never enough to prevent his own death." Grandpa's voice cracked. "I've done a pretty crappy job honoring his will."

Unsure whether to confirm or deny that, I gaped at the ruin my Grandfather had withered to. The slow beeping got louder, screeching above the orchestra of whirring and humming machines. José's damp sneakers squeaked as he shifted his feet in the hallway, interrupting the hospital symphony.

"So what exactly is José's role in all this?" I asked.

"He's my apprentice," sighed Grandpa. "And if you don't mind, I want a word alone with him."

"No." A tide of anger erased guilt like drawings in the sand. I pictured how sad José had been after I pushed him. *Enough people hurt me,* he said. What if Grandpa was one of them?

There was no magical Demon hunter academy, so the older generation trained the younger through apprenticeships, and the masters in the relationship were not known for being gentle. Yes, Grandpa was old, but in the world of hunters, you didn't need to be physically strong to hurt someone. If José was going to get in trouble, I couldn't leave him alone with Grandpa.

"Do you know who the Incubus was after?" I asked, hoping to buy more time. I knew it had been after me because it told me, but I wanted to see if Grandpa gave me a straight answer. "Was it after me, José, or random prey?"

Grandpa narrowed his eyes and stared at my nose. I stared back. I was getting my answer—Grandpa wasn't that sick. Then as if to contradict my thoughts, he coughed. I rolled my eyes. He tried to take a sip of water, but his cup was empty.

"Erin, please get me some water," he said between coughs.

José stepped into the room. "Is everything okay?"

"Have your apprentice get it."

Now José rolled his eyes. Grandpa shook his head and croaked "go" toward José. He knew I was just as stubborn as he was; I wasn't giving in. Yet he still tried to change the subject after he finished coughing and cleared his throat.

"Have you heard from Mel?"

"Yes. Who was the Demon after?"

"I was worried about her."

"Was it looking for Mel?"

"Erin, in the stories, remember there was a group called the Seven Stars?"

"Yes." They were actually seven giant families dedicated to protecting normal humans from supernatural predators. The McCormacks, who were actually the Evanstars, were the biggest, and they were in charge. If the names were the only thing Grandpa changed, then he was actually a regional leader—the boss of all the Demon hunters in the Northeast.

"Well, there have been more Demons in the area than usual. Last night there were three attacks within a fifty-mile radius. They've been targeting powerful people, not the ordinary humans they usually prey on."

"People like you?"

"Like us. Something strong is controlling them, and they are trying hard to take me out. They know you exist and that you don't know they're real. You're a weakness they're trying to exploit."

That was a better, scarier answer. It seemed honest, yet raised questions about my dreams. Sometimes, the nightmares of the end of the world had Demons in them but did the demons cause the chaos or come to feed on it?

"Erin, I'm exhausted and need to speak with José alone. He can tell you more over lunch. You should eat so you calm down. I need to sleep." Grandpa's voice was strained, and his eyes were looking more at the empty chairs than at me.

I stomped out of the room. I wanted to hit something, hug someone, and cry all at once, but I couldn't do any of those things alone in the chemical-scented hallway, so as I paced around, I took out my phone to call Mel. I had dozens of missed calls and texts from Sam, who apparently had not woken up when I yelled at her. I sent a quick text telling her where I was and then dialed Mel's number. I was relieved to hear her pick up after the second ring.

"Erin?"

"Hey, Mel."

"What's up?" She was a little out of breath.

"Umm, Grandpa's in Mercy Hospital." That seemed like the right place to start.

"Are you serious? For what?" Mel was talking too loud, as usual.

I turned down the volume on my phone and told her what I knew of how he got there.

"On my way" was the only thing Mel said before she hung up.

I shoved my phone into my pocket and ran my hands through my snarly curls. I'd figured out I wasn't hallucinating, but I hadn't exactly let myself think about what that meant. Many of Grandpa's stories were downright terrifying. Demons came in many shapes and sizes, but they all shared a common purpose of sowing fear, pain, and chaos among humans. They fed off negativity and thrived when people were miserable. Some were enormous with too many teeth and eyes. They ate people and destroyed things.

Others blended in with or possessed human bodies to cause harm in more subtle ways. Demons or witches already in this realm summoned some, while others slipped through where the veil between our worlds was thin.

In the stories, it was the job of the hunters to make sure the Demons stayed in Hell and didn't hurt people on Earth. When they were doing their job right, normal people didn't ever realize the Demons existed.

"Erin, how are you doing?" asked José.

"I think I'm okay."

"Want to go to the café and get some food?"

I slid my arm around him, smirked, and said, "So, Padawan, what secrets did your Jedi Master divulge unto your privileged ears?"

José played along...sort of.

"Well Mx. Evanstar, if they are secrets, then obviously I cannot pass them along to your innocent ears."

I snorted. "Innocent?"

I rolled my eyes and tried to glare, but simultaneously glaring and blushing didn't work, especially when the subject of the glare decided to lean in and kiss my forehead as one would do to a feisty kitten. At least it had distracted me for a few minutes. "Seriously, what did he say?"

"He pretty much gave me permission to answer your questions about Demons and the Stars, grilled me about why I arrived with you, and told me all the ways he could hurt me if I treated you the same as my previous girlfriends and boyfriends."

"That's all?" If he treated me like the other people he dated, then Grandpa wasn't going to be the one he needed to fear the most.

"Well, that's all I can tell you. Remember the secret part?"

I nodded and tried to smile, but my lips were stuck in a frown. I wanted things to work out with José. I neither wanted to become another person who hurt him nor get hurt myself.

Chapter Twelve

I'm sure every mother thinks this, but my daughter is truly amazing. When she is happy, she glows so bright I cannot look directly at her. Yesterday, while I was walking her home from school, we came across an injured kitten lying on the side of the road. Without a word, she knelt down and picked up the miserable creature. Light poured from her body until the kitten was whole, contentedly purring in her hands. She and the kitten spent the rest of the afternoon napping on my couch.

  —The journal of Lucile Evanstar, entry written 2004 and confined to the archives at a later date

Steel and glass stood between the food and me. A woman with a hairnet took orders at one end of the counter while another rang us up. I took out my wallet, but José stopped me. I let him pay since I was almost out of the money I had earned scooping ice cream the summer before.

"Your Grandpa's going to be okay." José sat down at a table by a window. "He's a tough old bastard who's survived much worse."

Half listening to José, I chewed on salty turkey and scanned the room. The café was generic: off-white floors with vomit-like speckles of orange; brown plastic tables and blue chairs. It was still early for lunch, so only two other tables were occupied. Both were out of earshot. I swallowed another bite. "So you're Grandpa's apprentice?"

"Yeah," he said.

"How's that?"

"It sucks."

"Why?"

"Everything about hunting sucks."

We ate in silence. I tried to focus on the food, but chewing was a mindless task. Grandpa had looked so frail, and the way he rushed me out of the room had been strange. Part of me wanted to go sit with him and pretend things were normal. Part of me wanted to scream at him.

"Why did he think I was better off not knowing?" I asked when the silence got to be too much.

"He loves you, but he didn't understand you or want you growing up around violence, especially since he doesn't understand your ADHD. He thought you'd get distracted mid-hunt and lose an arm...or your head."

"That was brilliant."

"Beating up half the football team isn't the same kind of violence. Have you ever seen a body? Not all dressed up at a funeral home, but freshly murdered." José tightened his grip on his fork as if he was ready to stab a Demon with it. "Have you ever seen someone's intestines dangling from their stomach? Or seen a man's skull shattered so his brains spilled out, all because you were too slow to stop the monster that wanted to eat him?"

I was frozen with my fork halfway to my mouth. I didn't shake my head or nod. I held his gaze while my throat constricted and my stomach churned.

"That's why hunting sucks," he muttered, finally breaking eye contact. "That is why Seamus didn't want you to be a hunter. One mistake can cost someone their life, and then you have to live with that failure forever."

José spent the next five minutes shoving food into his mouth as if it could erase the memory of the failures he kept from me. I moved bits of meat and potato around on my plate, but I'd lost my appetite. He eyed my leftovers. I pushed them over to him and watched him make them disappear. He didn't talk again until all the food was gone. "I didn't expect you to accept everything so easily."

"I used to believe the stories. It's like finding out Santa Claus does exist after all."

José laughed so hard mashed potatoes escaped his mouth. "He's real all right, but you don't want the kind of presents he brings. Accepting gifts from Faeries is never a good idea."

I stared while he tried to laugh and clean up the half-chewed potatoes splattered across the table like wet snow. I didn't ask for details about the real Santa because I was thinking more of Faeries in general. If I remembered right, Pixies and Mermaids were two out of dozens of Faerie species. Elves were another. Grandpa had never married, but he had fathered twins with an Elf Princess.

I stood up. Pieces of gray matter slithered around in my skull, exchanging information through electric charges that made my toes twitch. Those half-Elven twins were Mel's mom and my dad.

My dad had only been half human.

"Erin? What's wrong?" José's voice was distant.

I was frozen like a computer told to perform too many commands at once. I could accept that supernatural creatures existed. A small part of me had never truly stopped believing in them. Realizing I was a supernatural creature was something else entirely. Feeling a sudden urge to move, I took the trays to the trashcan.

Pointy ears and inhuman grace were probably the only things Grandpa's Elves had in common with the ones found in most of the fantasy novels I'd read. They were mostly human in shape, but their eyes were vibrant and feline. They were some of the most powerful creatures in Grandpa's stories and, thankfully, allied with the Demon hunters. They were ten times stronger than humans, more sensitive in all five human senses and in possession of senses humans didn't have, such as the ability to feel the life energy and emotion of other beings. They had eidetic memories, and the ability to move faster than sound and manipulate raw energy. A few were able to look backward and forward through time.

"Erin? Hello?"

I dropped the trays in the trash and watched José walk toward me. I stared until my eyes burned. The Elf Stone became visible on his head. His heartbeat became audible and the squeak of his sneakers became painful. The stench of rotten food was nauseating.

"Erin!" This time, it sounded as if José shouted through a megaphone.

I paced. In addition to José's pulse, I heard six other hearts beating around me, all on different rhythms. The lights, and the electricity that fed them, hummed overhead. Every voice was a missile assaulting my eardrums. I heard everything but understood nothing, swept up in a cacophonous current. It had happened before. Mom called it sensory processing disorder. I'd never imagined it was exacerbated by Elf hearing.

In one story, Grandpa explained that when Elves bred with humans, their offspring usually inherited some of the Elf's abilities. These powers were passed down for a few generations, getting weaker and weaker until, eventually, there wasn't enough Elf DNA left to sustain them. Being the second generation away from the Elf, I still had a lot of powers. My ability to see through illusions was one of them and I was willing to bet my dreams were another.

"Why are you ignoring me?" shouted José, putting his hands on my shoulders.

My hands flew to my throbbing ears. "Umm, I just realized something. I've got Elf genes. Lots of them."

"Well, you're an Evanstar."

"José, I literally have a Faerie Grandmother." I tried not giggle maniacally because "Faerie Grandmother" was so close to "Faerie Godmother." I really, really tried and failed miserably. If my Grandmother was an Elf, then Aunty Lucy, who was my Godmother, was half-Elf...so I had a half-Faerie Godmother.

"Your Grandmother is the Princess Niben, the youngest daughter of the Summer Queen," said José, interrupting my laughter with a serious tone. "I've met her. She's actually kind of scary but is probably why you were able to 'accidentally' turn a Demon's power against it. A purely human hunter needs lots of practice to learn it. Some can't do it at all."

"So it doesn't bother you that you're dating someone who's part Elf?" I asked, presently more concerned with how this affected my relationship than my fighting skills.

"Of course not." He pulled me into a hug.

"Are you part Elf or anything not human?" I asked before burying my face in his shoulder.

"No, though I'm surprised I don't have a half-Mermaid sibling by now," he snickered.

I joined his laughter, picking up my head when his chest bounced too hard. A shimmer of light caught my eye. After blinking a few times, I realized the light was coming from

Mel. She was leaning on the café's doorframes surrounded by an aura that looked dull compared to the blinding one I had seen on Thursday. She had a sword belted to her hip and her bell-bottoms were ripped in several places. Dark-red liquid was soaking her jeans around the tears. Either everyone in the hospital was blind, or Mel was doing something to hide her true appearance from them.

"Mel? Are you okay?" I said, pushing José out of my way. As I got closer to Mel, I realized the black splotch was not mascara, but a bruise surrounding her left eye. Across from it was a thin white scar I thought had healed years ago. Her upper lip was swollen and bleeding like someone had punched her.

"Where's Grandpa?" Mel uncrossed her arms and stood up straighter.

"What happened?" I said, staring into her swirling eyes. Those, combined with the glowing light told me Mel wasn't human, but Elves didn't have swirling eyes. While they did have auras, they didn't glow golden. The only things that did that were Angels.

She repeated her question.

"Upstairs."

She speed-walked to the elevators.

"Mel, you're bleeding."

"What floor?"

"Two."

"What happened to your leg?" José caught up and slid in the elevator seconds before the door closed.

"Long story," said Mel through clenched teeth.

"Stop being evasive." I crossed my arms and glared at her. She was acting strange and not in a good way. "You owe me explanations and apologies."

"I guess." She attempted to smile but achieved a constipated expression instead.

The elevator dinged. We were on the second floor.

"Which way?" asked Mel.

"Three doors to the left. What happened to your leg?"

"I can't tell you yet," she said, taking off toward Grandpa's room.

If she were going any faster, she'd be running. The red spot on her jeans was growing. I wished one of the nurses would notice it and grab her before she did any permanent damage. But they didn't notice, in fact, no one even looked directly at her. She wasn't only hiding her appearance from them. She was invisible to them.

"Amelia!" I shouted using her full first name as I skidded into Grandpa's room. "Do you realize your pants are soaked in blood?"

She turned around and stared at me with her head tilted as her too-loud voice seemed to echo inside my head. "Are you using Sight?"

"Umm, I think so." In Grandpa's stories, my father had Sight, courtesy of his Elf mother, but he always saw strange things; he couldn't turn it off.

Mel squinted. "Distracting, huh?"

"It is," I agreed.

A raspy cough from the bed caught our attention. Grandpa looked a lot sicker with Sight than he did with normal vision. His skin had a gray tint and his eyes were sunken in, surrounded by black circles. His bruises were darker and thorny black vines crept up his arms and onto his neck. When Mel touched his hand, the vines on his arm retreated halfway to his elbow as some of her light flowed into him. His eyes opened. They were a duller blue than they should have been. He coughed again and Mel took his cup off his tray, gently placing it in his hands. When she let go, the vines started creeping back toward his fingers.

I walked to the bed and stood next to Mel, who was focused on the vines.

"What are they?" I said while pointing at them.

"What are what?" Grandpa's voice was barely more than a whisper. I wished I'd never left to go eat.

I looked at Mel and met her eyes for a second.

"He can't see them."

I heard her speak, but her lips didn't move.

"You're just noticing now?" said Mel, but again, her lips didn't move. *I haven't said a word to you out loud since you left the elevator.*

I tilted my head. How did that work?

I'm not talking. I'm thinking at you.

That was kind of creepy, but a relief because I had heard her voice in my head Thursday.

I heard that. And yes, I was trying to communicate this way. I was forbidden from speaking to you about certain things, but I never promised not to think at you. I've been doing it for years, but you never heard me before.

I stared at her, thinking what I wanted to say: *Fine. So what are the things on Grandpa's arms and what the Hell are you?*

I am nothing to do with Hell, but the vines have very much to do with it. It's Demon magic and it's killing him.

Can you stop it?

Possibly

"What's going on?" José placed a hand on my shoulder. I jumped. He caught me, steadying us both and kept his arms wrapped around me.

"Umm, good question." I looked at Mel for an answer.

"Were you guys just talking in each other's heads?" asked José.

Mel nodded.

There was a cough. We all turned to face Grandpa at the same time.

"Amelia, am I dying?" His voice was barely a whisper, but I heard it as if my ear was against his mouth.

Mel sighed, shook her head, and then she managed three words: "You were poisoned."

"Obviously," whispered Grandpa. "The wards broke when the car crashed. I'd be dead already if your grandmother hadn't shown up. How long do I have?"

"By my Grandmother, you mean Princess Niben?" I asked. Grandpa couldn't be dying now. Not when there was so much he needed to tell me. It was pointless for Mel to even answer his question, if she could. Being accepted to medical school didn't make someone a doctor.

"Yes. She was here the whole time you were talking to me earlier. That was why I wanted you to leave." Grandpa closed his eyes tight and shook his head. "Amelia, you can speak to Erin freely now. You are no longer bound to your oath of secrecy."

A few sparkly tears dripped down Mel's faintly glowing cheek, but she didn't speak. She just reached out and put a hand on his, causing the vines to retreat. He seemed to relax for a minute then looked at José.

"You've passed your trial." He managed a smirk and took a drink from his cup.

José's face almost widened into a smile but stopped halfway there. "I banished it, but I didn't do a very good job. Erin did most of the work."

Mel grunted and squawked, squeezed her eyes closed and grabbed Grandpa's arm above the elbow, apparently struggling to eradicate the Demon poison. As she growled, light poured from her hand, surged up his arm, and made the vines disappear.

Grandpa managed a weak laugh. "José you've never been good at listening. Your task was simply to banish the Incubus. I never said you had to defeat it on your own or said how long it had to stay gone. You whined that I was giving you an impossible task."

José frowned. His foot tapped the floor behind me. "Thank you...but—"

"You've earned it," said Grandpa, a little louder. "Collaboration is part of being a hunter. That was a lesson you needed to learn."

In the stories, every hunter was given a trial or task at the end of his or her apprenticeship. When that was completed, the apprentice became an official hunter. There was no ceremony or celebration, simply a few words and a handshake. If the stories were accurate, then José just got a promotion.

Mel growled again, hands gripping Grandpa's shoulders, sending light to his chest. The black vines were gone from his arms, and the ones visible on his neck beneath the hospital gown were more of an ashen gray. Mel's light was dull and flickering. She took one of her hands and went to place it on his chest.

Grandpa pushed Mel's hand away from him. "Don't hurt yourself trying to save me; I'm an old man."

Mel put her hands right back on his chest. Light flowed into him, chasing the remaining black out of his body. The vines were gone, but he was still pasty and bruised. Mel stumbled backward. José caught her and helped her onto a chair. She was pale, and her light behaved like a nearly burnt-out bulb. When she sat down, I noticed her hands shaking. "Mel, are you okay? You're not glowing much."

She shook her head. "I might have pushed a little too hard. I need food and sleep."

I dug around in my cargo pockets until I pulled out a slightly crushed brownie all wrapped up in plastic. "Do you want chocolate?"

Mel's lips quivered into a weak smile. "How long has that been in your pocket?"

I looked down at the flattened brownie, thinking about the last time I wore these pants. "Sam and I went for a hike Wednesday afternoon. I think that's when I stuck it in my pocket."

Mel's skin looked a little better after she ate the brownie, but her light didn't get any brighter. Grandpa, on the other hand, was improving rapidly. I couldn't see any more vines, and the bruise on his face was already fading. He was breathing easier and had completely stopped coughing.

I heard footsteps behind me and turned around to see Dr. Estrella walking into the room. He wore dirty jeans, work boots, and a brown button-up flannel shirt. I tried to merge the two versions of him that I knew in my head: José's asshole dad and the goofy scientist/hunter. He walked right past me, José, and Mel without a hello or nod and stood at the foot of Grandpa's bed. "Seamus, what happened? Are you okay?"

"It's a long story, but I think I'll live, thanks to Mel." Grandpa smiled. "Did you manage to banish the Sirens that had been sinking those lobster boats?"

Dr. Estrella sighed and his shoulders seemed to lower. "Yes, but now I owe Beals Mermaid Colony a favor. I would've drowned without their help." He paused and glanced at Mel, who was curled up in a blue chair. "Are you okay?"

Mel shrugged. "I've been worse. I'll recover."

Dr. Estrella's eyes narrowed. "And what if you are attacked in the meantime?"

Mel's smile grew and she raised her eyebrows. "According to your son, Erin discovered some new skills last night."

"Demon-fighting skills," said José. "The Incubus attacked her with magic and they instinctively turned the energy against it."

Grandpa grinned like a pit bull. "Their father had a knack for that."

Mel yawned. She stretched her arms in the air, and she kept closing and reopening her eyes. "Erin, can you drive me back to your house? I can't stay awake and falling asleep here is a bad idea. Too many ghosts. Don't want to talk to them."

I nodded, looking for these alleged ghosts. I didn't see them.

"It takes more than Elf Sight to see ghosts," she said with a yawn. "Speaking of Sight, you should close yours. I doubt you'd be able to focus on driving with it open."

"How?" I asked, still staring at her. So far, every time I opened or closed it had been by accident.

"Just close your eyes and think about shutting it off. If you want to open it again, stare without blinking or let your eyes slide out of focus."

I closed my eyes, mentally willing everything to look normal. When I opened them, Mel wasn't glowing. Her eyes were human and hazel, her leg wasn't bleeding and the bruise on her eye was dripping mascara. I tilted my head and let my eyes slide out of focus. Mel's glowing form, swirling eyes and injuries all returned. For a second, I could've sworn I saw a transparent child tugging on her shirt.

Chapter Thirteen

TRUE SIGHT: The ability to see around illusions and falsehoods by looking through dimensions. This is possessed by most Fae species and some Demons. Hybrids often have the ability to turn their Sight on or off, depending on how far removed they are from the Fae ancestor. Heightened senses are often associated with opening one's Sight.
—The Demon Hunter Lexicon

Bullets of rain assaulted us on the brief walk from the car to the front door. I wasn't surprised to see Sam gone when I got inside since she had texted me saying her mom picked her up. The blankets were stripped off the furniture and piled next to the downstairs bathroom. Bessie's bowl was on the couch – a sign Sam fed her then left her alone to eat where she pleased.

Mel could barely stay upright, so José and I practically carried her up the stairs. When we got my room, José went back downstairs to wait while I helped Mel change. I opened my Sight when she took her torn jeans off so I could get a good look at the injuries she was ignoring.

"I'm fine," growled Mel while I stared at the three gashes made by either big claws or a small knife. "I heal quick. They'll close up while I sleep."

"You should at least put bandages on them so you don't bleed all over my bed," I said, unable to peel my eyes away from the angry red slashes.

"Fine." Mel fell backward onto my bed but kept her legs hanging over the edge. I walked to the bathroom, where I found a roll of gauze and tape in the medicine cabinet.

Back in my room, I arranged my supplies on the floor and knelt down at the edge of the bed. I still had a lot of questions boiling in my head, so I decided to ask Mel one while I worked. "Are we really cousins?"

"Yes."

"Right. So what was your dad? Your biological one, not your stepdad."

"You figured it out when you Saw me at the hospital."

I hadn't voiced my thoughts about what she was when I had opened my Sight, which meant she had been reading my mind. "Mel, do you always—"

"Hear people's thoughts? Yes, unless I make an effort to block people out. I'm too tired to bother right now."

"Your dad was an Angel?" I thought about the few Angel stories I knew. My dad had occasionally glimpsed them at Mass and in some of his more intense fights. They were always huge—at least ten feet tall—and surrounded by white-hot light. I couldn't even begin to picture how Aunty Lucy had managed to get herself pregnant by one or understand how that was allowed. The angels never did anything in the stories, and when I asked Grandpa why, he told me it was because they were only allowed to watch. Interfering messed with the balance of power and could lead to a war between Heaven and Hell, ending the world as we know it. He said it would be like the stuff in the book of Revelations. Was that what my dreams—

"Erin, your thoughts are giving me a headache." Mel's eyes were wet with tears and her now bandaged legs were quivering.

"Sorry," I muttered as I taped the last piece of gauze in place. "I didn't mean to upset you. I just want to understand."

"It's okay." Mel rolled the rest of the way into my bed where she proceeded to bury herself in my blankets. "I'm part of the balance. If an Incubus successfully creates a child with a human, then an angel is allowed to reproduce with a human. There's almost always an equal number of half Angels and half Demons, but it can be dangerous for a human to have sex with an angel. A woman is more likely to survive and enjoy the encounter is she's half Elf like my mom. At the time, Mom wanted a kid but not a relationship, so it was a win-win. Trust me, as a telepath with little respect for privacy, I know my mom enjoyed making me. Whenever she thinks —"

"Enough, TMI." I glared at Mel who was snickering from under my blankets. "I don't want to know about my aunt's sex life."

Mel giggled. "Be careful what you think."

I continued glaring.

Mel peeked under the covers. "You suck at first aid."

"Well, at least your blood isn't leaking over my Star Wars sheets."

"Check me on every half hour, but don't wake me up unless you think my light gets dimmer."

She made squeaky snoring sounds before I asked anything else. I leaned over her face and let my fingers hover above the scar on her cheek. It didn't show up with normal sight. I thought it had healed and vanished a long time ago, but there it was, marring otherwise perfect skin.

Curious if I had scars that were only visible with my Sight, I stepped back and pulled my shirt up over my head. My skin was darker, as if the pigment from my freckles bled out and been smoothed into the white. In the normal sight, I had no scars. There should have been thin white lines all over my arms and stomach. The other person I knew who cut how I used to had so many it looked like she battled feral cats for fun.

I unbuttoned my pants and slid them down. Only one of the cuts I made on my leg had scarred. It stood out in stark contrast to the darker version of my skin: a pale line, deep and jagged, stopping just short of my femoral artery. I glanced back over at Mel's faintly glowing body almost certain she had healed the other cuts so they wouldn't scar but left me that one as a reminder of what I tried to do.

Desperate for a distraction from that memory, I turned around, looked in my mirror, and barely managed not to scream. My hair resembled sparking orange flames writhing around green leaves more than its usual dark red. My irises were more feline oval than round and the color of birch leaves. The tips of my ears rose up in sharp points. I wasn't as alien as Mel, but I looked less than 75% human, not the other way around as I had been led to believe. Either Faerie DNA didn't behave the same as human DNA, or I was missing a lot of information about my family. I added it to the long list of questions I needed to ask Mel and Grandpa when they got better and stood in my boxers, gaping at my reflection, until there was a knock on the door.

"Is everything okay?" asked José.

"Hold on," I said, hurrying to pull my pants and shirt back on.

"Your shirt is on backward," said José as I stepped out into the hallway.

I gently closed the door behind me and walked down the stairs. He followed, saying, "Erin what's wrong?"

When I got downstairs where I didn't have to worry if our voices woke Mel, I turned to him and asked what I looked like.

"Beautiful," he smiled.

"That's not what I meant. What color is my skin?" I moved my face closer to his.

His eyes widened and his cheeks turned red. The gem on his head glowed green. "Did you look at yourself with your Sight?"

I nodded and paced around the room. "I look like an Elf! Not a quarter Elf and three-quarters human. It's the opposite. And without my Sight, I always looked human with all those stupid freckles, and it's not as if I were glamouring myself to have freckles. If I was going to glamour myself, I'd be sun tanned all the time with no freckles, and I'd be skinnier with broader shoulders and smaller, almost non-existent boobs. I could actually look androgynous, and only be more male or female when I felt like it!"

"Well, you're a little more than a quarter Elf, because your Grandpa is also a quarter Elf," said José as he tried to follow me around the room. "Erin, you're body is perfect... and I adore your boobs exactly the way they are."

I wanted to smack him for talking about my boobs, but smacking people was bad. Even thinking of hitting José was wrong on so many levels, but the thought was there. Dark and violent thoughts lurked in my mind no matter how bad I wanted to get rid of them. I took a few very slow and deep breaths until I was calm enough to face José. "Which me is real?"

"Both of them. Do you know how your Sight works?" He walked closer.

"Yeah, but I'm not creating an illusion to look human." The heat of his hands made me feel calmer and human, but it also sent distracting messages to a different part of my body.

"I know. You don't need to yet. Both versions of you still exist at the same time. When you get as old as Sister Marie, you might have to because the human DNA ages quicker than the Elf DNA and the Elf starts to bleed through. Right now, all that shows through are pieces of pigment the color of your grandmother's skin—they're not technically freckles. The older you get, the more they will show."

I stared into his eyes. "Can you see both versions of me?"

"Yes," he said cautiously.

"Which one is better?" I asked, closing the space between us.

"They're equally gorgeous," he said as his hands slid up my back. "Can I kiss you?"

"Which me?"

"Whichever one you want."

"You can't feel me up and you can't take my clothes my off," I said before grabbing his face and devouring his lips.

His hands slid from my hips to my back, crushing my body against his. Heat poured from him to me, making me want to eliminate any space between us. My legs wobbled, so I had to cling to his shoulders to stay standing. It was a lot of work to focus on remaining upright with my lips moving so fast and my body so hot. It would be easier to fall over backward and drag him down with me and climb on top of him, but that might give him the wrong idea. Kissing was fun, but I wasn't sure if I'd like anything more, so I held on tighter, afraid to go further but unwilling to stop.

His grip on me tightened as well. His hand slid up my neck, causing me to shiver while the other crept closer and closer to my ass. Perhaps telling him not to feel me up hadn't been specific enough. I should have told him not to feel me up or down. My heart skipped a beat when his hand squeezed a cheek and pushed forward.

Angry shocks traveled up my body, short-circuiting my brain. Rage reared its head. He had no right to do that. My stomach clenched. My arms twitched, wanting to shove him. I couldn't. I shouldn't want to.

"No," I croaked as my arms and hands cramped. He let go. I yanked my hands off of him. I blinked. Fingernail-sized crescents marred his neck. I opened my mouth to apologize, but I couldn't breathe enough to form words. I was freezing cold. Shivering. Lightheaded from a lack of oxygen. I stopped myself from pushing him, but I still hurt him. I was a monster like his dad.

"Erin, what happened?"

José held his hand out to me, but I backed away. Why wasn't he mad?

"Why did you panic again?"

I wasn't getting enough air to answer him. I didn't want to get enough air. He'd be better off of if I stopped breathing.

"Erin, on the count of three, I want you to take a deep breath with me."

I shook my head. I deserved the burning in my lungs and the dizziness it caused.

"Erin, please. Let me help you."

"Don't...deserve...help."

His eyes widened. His jaw clenched. His hands tightened to fists. "Erin, breathe."

He started counting. Something about how steady his voice was despite the anger seeping in broke my resistance.

When he got to three, he stopped counting and took a deep breath and slowly exhaled. He repeated it. I copied him. After the seventh repetition, the feeling returned to my hands.

"I'm sorry," I whispered.

Awkward tension blanketed the space between us while he waited for an explanation I didn't want to give. I didn't want him to know what someone else tried to do to me, and how toxic the relationship with that boy had gotten. I didn't want to say close I had come to murdering that boy. I didn't want to remember the guilt I had felt days later when I stood alone in the woods with a knife pressed against my artery.

"Erin, it's okay," said José.

"No, it isn't."

"Please, Erin, tell me what's going in your head."

"I don't want to talk about it." I stared at the floor.

He nodded. His lips quivered into a frown. "If you don't want to talk, I'd like to take a shower. I'm still wet from the rain."

"Of course," I said relieved he was changing the subject. "There's a dryer behind the folding doors in the downstairs bathroom. You can throw your clothes in while you shower."

He took his shirt off and walked toward the bathroom. His back was covered in angry splotches of black and blue. The monster in me roared with a need to hurt whoever did that to him trumping the sick guilt I felt for cutting him with my fingernails.

"José," I called right before he got to the door.

He paused and turned around. His front side looked just as bad. He had black and blues above his hips, around his ribs, and on his shoulders. He had scars too—one raised pink line cut across his six-pack and three jagged lines disfigured his shoulder.

"Were you going to say something?" he asked, staring at me with his head tilted.

"What happened to you?" I couldn't look away from his bruises.

"Thursday was rough." He frowned, staring at his injuries.

"Is that all from your Dad?" I moved closer to get a better look.

"No." His eyes closed and he took very slow deliberate breaths.

"Then who?" I gently ran my fingers over his shoulder and chest.

His hands balled into fists. "I want to take a shower."

"Will you tell me after?" I asked, trying to keep my voice steady. I wanted to find who or what made him so bruised, so I could make sure they or it got equally bruised.

"I'll tell you later, if you tell me why you panicked. I want to understand."

Before I said yes or no, he went into the bathroom and closed the door. I stared at the door's peeling white paint. Through it, I heard the clothes tumble in the dryer, the water running, and sobbing. Two monsters battled in my stomach: Rage and Guilt. They savaged each other with sharp claws and teeth. They trampled the lining of my stomach, tearing flesh as they battled.

When my limbs began to twitch, I paced around the house until I found myself staring at the knife block on the kitchen counter. I hadn't cut in nearly two years, but I couldn't stand the twisted rage I felt inside me. My hand closed around the steel hilt of the paring knife and slowly pulled it from the sheath. I let its sharp edge run over the skin of my palm, but didn't press down hard enough to cut. My stomach was the battleground, not my hand.

I heard the clink of claws on the tile floor as I lifted my shirt up. Bessie barked as she sat down next to me, staring with her big brown eyes. I took a deep breath. She barked again. I rolled my eyes. She was a dog. She couldn't tell anyone what she saw, so I lowered the knife to my stomach. Her barking got louder. I moved the knife away, and she quieted down. She scooted closer and licked my stomach.

I put the knife on the counter so I could push her away, but before I had the chance, she put both paws on my shoulder and proceeded to bathe my face in slobber. I put my hands on her to make her move, but they wrapped around her neck in a hug when I realized how she smart she was. She had known what I was going to do and knew it was wrong when I didn't. She just stopped me from relapsing to a habit I had fought hard to break. I buried my face in her fur, crying until the rush of tears drowned the raging monsters.

WHEN THE TEARS finally stopped, I wandered into the living room, searching for a task to take my mind off how bad I was at being José's partner. I sent Sam a text thanking her for cleaning up and feeding Bessie. She asked how Grandpa was and told me I could call her if I wanted to talk. I was tempted to, but there was too much I didn't want to tell her. Sam didn't need to know about Ricky. She didn't need to know how my temper poisoned my fledgling relationship with José. I had no clue how she'd react to me telling her Demons or other supernatural creatures exist.

No one had explicitly told me I had to keep it a secret, but it was obviously something most people didn't believe in. Sam had a fascination with the supernatural, but as far as I knew, it was limited to Wicca, spells she had no faith in, and never-executed plans to go ghost hunting. Knowing Sam, if I told her Demons existed and she actually believed me, she'd want to meet one. She was better off not knowing.

I didn't call her. When she called me, I didn't answer.

I wound up on the couch conjugating verbs out of my Spanish textbook. That's where I was when José emerged from the steamy bathroom with wet hair, dry clothes, and red, puffy eyes. He plopped down next to me but didn't speak until I grumbled at my textbook. He explained what I doing wrong and helped me finish the rest of the assigned exercises, but I couldn't stop thinking of his bruises.

I checked on Mel. Her aura was a little brighter. When I returned downstairs, José and I worked on homework from our Biology and English classes. I tried to act like nothing weird had happened, but we were both tense and neither of us was smiling. After we ran out of homework, I checked on Mel again and cleaned up the dishes from the night before. José helped with the latter, but he wasn't talking, and he couldn't stop frowning.

I started the dishwasher, desperate to end the silence. He sat down at the table but didn't answer me. His frown grew. His heart beat faster.

I sank onto the chair next to him. "You want to tell me what happened on Thursday?"

"You promise you'll tell me why you panic when I touch you?"

I stared at his quivering lips for a long time before I answered. I hated thinking of what happened with Ricky, let alone talking about it, but José deserved to know the truth. Plus, I really wanted to know how José got so bruised, so I slowly reached forward until my fingers found his stubbly jaw and tilted his head up, so his eyes were looking into mine. "I promise that if you tell me about the bruises, I will tell you why I panic."

"I already told you what happened with my dad," he muttered.

"Yeah. I dreamed a good chunk of it Wednesday. He didn't hit you on the back."

"No. Not in the first fight." José stared past me with a zombie-esque look. "He was being a hypocrite, I called him out on it, and he smacked me. I tried to fight back, wimped out, and wound up with a broken nose. It was nothing."

"That's not nothing." I tightened my grip on the table, letting my nails sink into wood, not skin.

"Mel called a few hours later. The Incubus had followed her to her mother's and kept trying to talk her into 'joining him' but wouldn't tell her what she'd be joining. She couldn't get it to give up any more information or provoke it into attacking her. She's not supposed to fight Demons unless they attack her directly, or she catches them harming a human, so she called us." José paused to catch his breath. "Dad refused to go with me, even though Seamus was Downeast and Sister Marie was occupied on another hunt. He told me I needed to find courage and learn to hunt solo. Since banishing the Incubus was the last part of my trials, I didn't argue with him, even though I should have. I didn't want another fight."

"Is it normal to hunt alone?" It had taken all of my concentration to defeat the Incubus. Had the second Demon not been occupied with José, I'm not sure I could've won. Of course, someone who had been trained to hunt Demons might be better at it.

"Sometimes hunters have to go out alone, but not against things that are intelligent like the Incubus. I had Mel to back me up, so I thought it'd be okay."

"I'm guessing it wasn't." I put my hand over his but made sure my nails were touching the table, not his skin.

"The Incubus led us on a wild goose chase across three states. With another person, we would've stood a better chance at trapping him, but it was only Mel and me. By the time we caught up to him at a closed water park, he was torturing a teenage girl. A redhead. For a minute, I thought it was you."

"I'm not a girl," I growled and pictured shoving my staff through the Incubus's face.

"I didn't mean to imply you were. She just had the same hair color, so from a distance, you were the first person that came to mind."

I nodded and waited.

"We fought him," continued José "Mel helped, but he summoned a dozen Crawlers to distract us. In the end, both me and his victim wound up stabbed through the stomach, leaving Mel able to either follow him or save us."

"She healed you."

He nodded, but he looked like he was going to throw up. "She healed us before tending her own injuries."

"Did you get the other bruises in that fight?"

His arm trembled. "It was my fault that girl got hurt. I wasn't good enough. I knew that from the start. I said as much to Dad when I got home. Told him if he'd come with me, things would've been different. Then he really kicked my ass. I let him. I deserved it."

"Don't you ever say that. You do not deserve a beating, ever!" Ripping my hand away from his, I stood up and paced around the kitchen.

"Says the person who shoved me across a room and clawed my neck."

"I'm sorry." I ran my hands through my hair. There wasn't much, but I managed to twine my fingers around some curls and pulled. The pain wasn't enough to ease the guilt or the urge to break things. I cupped my hands around my neck and squeezed until blood oozed out. My anger seemed to drip out with it, making me light and calm enough to hug José.

"Will you tell me now?" His voice crackled, so I hugged him tighter. "You're going to tell me, right?" he asked, pulling back enough to see my face but not the blood dribbling down my neck.

"You remember Ricky?" My voice was a hissing whisper and my eyes were locked with José's. If he kept making eye contact, he wouldn't see the blood.

José grunted. "The control freak? You had to make a fake Facebook account to talk to me while you were dating him."

"We went to the beach after his prom. He tried to rape me. I tried to kill him." My voice was deep and raspy as I forced each word out of my tight throat. Part of me wished Mel hadn't stopped me from bashing Ricky's skull with that rock. Another part of me was so repulsed by that desire that I wanted to bash in my own skull to protect the world from me.

José swallowed hard. "How close did he get?"

"Do you truly want to know?"

José's chocolate eyes, wet with tears, stared into mine for an eternity before he spoke. "You need to tell me or it will always be between us, holding you back."

He put his arm around my waist and guided me back over to the table. I told my story in a low monotone: "After walking far past the houses and onto the preserve, where there were no houses or witnesses, we made out. It was fine until he tried to feel me up. I pushed his hand away. He shoved it back and squeezed. I punched him in the face. He grabbed me and smothered my protest with his bloody mouth. I pushed him away and he tackled me."

I paused, breathing slow, lodging my fingernails into the seat of my chair. "In seconds, Ricky pinned me to the sand, ripped my shirt open, and yanked my pants down." My throat tightened, but I kept talking. "He covered my mouth so I couldn't breathe."

My grip on José's hands got tighter as I moved into the part where I started to fight back. "I don't remember all the details," I said through clenched teeth. "I just know that I flipped him over. We grappled, like Judo but not sparring. We meant to hurt each other. The more he hurt me, the angrier I got. I kept hitting him for a long time after he stopped defending himself. I found a big rock to kill him with. I didn't hesitate. It was halfway to his skull when Mel grabbed me. I was furious. I fought her so I could get back to killing him. She had to knock me out cold."

José swallowed hard, but he didn't speak.

"Don't ever tell me I'm not a monster. Don't tell me I'm a good person." I let go of him, slowly backing away.

"Why do you both feel ready to commit murder?" asked Mel, stumbling into the painfully silent kitchen.

"I told him," I said in a flat voice and thought about our conversation.

Mel swayed. She had to grip the counter for support. "Erin, take a deep breath and think of something else."

I tried. It didn't work. I couldn't stop thinking about how I had wanted to kill Ricky and how I wanted to kill Dr. Estrella for beating José to the point where he thought he deserved it. I was landmine ready to blow up the next person who stepped on me.

Erin, you're not going to hurt anyone. Take a deep breath. Count to ten. Picture yourself down the cape with the sun baking your shoulders while cool water kisses your toes.

I counted as I inhaled, but it wasn't enough. I was shaking with the need to hurt. I kept backing up, edging closer to the knife I'd left on the kitchen counter. The little cut on my neck had helped, but I need to make a larger one to let the monsters out.

Bessie charged into the room, barking, but it didn't stop me this time. Short of hurting someone, cutting was the only way to release the rage that had built up inside me. I'd try one quick slice across my stomach with the little paring knife, and if that didn't work, well, I'd cut deeper.

"Erin, no!" Mel was shaking, barely staying upright. She couldn't stop me.

"What's going on?" asked José.

I closed the distance between the counter and me.

"They want to cut," gasped Mel.

I heard stomping. My hand closed around the cool, stainless steel hilt. José's arms closed around my waist and pulled me back against his body. The knife clattered to the counter and we both fell backward. I tried to roll away, but his arms tightened around me like snakes.

I growled, "You're going to get hurt if you don't let go."

"No, I'm not. You're not going to hurt me. You're not going to hurt yourself," he said in a surprisingly steady voice. "I trust you, Erin. I trust you not to hurt me."

His words were needles stabbing the hot air balloon my chest had become. My rage deflated into sobs that shook my whole body. His grip loosened enough for me to roll to my side. He curled his body around mine and just held me.

Chapter Fourteen

I'm not nearly as skilled as my sister when it comes to weaving illusions, but today, I raced a bullet and won.
—The hunting log of Liam Evanstar, 1988, confined to the archives after his death.

When I finally got myself under control, I wanted to run off to my room, hide under a mountain of blankets and never come out again. Unfortunately, Mel had other plans. She was hungry and still too weak to cook. She had managed to get the mixing bowls and waffle iron out while I was crying, but claimed she was too dizzy to get the ingredients out of the higher cupboard. Apparently, after expending 95% of her body's energy in a healing and having her mind exposed to her cousin's emotional breakdown, she needed chocolate chip waffles and bacon.

"You'll feel better after you eat," she said with her feet on the table.

"I don't know if I can eat." I watched José rummage through the fridge. He probably thought I was a complete nut job.

"He doesn't think that," said Mel, apparently still reading our minds. "He just realized you're a little more complicated than he thought. He still wants to be with you and even feels like you bonded in some weird emo way. Something about being emotionally naked."

Things clattered in the fridge. When José emerged, his cheeks were red.

Mel's eyes gleamed with mischief as she smiled. "Shield your mind if you don't want me reading it."

He shook his head, put the eggs on the counter and kissed my cheek. "Do you want help cooking these?"

"No. It's easier to focus without help." I turned to Mel. "How many batches should I make?"

She gazed at the ceiling. "I need at least three waffles. You, Mike, and José will eat two each. And don't forget the bacon."

"Mike's coming?" Mike, Mel's fiancé, did have a big appetite, but the four of us were not going to eat three batches of waffles. I wasn't even sure I could force any food into my stomach, so I began measuring out ingredients for two batches: one for Mel and one for the rest of us.

"You need more food than you think," said Mel. "Anyway, Mike dropped my mom off at the hospital so she could visit Grandpa. He'll be here any minute."

Bessie barked. Through the window, I saw a gray Delorean's doors lift up, revealing a pair of converse chucks. Tight jeans, a plaid button-up, and a mess of honey curls that were sticking up in the fashion of Albert Einstein followed the shoes.

"Does he know what you are?" I put the egg whites aside, focusing my attention on Mike. Was he something supernatural too?

"He's human, but he knows all about me, and he's figured out all the physics behind Demon hunting, so he can make weapons for the hunters under Grandpa's command."

"Right, so he's the hunter's token geek?"

"You could say that," said Mike as he and José entered the kitchen.

A second later, Mel tackled him with a hug. He held on to her tight and ran his fingers through her wild curls. "I love you."

"I love you, too." She clung to him as if she hadn't seen him in years.

It feels like years to me. Mel's voice was accompanied by a sad giggle. *You'll understand one day.*

"How are you?" he asked when she was done smothering him.

"Exhausted." She leaned her forehead against his.

I pulled my attention away from the love fest to finish cooking. It got a little harder to concentrate when the conversation turned to more normal things, such as comic books, weather, and TV shows. I measured the vanilla wrong, covered my face in flour and dropped a piece of bacon right into Bessie's open mouth.

Every time I looked at the table, Mike was touching Mel. With my sight open, I saw that Mel had definitely gotten brighter since he arrived. Mike was glowing a little himself. As he touched her, his borrowed light seemed to be returning to its rightful owner. I wondered if Mel had done that on purpose.

I nearly burned myself on the pan when Mel's cheeks got red and her giggling filled my head. Soon her coy voice was responding to my musings. *It just kind of happens. People's auras mix when they make love.*

My own cheeks got hot and I forgot what I was supposed to be doing.

Feeding me bacon, thought Mel.

I was going to have to learn how to keep Mel from hearing my thoughts and from randomly inserting hers into my brain.

It's not easy. It actually takes quite a bit of energy to wall your mind off but is a fantastic skill to have if you're fighting a Demon that wants to beat you by controlling your thoughts. That was one of the reasons why your dad was so successful—because his mind kicked butt, metaphorically speaking. A brain literally kicking a butt would be pretty weird.

I couldn't help but laugh at the image that last thing conjured.

"You're doing it again. Can't you two talk out loud? Or at least include me in the mental loop?" asked José through a mouthful of waffle.

"I was thinking. She just kind of put her two-cents in." I emptied the last of the bacon onto a plate and stuffed a piece into my mouth. I nearly choked laughing as the plate was replaced by an image of two pennies being squished into gray matter. "Mel, that's gross. How did you even do that?"

It's a simple glamour. Open your sight, she responded.

I did. My waffle looked normal. *Can I do that?*

Yes. Look at the blueberries in José's waffles. Focus on them with all your senses until you're thinking of nothing but the blueberries. Look at their shape and size; focus on their smell.

At first, it was hard to ignore José and Mike's argument about what kind of weapons drones needed to effectively combat Trolls, which contrary to common folklore, were Demons, not Faeries. However, as I continued to stare at blue blobs and fell into a hyper-focused state, the conversation faded away with the rest of the room until my attention was completely occupied by those berries.

Now feel them with your mind. Don't tell me you can't. Just breath slow and focus on feeling.

I took my next few breaths as slowly as possible. Time seemed to stand still. José's fork crept toward his plate.

Good. Your perception is slowed; now feel the berries!

I didn't really understand what she meant by feel, so I pictured my mind touching everything in the room; it was instantly overloaded with buzzing heat. The hottest, most intense energy came from the people. Electricity hummed in the walls and heat lingered on the stove burners.

Focus on the berries.

I let them fill my eyes and attention. The burners were cooler than the people but warmer than the table and drinks. They didn't buzz like the people.

Perfect! Now think of how you want them to look. Feel them, and send your own energy out to shape them.

I mentally reached out, attempting to turn the berries red and stretch them into hearts and felt a tiny bit of heat leave my body. I yawned. José coughed and sputtered. I opened my eyes. He spit out his waffles with a look of pure disgust on his face.

"Wait a minute, did you just glamour my pancakes?" he looked up at me. "They're bleeding."

"It was supposed to be cute little hearts."

"They look more anatomical than cute." The creases eased out of his face. He smirked. "Still, it's impressive that you were able to alter their appearance at all."

"Erin learns quickly when they actually pay attention." Mel's smug smile brightened her light. "They figured out how to slow their perception of time, feel auras, and create illusions."

José's grimace transformed to a smile. "If you can slow your perception, then you can move super fast.

"Like having a hyperdrive in your brain," added Mike.

"I've been trying to learn that for a long time without much luck," continued José.

"You can't stay fast for too long. You can hurt yourself if you're not careful," warned Mel as she scooped another waffle onto her plate.

I practiced more while we finished eating. I glamoured Mike's waffle to Jigglypuff and managed to make Bessie look like a big pig, which was appropriate because she was being an obnoxious beggar. I wanted to try moving super fast, but everyone agreed the house was not the place to experiment with that ability.

Chapter Fifteen

CRAWLER: A low-level Demon with the mental capabilities of a feral dog. While these foul creatures are capable of walking upright, they prefer to scurry on all four (sometimes six) of their legs. They are not skilled at materializing on earth and often merge with each other, resulting in mutated creatures with additional eyes, teeth, and appendages.

Crawlers consume human flesh. Uncontrolled, they will rampage through the streets devouring anyone they encounter. However, more powerful Demons have been known to use Crawlers as assassins or cannon fodder when they have a need for such a thing.
    —The Demon Hunter Lexicon

The heavy rain eroded my hope for an early spring. It was starting to freeze, coating the road with a shiny layer of ice as I followed Mike's Delorean. My beefy tires and four-wheel drive went a long way in a snowstorm, but they didn't do much when the road decided to become an ice skating rink.

Mom called as I was sliding across an intersection. José picked up, told her what was going on, and asked if she wanted me to call back when we got to the hospital. She didn't want me to call unless it was an emergency. Apparently, by then, she'd be out to dinner and unable to talk.

"Typical," I muttered when José got off the phone with her.

"I'd take her over my dad any day." José put his hand on my leg and stayed silent for the remainder of the drive. I wanted to say something comforting, to tell him his dad wasn't all that bad, but anything along those lines would've been a lie.

When we got to Grandpa's room, he was sitting up. He still had tubes in his arm, but color had returned to his cheeks. His voice was back to its normal volume—a few notches below shouting. He was too absorbed in his argument with Aunty Lucy to notice the new company.

"I hate hospitals," he scowled. "We're experiencing the biggest surge in Demon activity since the sixties, and I'm stuck on my butt in an unprotected hospital."

Aunty Lucy shook her head. "The doctors need to make sure there aren't any complications."

Grandpa grunted. "I'm fine. I should be out fighting, not letting these idiots fuss over me."

Aunty Lucy leaned back and crossed her arms. She was plump, with pale skin, covered with constellations of freckles. Poufy red and gray curls crowned her head. "You could still get an infection in that gash on your leg.

Grandpa's eyes narrowed. "I'm leaving first thing in the morning."

"Hi, Grandpa, how are you feeling?" I asked before the argument could go any further. I plastered a smile on my face, hoping that if I looked happy, I'd feel it, even though I was pretty sure whoever told me to try that trick was an idiot.

"Old," growled Grandpa.

Aunty Lucy wheeled around and beamed when she saw Mel. "I was so worried about you."

"Erin took good care of me." Mel gave her mother a brief hug, then sat on the edge of Grandpa's bed. She rattled off details of injuries that still needed to be treated by doctors since she was too drained to heal them. I opened my Sight, trying to figure out how she knew everything about his injuries. Grandpa looked the same but with fewer wrinkles and very subtle points at the tips of his ears. Mel's glow was still very faint and I wished I could see through her pants to assess her injuries. She snickered something about x-ray vision in response to my thoughts and told me to stop distracting her, so I turned my attention to the others in the room.

Mel shouted a mental warning, but it was too late. I was already staring at the two shriveled pieces of blackened flesh that had once been Aunty Lucy's legs. They dangled from her knees like strings of hot dogs left on the grill too long, thrown in the trash to rot and then dragged into a tree by a raccoon.

"You remember the story of Liza and the Kraken?" Grandpa's voice sliced through my sick fascination.

"Cursed, acidic saliva," I said, remembering the story. Aunty Lucy had disguised herself as bait while my dad planned to cut off all the Kraken's tentacles with his super speed when the Demon attacked. It would have worked if the Kraken had been alone, but it hadn't, and by the time my father killed the Crawlers, he'd lost precious time. He got seven out of eight legs but didn't quite cut off the eighth before the tentacle wrapped around Aunty Lucy's legs, partially disintegrating them. I remember asking Grandpa why he hadn't stabbed it in the head, but Grandpa told me Krakens had a brain at the end of each tentacle and the only way to kill them was cut off all the legs.

"I'm hungry," said Mel, getting up from Grandpa's bed. "Have you eaten, Mom?"

Aunty Lucy rolled her eyes and glared at her daughter.

"I'm sorry for staring," I muttered, turning off my Sight.

"Don't worry," said Aunty Lucy.

"That Kraken story always makes me crave calamari," said Mel with an impish grin. "I pretend I'm eating the thing that hurt Mom."

"Let's get pizza," said Mike, mitigating the drama of a family he wasn't quite part of yet.

"Erin and I will keep an eye on Seamus until the next watch gets here," said José.

"I don't need watching," said Grandpa.

"You do," said everyone else.

"Mel needs watching," said Grandpa.

"I have Mom and Mike," she said. "Plus, the Demons know you're weak. They don't usually risk attacking me unless they know I'm out of gas."

"If they see you, they'll know."

"If they get that close, then they'll get vaporized," said Mike.

"Last time you tried to vaporize a Demon, you vaporized the whole room," said Grandpa.

"That was three attempts ago," whined Mike.

"We're going. End of story." Mel grabbed the handles of Aunty Lucy's wheelchair and pushed her out of the room at a jog. Mike dropped his argument and followed, leaving me alone with Grandpa and José.

"Well, at least there's been some good entertainment here," muttered Grandpa with a wrinkled grin.

I stared, caught between the nasty things I wanted to say and the concern I felt about seeing him weak in the hospital bed.

"How are you doing?" asked José while I decided whether to be nice or not.

"I've been better," said Grandpa. "But I'm years better than I was this morning. How's Erin doing?"

"I'm standing right here," I said through clenched teeth.

"But your mind was elsewhere," he said. "And there isn't time for you to be inattentive. The Demons know you're a threat now. Next time they come for you, it will be in numbers."

"Well, I'd be better prepared to defend myself if you hadn't let me think your stories were fiction all my life."

José laughed.

I glared at him. There was nothing funny about being lied to by the one family member who actually acted as if he cared.

"Can I hug you?" asked José.

I nodded. His arms twined around my waist like thick vines strangling my rage. "Erin, you aren't exactly defenseless. Do you know how many times I've fought that Incubus and got my butt handed to me?"

I shrugged.

"Six times. He's faster, stronger, and more skilled. I can't beat him. Heck, Dad and I couldn't beat him together. Dad blamed me, but he blames me for everything. Mel's the only one who can hold her own against him in a fight. You defeated him in ten minutes. Ten. Minutes. I've never seen anyone fight how you do, at least, not anyone human."

I pulled away, suddenly uncomfortable in my own skin. "How human am I?"

"Human enough," said Grandpa. "How much detail do you remember from the stories?"

"Some. I remember a lot of fighting."

"They're all fighting. I'll quiz you." He hit the buttons on his bed so he was sitting up straighter. "How do you kill a Troll?"

"Heat." There had been at least three stories involving Trolls—massive Demons that savored the feeling of human bones crunching between their tombstone teeth. Rocket-powered grenade launchers were Grandpa's weapon of choice when fighting them, but those were kind of hard to conceal. "You blow it up. And if that doesn't work, cut it up with a super-hot sword. Or electrocute it. Didn't you hook one up to a car battery once?"

"I did, but what would you use if you were alone in the woods without any weapons, electricity, or means to start a fire?" He leaned forward, now with a glimmer of excitement making the blue in his eyes deepen.

"Magic. I could turn its own power against it like I did with the Incubus."

Grandpa shook his head. "You only got away with that because the Incubus didn't know you were capable of such a feat. What else can you do?"

"Can I make my own weapon?" Excitement shook my legs; I paced around the room. I loved the stories, not just because Grandpa was skilled at creating suspense, but also because the hunters could do so many cool things, violent things they didn't get in trouble for.

"What can you make it out of if you are in the middle of nowhere?"

"Water?" It was everything—in the air, in the trees, and in the ground.

"Show me."

"Seamus, are you sure that's a good idea?" asked José. "It takes a lot of energy to change the state of matter. That's completely different than turning a volley of magic around."

"I know." Mischief took decades off of Grandpa's face. "But they know the theory behind it. I want to see them put it to use."

"But—

"Don't say it. I know they can do it."

José nodded, but he clenched his jaw and took a few steps away from me. In theory, I did know how to turn water vapor into ice. Grandpa had been very detailed when telling stories, more specific than he actually needed to be if he'd just been trying to entertain me, so I ignored José's nervous pulse and closed my eyes.

Magic was simply energy. Call it chi, the force, or whatever you want. Everything had energy and the laws of physics applied. I couldn't make something out of nothing, but I could change the state of things.

Taking a deep breath, I imagined pictures of the Mickey Mouse-like water molecules from last year's chemistry textbook. I felt them floating in the air around me, but I couldn't touch them. They were too small, and they were moving too fast in their gaseous form. I paced faster and breathing slower. That was what my dad had done in the stories when he wanted to move super fast. The breathing part worked for me when Mel was teaching me how to work a glamour. I hoped I had better luck with this than my attempt to put hearts on José pancakes.

"Seamus, are you sure—"

"Hush," hissed Grandpa.

José's sneakers squealed as he crossed the room. Grandpa continued talking in a whisper, telling José to let me concentrate, then he shut up, and all I heard was beating hearts, whooshing air and humming electricity. The sounds were reminded me of weird classical music aiding my focus. My pacing turned into a rhythm that matched them as I tried to focus on feeling the molecules instead of Seeing them. Grandpa and José were balls of fire resting beside the bed. Their tiny pieces danced and worked, keeping the furnace of the bodies alive. Electricity surged all around me:

raw power, lightning imprisoned by copper and rubber. It wanted out. I reached toward the ceiling, where the electricity was flowing into gas, exciting molecules so they turned to light, and sparks jumped out at me, shattering the glass.

"Erin, you can stop," said José at the same time Grandpa shouted, "Stay focused on the water molecules!"

Their voices were loud enough to make my ears throb, but at the same time, they seemed far away as if they were muffled by fabric and water. I pulled my hand away from the light, keeping the sparks that had already come to me. I ignored the captive voltage and focused on the air. I pulled energy from the water molecules the same way I had pulled energy from the light and they slowed down. I let go of volts as the ice formed around them, locking them in the center of a long blade. I didn't know how long it would last before it melted, but I thought if I hit a Demon with it, then it should do some serious damage, especially since Demons and electricity don't mix.

"I told you they could do it," said Grandpa.

"I told you it was a bad idea," said José. "It's freezing in here, and the light broke."

"They did it. It was worth it."

I stopped moving and opened my eyes. The room was spinning. José was a brown blur among sterile white and steal. The only way to tell Grandpa apart from the rest was by the swirl of bright blue from his eyes.

"It's not worth it if they fall on the sword and impale themselves," said José.

His feet thundered across the room. I dropped the sword and watched it shatter into thousands of sparkling shards. They melted into a golden puddle right before I fell into a wall of pulsating heat.

I blinked.

José's face was mere inches away from mine and his hands were on my cheeks, holding my head up. I was sitting in a chair, across the room from where I had been standing a few minutes before.

"Erin, focus on my eyes. Breathe with me. Focus on the present."

I did what he said. He was the one that had been training to hunt Demons his whole life. I'd only been told stories.

"How are you feeling?" he asked after I synced my breathing with his.

"Tired. A little dizzy, like I didn't eat enough. A burger would be really good right now." I pushed myself up to my feet, tripped over José's shoes, and landed in the puddle I'd made.

I got back on my feet and kept pacing.

"Erin, you might want to rest a little bit," said Grandpa.

"Need to move." I paced circles around the puddle and broken glass while I tried to process what I'd done. I'd shattered a light with my mind, called electricity to me, and made a sword out of water vapor. Before that, I had created a visible illusion. I wasn't just part of some kind of hypersensitive species; I could create lethal weapons and summon electricity with a mere thought. I was terrifying, dangerous.

After nearly killing Ricky and myself, I spent two weeks in a psychiatric hospital. The staff knew I had attempted suicide after being sexually assaulted. They knew I fought off my attacker, but they never learned how close I had come to killing him. Thankfully, the hospital staff was competent, and even without the whole story, they realized two things: I was going to have a hard time trusting people in the future, and I was afraid that lack of trust would lead me to physically harm someone who didn't deserve it.

My therapist brought me superhero comic books with powerful people who were heroes, not villains. When they'd convinced me I was gifted, not dangerous, they sent me back out to the world. By then Mom had gotten her new job, packed up all my stuff and moved to Portland, claiming a "fresh start" was exactly what we needed.

"Erin? You still in there?" asked Grandpa. His bed was as upright as it went; his hand hovered over his emergency call button.

I nodded. "I need to get this right."

"You can try again tomorrow," said José.

I shook my head, already letting my eyes slide back out of focus. I watched the puddle on the floor and the stray pieces of energy hovering around it, picturing the particles too small for naked eyes to see. Mentally, I located millions of atoms buzzing like a colony of bees. I sucked their energy out with an imagined straw until I felt them slow down. I reached out with my own energy, guiding them around glowing heat as they locked into a crystalline grid. This time, the ice took the shape of a luminous sword worthy of any comic-book hero...or anti-hero.

Chapter Sixteen

I curse the imbecile who convinced mortals that Trolls were cute little Faeries.
　　—Princess Niben, 1967

Practice and persistence were what got me my black belt and made me such a good fighter, so I knew they would also be how I mastered whatever powers I inherited from Niben. I melted and reformed the sword dozens of times in different shapes and sizes until I successfully made a basic knife in less than a minute. I only stopped because when Sister Marie arrived, she, Grandpa, and José all teamed up and convinced me to stop.

By the time we left to head back to my house, where Grandpa had surprisingly given José permission to stay, I was so tired I was bouncing off the walls and talking like a chipmunk on speed.

"I could make an ice lightsaber," I told José as I skipped down the sterile hallway. "I'd be the love child of Legolas and Yoda."

"That makes no sense," said José between giggles.

"Shhh," I said as we stepped out of the dry hospital and into a dank parking garage. "Impossible, there is no. Only possible."

"That doesn't make sense either," said José, pausing to scratch his head.

I wrapped my arms around him, deciding if I wanted to dance or kiss him, but froze when the hood of a silver sedan triggered an overpowering wave of déjà vu. I inhaled slowly, choking on the stench of cigarette smoke and rotten eggs.

"I smell Troll," said José.

"Get down!" I screamed, tackling him to the ground as a chakram whizzed by. We were both on our feet in seconds. He pulled a knife from his hoodie, one Sister Marie had brought to the hospital for him, and charged toward a six-foot-tall, four-armed Demon until the knife was buried to the hilt in its gut. The Demon exploded into a flurry of white flakes. José spun, getting his blade up in time to cut the wrist of a shorter, humanoid Demon that had a spike in the middle of its head.

I rushed to help José but was blocked as a spider-like creature materialized in front of me. I raised my hand to block the spindly Spike. It was like grabbing a metal pole on a frigid January day. My palm burned from the cold when I wrapped my hand around the limb and held it away from my face. I used my free hand to punch it in the eye.

It stumbled back, then spun and kicked me in the stomach. Air rushed out of my lungs as I fell into a putrid puddle of water and motor oil. I took my next breath as slow as possible, begging time to slow down. The advancing Demon became sluggish. I grinned as I pulled energy from the puddle. By the time the monster was on me, I had a hiltless blade of white and black in my hand.

I shoved it into the Demon's eye.

The force of both the Demon and knife exploding sent me stumbling into a wall with the spray of black and white guts. Everything spun as I struggled to stay on my feet, and time returned to normal. If this battle stayed true to my dream, we had to fight three more Demons. I looked for José and saw him swinging his knife at two more of the Demons with spiked heads. I started rushing to help when I remembered the knife hidden under the driver's seat in my car. I knew from my dreams that if I got to it before the largest Demon arrived, the fight would end quickly.

I ran. I almost made it before a warty, scarred mass of fist and muscle materialized two feet in front of me. The Troll had the build of an NFL player but was over seven feet tall. It roared like T. rex; the stench of rotten eggs almost made me pass out. I ducked as it swung one meaty fist at me. I jabbed my own into its abdomen, hoping I'd buy myself enough time to make another ice knife. It laughed. I tried to breathe slow and find more water molecules, but my head spun from the stench of the Troll's noxious breath. It swung at me, forcing me to duck or allow my skull to be pulverized.

I backed away, struggling to focus on making ice. I smiled when I finally felt something cold in my hand and jumped onto the hood of an SUV. I crouched, feigning a jump toward my car. When I saw the Troll getting ready to block me, I leaped at it, hoping to sink the ice knife into one of its eyes. I missed, stabbing its shoulder instead. It roared in pain, but it didn't explode. I scrambled to my feet and didn't quite make it to my car before the thing grabbed me and threw me into the hood of an oversized pickup, causing the alarm to go off.

Pain shot up from my shoulders to my head and down my back to my hips. I closed my eyes and took a slow breath, willing everything to slow motion again. When I opened them, the Demon was gradually pulling its meaty fist back, raising it higher and higher above its head. I knew exactly what I needed to do next. It seemed impossible, but I had done this half a dozen times in my dreams over the past week.

I closed my eyes again and pictured the car battery a foot below me in the engine of the truck, calling all its captive electricity to me. The hood heated up. My body shook. I ignored the pain and willed all the energy to travel up my arm and out into an imaginary blaster. I opened my eyes. A gray pistol materialized in my hand and pulled the trigger. A blue bolt of energy collided with the Demon's shoulder. The pistol didn't vanish, so I adjusted my aim and shot again and again and again until all that was left of the Troll was a smoking heap of ash and black slime.

Smiling, I slid off the hood, pain shooting through my body when my feet hit the ground. The garage rocked like it was being tossed in a tempest. I shook my head until my eyes focused and stumbled forward.

José ducked a punch from one Demon while he failed to slit the throat of the other. The blaster was still in my hand, so I shot the Demon on the right. Its head exploded. José backed away from the remaining one and I pulled the trigger again. The bolt hit it in the gut and goo spilled onto the concrete. The blaster vanished.

José stared at me while we both caught our breath. His lips quivered as he moved forward. "How did you—"

He stopped short as eerie bell-like laughter echoed through the dizzy garage. The air in front of us shimmered with heat. Something wearing a big pine-green cloak materialized in the center of the ripple. Its laugh was both creepy and inviting. It wanted me to start laughing, to be happy and forget about the burning skin on my back and the ache in my head. It scared me, so I muffled the sound. I imagined building stonewalls and metal blast doors and powering up deflector shields. I even pictured a big beast, a mash-up of Bessie and a bear, hitting a switch to divert more power to them, and the creepy magical laughter was replaced with a deep bark. I smiled, realizing I had just figured out how to shield.

The cloaked figure slowly lifted its hands up and removed the hood. The face the cowl had been hiding almost looked human. Her skin was warm reddish brown, and her hair was fiery red. Her almond-shaped eyes were the color of green grass and birch leaves. Her black pupils looked more feline than a human. She had a high jawline and her pointy ears were at least six inches tall. She smiled with her lips pressed together and shook her head.

"People thought Seamus was an idiot for not properly training you as a hunter, but I say he was a genius. Your father was one of the most talented hunters of this age and with all his practice and training, he never could have pulled off that stunt you did with the car battery. José can't decide if he is more jealous or aroused by your talents."

"Who are you?" I asked, gaping at the Elf woman.

She tilted her head. I felt like her eyes saw through mine into my brain. "Your resemblance to Liam is strong."

I told the imaginary Bessie-beast to send more power to the shields. I was going to repeat my question, but José spoke first. "Princess Niben, were you watching the whole fight?"

"I arrived with the intention of assisting you, but it clearly wasn't necessary, so I elected to sit back and watch the show. It was quite amusing. Demons rarely work together, and my grandchild has such style," she said with a sly smile.

"I'm your grandchild?" Grandpa had told me stories of my grandmother, but I had not expected to meet the nature-loving Elf princess in the middle of an urban parking garage.

She grinned at me. "After Liam died, Seamus claimed a mortal disorder made you incapable of hunting. He made me swear to stay away from you unless you discovered the truth on your own and made my people take a similar oath. I thought he was quite mad, overtaken by grief. Now, I doubt his intention was ever as he said."

"I don't understand."

Princess Niben was close enough that I saw past her to José standing amid the Demon guts with his arms crossed. He was watching intently but didn't look ready to attack. She leaned toward me so her face was inches away from mine "You are not limited like the rest of them. He made sure you knew how to fight with your hands and told you stories about his own adventures so you knew what magic, hunters, Demons and Faerie Folk are. But he never taught you any of the guidelines for using magic. You let instinct and imagination guide you. He didn't leave you defenseless. Whether he acted on fear or was more aware of how you learn than he lets on, he made you more powerful than any training could have."

"Princess Niben, what are your intentions toward Erin?" asked José.

The Elf woman turned her back on me. "I was on my way to check on Seamus and intended to properly introduce myself to Erin and ensure they did not get killed by the juvenile Troll. I'll leave you in peace."

My grandmother vanished, leaving José and me alone with a big pile of quivering Demon goop. José's arms were around me in seconds hugging me so tight I could barely breathe. He didn't even kiss me. He just held me as close and as tight as possible while his heart thundered in his chest. When he finally got his breathing under control and his heart rate down, he hoisted my wobbling body onto the hood of the Jeep and looked me over. "Are you okay?"

"If I wasn't, I would have passed out while you were hugging me. Are you?"

"I'll have a few more bruises in the morning, but otherwise I'm unhurt, I'm really shaken. I've never fought so many of them at the same time without Dad or Seamus. If you hadn't conjured up that blaster, we'd both be dead. When I saw the Troll throw you onto the car, I thought for sure I was going to lose you. I love—"

I kissed him before he finished his sentence. He resisted for half a second, and then his lips parted and he pulled me close again. I wrapped my legs around his hips, dug my hands into his shoulders and kept kissing him while one of his hands roamed down to my lower back and the other ran up to my neck and cupped the back of my head. I was too hyped up from the fight to be afraid. I got lost in the movement of our lips and the sounds of our bodies for a few minutes before I remembered another dream and pulled away. "You should do that thing where you speak Latin and make the goop go away. The big pile is kind of twitching and I don't want to fight it again."

He stared at me with a big dopey smile on his face.

"What?" I asked, tilting my head.

"You didn't panic."

I yawned. I hadn't been nervous at all. In fact, now that the adrenaline rush was starting to wear off, I just wanted to sleep. José walked away and shouted Latin spells at the piles of goop, so I curled up in the passenger seat of my car and closed my eyes. I was asleep before he got back.

Chapter Seventeen

I opened my Sight at the rally and saw a shadow over Hitler and his guards. Half of them were Demons; half of them were possessed. At first, I thought the shadow was attached to or possessing him, but then, when I got closer, I realized it was him. The man we all see is nothing more than a strong glamour created by a Fallen Angel, possibly one of Lucifer's lieutenants. He must be stopped at all costs, or in a few years, there will not be a world left for us to live in.

    —A letter from German Lt. Albert Adlersflugel to Spanish General Eduardo Estrella, 1944. Copies sent to all hunter archive locations

I couldn't stop yawning as I made the short trek from the Jeep's parking spot to my front door. As soon as I was inside, a mass of fur and slobber jumped up on her hind legs, knocked me into José, and proceeded to lick my face. Mel wasn't far behind Bessie, pulling me into a bone-crushing hug that stung the raw skin on my back. "I'm so glad you're home."

I patted her on the back while she strangled me, laughing and crying at the same time.

"Erin, I'm sorry I couldn't help you. I felt you get hurt and wanted to go, but I'm still too weak. I called Sister Marie and Pedro, but both of them were busy fending off Demon attacks themselves, so I called our grandmother to go help." When the last word spilled out, she finally loosened her grip.

"Niben wasn't exactly helpful," muttered José.

"Is Grandpa alright?" I pushed Mel back, holding on to her shoulders while Bessie tried to get between us.

Mel nodded and sniffled. "Two Crawlers attacked together. Sister Marie got rid of them pretty easily. You and José had a much tougher fight. How are you feeling?"

"I'm fine. It was like that parking garage dream I told you about. How did you even know it was happening?" I scratched Bessie behind the ears so she'd stop hitting me with her nose.

"I always know when you get hurt." Mel's eyes got wide as she sniffled a few times. I felt her mind reach out to mine and touch my shields. I heard my imaginary Bessie-beast growl when Mel got close.

Laughter conquered Mel's sniffles. She giggled her way over to the couch and plopped down next to Mike, who was furiously typing on his laptop. I watched for a minute, wondering if I should ask her if she was okay. When Mike put the computer down, he wrapped her up in his arms and used his sleeve to wipe what was left of her tears. I decided she didn't need me, too.

I greeted Aunty Lucy then glanced over at José and noticed him texting. I pictured myself dismantling the wall I had built around my mind and told Bessie-beast to power the shields down before directing a thought at Mel. *Do you spy on everyone? Or only me?*

I always sense things about people I'm close to, like you, Mom, and Mike.

Right. So no one you care for has privacy, I thought and then rushed to the bathroom to answer the call of nature. Afterward, I started the laundry so everyone would have clean sheets and blankets. My phone beeped when I closed the closet door that hid the washer from the rest of the bathroom. I dug it out of my pocket and frowned at the now cracked screen. The battery icon was red and there was a notification from Sam: a text asking me if I wanted to meet her and a friend from out of town for dinner.

I replied telling her I was too tired. She sent me a link to the restaurant's dessert menu, hoping to change my mind. The triple chocolate cake tempted me, but I couldn't go, even if I had the energy.

As an afterthought, I sent her another text: *It isn't the stalker guy from downtown, right?*

Just someone I normally only get to talk to online, she replied.

I started typing another message, but my phone shut itself off. Next time Mel or Grandpa felt inclined to teach me things, I'd have to ask how to stop accidentally pulling energy from cell phone's battery.

I walked out and stood halfway to the couch, where Mel and Mike were snuggling. Aunty Lucy was in the oversized armchair. José stood beside, her telling her about the attack and the strange visit from my grandmother.

"Typical Niben." Aunty Lucy crinkled her eyebrows.

"Yeah. She was too amused by Erin's fighting style to do anything but watch."

"She did have a creepy laugh." I walked closer to the chair. "I felt like it was trying to make me sleepy and complacent, so I figured out a way to block her out. I thought she was going to try to abduct us or something."

Aunty Lucy turned her wrinkled stare to me. "Perhaps she was trying to teach you to shield."

"I have no clue. Do you think I'll see her again?"

"Yes, but right now, I'm more concerned about the Demons. Last time we saw two Spikes in the same area, they were more interested in fighting each other than me.

Juvenile Trolls hate working with other Demons. If they were all cooperating in a group of five, then someone or something else was controlling them. We need to find out who or what it is."

"Are they trying to end the world?"

Aunty Lucy cocked her head. "Why are you asking that?"

"Their dreams," said Mel. "When it was just floods and storms, I thought Erin was seeing the result of climate change, but then they saw demons burning down cities. The next time they had a flood dream, I paid attention to the details. It didn't look like something happening fifty years in the future."

"You read my mind when I'm sleeping?" I asked even though logic told me I should be more worried about the content of the dreams.

"Sometimes," Mel admitted. "I've actually prevented some of the things you saw. I stopped someone from killing themselves and stopped a bank robbery before it happened."

"I stopped the robbery," said Mike. "They were hacking the bank, not physically breaking into the vault."

"It doesn't matter which one of you did it," said Aunty Lucy. "I want to know why Amelia fails to mention the apocalyptic part of Erin's dreams when she talks about them."

"It was mere conjecture. I didn't want to worry you over nothing, but now demons are after Erin specifically."

"Right. What is the real reason you hid it?"

Mel glared at the ceiling.

I opened my mouth to speak, but Aunty Lucy shushed me.

"Some prophecies are self-fulfilling."

No one spoke. Mel got up and paced around the room, eventually stopping in front of her mother. They glared at each other, probably having a conversation no one else could hear. The skin above their brows creased. Mel's hands balled into fists. She threw her hands in the air and spoke out loud.

"He loves me as much as you do. What if I dig into too much, get in trouble, and he upsets the balance trying to save me? Erin's visions are probable futures. Sometimes, by seeing and reacting to them, we make them more likely to happen!"

"When did they start dreaming Armageddon?" asked Aunty Lucy.

"I didn't say it was Armageddon."

"When?"

"A week or two ago," I said.

"That's when the activity increased," said José.

I made eye contact with him. "It can't be a coincidence."

José sat down on the couch next to Mike, pointing at the screen while Mike typed. Mel and Aunty Lucy dropped their voices to whispers and continued their argument.

José and Mike talked about something on the computer.

I couldn't focus on listening to both conversations and found myself staring at the screen on Mike's laptop. It was a map of the New England states plus New York and New Jersey. The states were covered with different colored dots. José got up, grabbed his backpack, and carried it upstairs. When I lost sight of him, I stared at the empty hall listening to everything and hearing nothing until Mike shouted incoherent words in my ear.

"What?" I asked, blinking at his glasses.

"Do you want to know about the map?" he asked.

I nodded. When I saw Mel's faint glow, I realized he wasn't actually shouting. I'd accidentally turned my hearing up and my Sight on.

"The black dots are Demon energies. The white are Angels. The hunters are colored based on their specialties. The same is true for Fae-hybrids. My sensors can detect Demon and Angel energy, but human auras are too dull, so I track the GPS in their phones." He stopped talking long enough to zoom in over Portland. "These two yellow lights are Sister Marie and Seamus."

There was black dot near them, but it vanished a few seconds later.

"Did one of them just banish a Demon?" I asked.

"Looks like it." Mel looked over Mike's shoulder. "Zoom in on where we are."

Mike did. There was a yellow dot, an orange one, a green and white swirl, and a question mark. A white dot hovered outside the house. A black one popped up for a few seconds, moved toward the house, and vanished.

"The wards just disintegrated that Demon." Mel smirked, apparently done arguing with her mother. She pointed at the dots in the house. "You're the question mark because you're not technically a hunter, but you're part Elf. The white and yellow one is me because I'm half Angel, but I'm also an Evanstar."

I pointed at the all-white dot. "Is that an Angel?"

"My dad usually has someone watching over me," said Mel.

Mike zoomed back out. "Usually, there will be only one or two black dots at a time in an area. Occasionally, something powerful such as a Kraken or Mature Troll will summon Crawlers to work for it, but most Demons hunt alone. Look at how much black is on the map tonight."

All over the area, groups of two or three colored dots were surrounded by anywhere from five to ten black dots.

"That's worse than Thursday," said José, walking back into the room.

"Yeah." Mike zoomed back into Maine and stopped over a cluster of black and blue just south of Portland. He let his mouse hover over the black until it said "Crawler" then hovered over the blue until it said Pedro Estrella. "This is the third group of Demons Pedro's fought tonight."

A slight smile crept across my face as I pictured José's dad getting eaten by a horde of bloodthirsty Demons.

"We need to catch a Demon and interrogate it," said Aunty Lucy. "It might give us some insight into what is going on and if it is related to Erin's dreams."

"Then why haven't you guys done that?" I asked, recalling stories where my dad trapped a Demon to find out where it was hiding its human livestock.

"It's a lot harder to catch a Demon intact than destroy it, especially when there are a lot of them." José looked down at his phone and frowned. "Sister Marie is painting a Star Trap on the floor in Seamus's hospital room. They summoned a troop of Pixies to hide it for them in exchange for an entire vending machine's worth of candy bars."

"Oh dear," said Aunty Lucy. "So much for Seamus getting any rest."

EVERYONE SPENT THE next few hours huddled around Mike's computer watching the activity and reading through the small portion of the archives the hunters had managed to digitize. Mike put a TV show on while they worked, claiming the background noise helped him concentrate, but it had the opposite effect on me. I found myself more interested in watching smuggler space-cowboys avoid the alliance than the conversation on the best ways to trap Demons and stop what might be controlling them. Before I got completely lost in the "'verse," I did learn that the hunters only knew of three things that might be controlling the Demons: A Fallen Angel, a human Witch, or a rogue Elf.

As far as I knew from the stories, there hadn't been any Fallen on earth since the 1940s, and it had taken a considerable amount of collaboration between hunters and Elves to get rid of the one who wreaked havoc during WWII. Witches were equally rare, and while they were a lot less powerful than the Fallen, the hunters never knew what to do with them. They didn't like killing things that weren't Demons, but they had no prisons. Rogue Elves, also rare, were technically the responsibility of their queens, which made the situation complicated and delicate. Executing or harming an Elf, even a rogue one, could jeopardize the alliance between hunters and Elves. Supposedly, any one of them could be leading the demons with some kind of apocalyptic endgame and until we had more information, all we could do was react.

WHEN THE LAUNDRY was done and the conversations had died down, José and I changed the guest-bed's sheets. Mike literally carried a snoring Mel up to it. Our next task was to unfold the couch for Aunty Lucy. Once the cushions were off, we pulled the bottom portion out revealing a queen-sized mattress. We got that covered in sheets and José helped Aunty Lucy out of the armchair and back into her wheelchair. "I can get from my chair to that bed and back no problem. You kids can head upstairs."

José and I looked at each other then back to her.

She winked at us. "Don't worry; I won't tell Seamus."

I shook my head, too tired to respond, bent down, and gave her hug. She looked squishy, but her shoulders were rock solid. "Good night, Aunty. Sleep well."

She squeezed me a little too tight. "Good night, Erin. If you dream, tell me about it in the morning."

José followed me upstairs. "So you're really letting me sleep with you?"

"Just sleeping," I said as we reached the top. "No kissing while we are lying down. Your hands stay outside my clothing and don't go below my waist or near my chest."

"You can trust me," he said as he followed me into my room. "I promise. I'm never going to make you do anything you don't want to."

I wanted to believe him. I wanted to trust him. If he slept in the same bed as me and not even kiss me, then perhaps it would be easier to trust him in the future.

When we got up to my room, I dug a pair of Hulk pajama pants and a matching top out of my drawer and went into the bathroom to change. When I got back, José was lying on my bed, under the blankets with his hands under his head. I climbed in, wrapped one arm around his torso and plopped my head on his shoulder. I closed my eyes listening to his lungs fill with air. When he wrapped one of his arms around my back, my muscles and bones turned mushy. Currents of dreams swept me away before I said goodnight.

I WAS SIXTEEN staring out across a lake on a hot summer afternoon. Glistening sun burned my eyes. Mosquitoes attacked my skin while I pressed a knife into my leg. Blood slowly pooled around the blade as I moved it closer and closer to my femoral artery. It was almost over. No more guilt. No more nauseous cold sweats thinking of what happened on the beach. No more not being good enough. The world would be safer without me. Less than an inch and the blood would spurt until I couldn't feel at all.

Crunching sticks distracted me. A small hand grabbed my shoulder and jerked me around. "Erin! Holy crap, do you know what you were about to cut?"

"Yes," I said in a flat gray voice.

Mel slapped me.

I growled at the stinging skin on my face and swung at her with my knife.

I found myself in Times Square, surrounded by thousands of bodies what we're all moving forward, screaming, yelling, and trampling each other, pursued by a horde of demons. A small figure with blonde curls fell to the ground and became an unrecognizable heap of blood, guts, and flesh.

A pale woman stood in the woods, alone and naked. She cut her hand with a black knife and let the blood drip into a stone bowl. The Incubus materialized in front of her, knelt down, and drank the blood from the bowl. When he finished, he wrapped his arms around her.

I was falling. White icy hands grabbed me. I twisted, kicked, and screamed. Hands closed around every part of my body; I couldn't move. They dragged me over rocks into a freezing ocean. I kept yelling. They pulled me deeper and deeper until there was no warmth left. I screeched and choked. My lungs burned as they filled with water.

I was alone in the dark. Electricity made my body convulse, but I couldn't make my mind do anything with it. Cold iron cuffs burned my wrists. Something hard hit my stomach, my face, and my back. Cold metal clamps dug into my toes. The cycle repeated itself over and over again until all I knew was darkness and pain.

"ERIN, WAKE UP, please wake up."

I gasped. Warm air filled my lungs. Hands were rubbed my sides. José's face was less than an inch below mine. My cheeks were wet and everything hurt.

"Erin, are you okay?"

My brain felt like shredded ribbons. I kept reminding myself that no one had hurt me. It was only a dream. My throat burned and tears wet my cheeks. I buried my face in his neck and tried to hold back the sobs. The more I felt his body heat, the less I felt the cold iron cuffs and icy hands, but it wasn't enough to stop the tears. The beating, the electrocution, and the cold hadn't been quick flashes but had dragged on forever.

"Erin, I love you."

I cried harder because I wasn't sure if I believed it. I felt guilty for doubting him, but the whole weekend had been so surreal. My world had just turned upside down. José and I fought Demons together, but I also shoved him across a room. I was another person who was going to abuse him, not someone he should love.

There was a knock on the door. "Erin, it's Mel, can I come in?"

"Yes." I rolled off José and sat up as Mel walked in the room wearing my pj pants and one of Mike's Star Wars T-shirts. I opened my Sight and stared at the scar on her face. That was the only time I cut her, but it hadn't been the first time I had hurt her. I remembered at least three different times I had gotten mad and punched her in the face. I was no better than Dr. Estrella.

Only if you choose to be. Mel's voice was a gentle breeze, rustling half-dead branches in my brain. Despite her smile, her eyes looked sad. I recognized those eyes; I had seen them years before, and last night in my dreams, alongside a buggy lake.

Chapter Eighteen

I've always seen angels watching over us. Occasionally, they speak to me. I never knew they could interact more than that, until I found out my sister, Lucy, got pregnant by one. Today, when Grace and I were at Amelia's baptism, I realized what the light that always clings to Grace's hair is. I'm terrified and amazed. I don't know how she can deny what she is and deny what stands in front of her. I need to tell her the truth before I propose.

—The journal of Liam Evanstar 1999. Confined to the archives after his death

The first thing I heard when I turned the water off was the pop and sizzle of my favorite food. I smelled salty goodness next, so I dried off quickly. I stepped into an old pair of black cargo pants then twisted to examine my shoulders in the mirror. They were sunburn red with odd shaped black and blues. Frowning, I rubbed green aloe gel over the red area before covering it with a green flannel button-up. My stomach growled, so I followed my nose to the bacon.

Mel's wild curls tried to escape from a messy bun while she flipped sizzling strips of heaven. Everyone else was sitting at the table, sipping from steaming mugs. I sank into an empty chair and rested my head on the cool wood until Mel plopped a plate of bacon and eggs in front of me. It was gone in less than five minutes. I helped myself to seconds and took my time eating them.

"Dad managed to catch a Demon last night after he met up with Seamus and Sister Marie at the hospital," said José, half smiling, half frowning at his phone. "And Seamus is being discharged."

"Did they learn anything?" asked Aunty Lucy between mouthfuls of toast.

"Well, at first, the Demon rambled out how awesomely terrifying its master was but didn't say who or what it was. After more persuasion, it admitted there was a 'reward' for any demon that killed Seamus or captured Erin alive."

"Alive?" I nearly choked as sharp bacon cut into my contracting throat.

"Did this Demon say what it wants with them?" asked Aunty Lucy.

José typed, presumably conveying Aunty Lucy's question via text. I swallowed and then proposed an answer of my own. "They want to torture me. I dreamed it last night."

"Do *you* know why?" José didn't look up from his screen. "The Demon didn't tell."

"I'm not sure," I said and described the dream to them, reliving each torturous second while I told them what the Incubus had said to me the two times I'd fought it.

"Why didn't you tell us what it said sooner?" asked Aunty Lucy.

I stared at the remains of my scrambled eggs and poked them with my fork. "A lot was going on, and it seemed like he was just being a cliché villain. I didn't think to mention it."

Words flew across the room as everyone speculated why the Demons wanted me on their side. They seemed more concerned with that than how in the same set of dreams, I saw apocalyptic chaos. Did the demons need me to bring on some kind of Armageddon? Did the Incubus think if he hurt me enough, I'd destroy the world in my rage? Maybe he knew more about my power than I did and understood my nature better than my family did.

It's possible, whispered Mel in my mind. *But our family can't wrap their heads around the idea of demons turning you to their cause, so Grandpa, my mom, and José are seeing two separate problems: keep you safe and figure out who wants to conquer the world and why.*

My stomach ached. Anxiety twined around my insides. I slipped my leftovers to Bessie and closed my eyes. It didn't matter if the Incubus wanted to turn me evil or use me to get to Grandpa. I planned to annihilate the monster next time I saw him, and if that failed, well, I had no intention of letting him take me alive.

AT ELEVEN, WE left for Mass. The sun was out and everything was coated with an inch of soggy snow. Mel and Mike promised there were no Demons outside, but I couldn't shake the feeling of cold hands and the Incubus's fists. I looked around cautiously. Too nervous to clean off my car, I clambered in, turned the wipers on, and watched big chunks of snow fall off a maple while José cleaned the side windows with his shirtsleeves.

The door squeaked. José climbed into the passenger seat. "You seem quiet."

I put the car in drive. My world was falling apart like snow too wet and heavy to stay on the branches. There were real monsters out there that I could hurt without feeling guilty, but some of them were stronger than me, and they wanted to do bad things to me.

"What's wrong?" he asked.

I glared at him as I pulled onto the street. "Everything. The vision felt too real."

José squeezed my leg and did his best Yoda impersonation. "Always in motion, the future is. Happen, do all your dreams?"

"You'd be dead if they did," I admitted with a slight smile. "I guess I can change some things if I know enough about them."

"Then don't ignore the dreams. Decipher them so you can change what you see."

"You think I can do that?" My dad had dreamed the future too. It had saved Grandpa from getting paralyzed by a Troll but hadn't saved my dad from getting eaten.

"Of course. What's the point of being a prophet if you can't change the future?"

"Prophet sounds too biblical," I muttered. Life was full of pointless things: high school, cookies without chocolate, and frilly dresses. Who was to say my dreams were more useful than math class?

ST. PATRICK'S CHURCH was on the same property as the school, but set back on the right-hand corner of the land. Its shimmering gray stone and towering steeple made it look like a raw-diamond pendant for the campus. Inside, oak pews encased three aisles. Life-size bible scenes caught sunlight as it poured through the stained glass window, projecting red, blue, and green shapes all across the shining floor and pews. Olivewood carvings hung on the wall, reminding the congregation how Jesus suffered during his crucifixion. I dipped my fingers in a basin of Holy Water and then followed Mel right down to the front pew, which was shorter than the rest so a wheelchair could park next to it without blocking the aisle. Grandpa, Sister Marie, and Dr. Estrella were waiting for us.

"You three appear to have had a rough night," said Aunty Lucy, wheeling up alongside the pew.

"Only a few scratches." Dr. Estrella frowned at his bandaged hand, and I couldn't help but grin. I genuinely hoped it was broken, or permanently damaged so he couldn't hit José with it.

If you don't want to become him, you're going to need to learn to forgive. Mel's voice fluttered through my head like a butterfly whose wings jumbled my gray matter. I tried to ignore her and looked around the church. The front pews were filled with the elderly while the middle hosted families. Among them were several students from my class, including Jenny Dunn. Her icy eyes narrowed as she bore her teeth in a fake smile: non-verbal teenage code for "I hate your guts."

Sam's parents walked in with Sam trailing behind them. Her hair was flat instead of spiked, and as she got closer, I saw dark circles under her eyes and traces of smudged makeup. Her black T-shirt was wrinkled and grass stained the knees of her jeans.

Apparently, she'd had a rather wild night.

When she saw me staring, she smiled and winked at me before following her parents into one of the middle pews.

"Sunshine, you in there?"

"Yeah. Just spacing." I tore my eyes away from Sam and looked at Grandpa. "How are you feeling?"

"Better than last night," he said with a grin. A closer examination told me it was forced: he winced every time he inhaled and was clutching his cane even though he was sitting down.

Organ music smothered the conversation, the cantor announced that Fr. McPherson was saying Mass and the opening hymn was on page 325. I tried to only listen to the music, but I was worried about Grandpa, and Jenny Dunn. What if he didn't get better? What was Jenny going to do to me in school tomorrow? Did learning I was Demon hunter count as an excused absence? The questions rolled on and on until Mel interrupted.

Open your sight.

Why? I thought back at her.

It's beautiful. You'll understand when you see it.

Realizing she wasn't going to tell me what "it" was, I took a deep breath and let my eyes slide out of focus until my Sight opened. Everything on the altar glowed, dusted by golden and white light that was emitted by two majestic creatures. Their skin was liquid light. Their robes shimmered and feathered wings glistened like freshly fallen snow.

They're angels, said Mel. *Real ones.*

A faint glow surrounded the priest as he processed down the aisle. Its brightness increased as he got closer to the altar. Eventually, it merged with the angelic glow and consumed them.

Keep looking.

Light flowed off of the altar, sliding around some people and through others. It slid right into Mel, amplifying her light until I couldn't look directly at her. It brushed the top of José's and Grandpa's heads, lingering long enough to give them the tiniest glow, but it seemed to actively avoid Dr. Estrella. That pattern held throughout the church. A lot of the older people seemed to be sucking up as much of the light as they could get. It twined around others, like Sam, trying and failing to find a way in. The light slid away from

Sam the way water beaded off oil. The light avoided Jenny Dunn as much as it avoided José's dad.

That's because they're both full of rage. It's avoiding you too.

Does it matter if it avoids me or not?

It can make you stronger if you let it.

Then how do I let it?

Let go of your anger.

How?

Mel didn't answer. She and her butterfly thoughts were gone, once again leaving my brain mushy in their wake. While the priest rambled on about Lenten sacrifice, I tried to identify exactly what angered me the most. Not all the therapists I had worked with had been equally proficient, but I was pretty sure they all agreed that, in order to solve a problem, I had to know what its root was. Getting rid of all the anger would take time, but maybe, if I pinpointed one problem and loosen the knot a little, I could let some of the light in today.

I looked down at my hands, which were balled into cramped fists. I forced myself to open them. Some of the things that made me angry were obvious, like the fact that my family hid things from me. Time was the only thing that was going to ease that hurt. I needed to focus on the subtler threads, like José. I was still hurt that he had slept with Jenny Dunn only a week ago, even though he was supposedly in love with me. He should have been trying to woo me, not get over me. I didn't think what he did was right, but I could try to see it from his point of view.

He lived in a nightmare, hunting monsters he wasn't strong enough to fight, and people got hurt as a result. His father beat him. I was unpredictable, sometimes his best friend, sometimes ignoring him, or even being cruel in my attempts to prove the lie: that I didn't have feelings for him beyond that of a brother. It made sense that he sought some kind of distraction or release. For some people, that might have been a drug. For him, it had been anyone who was attracted to him, like Jenny, and Jenny was a lot easier to quit than heroin. I could forgive him that.

I took his hand. I was probably being more literal than necessary, but as the congregation spoke the apostle's creed, I shouted the prayer, imagining that one hurt leaving with my words. My chest felt lighter. The knot of anger loosened enough to let a sliver of light in. It surged through that crack, pouring through my veins until my muscles felt tougher and my body so light I was afraid I might float away.

As the Mass moved on to the Liturgy of the Eucharist, I was able to focus. I let the words, music, and thud of a hundred beating hearts fill my head. When the priest consecrated the bread and wine, it exploded with a light brighter than any I'd ever seen. I welcomed it inside me, letting it burn the shadows and expose the monsters, chasing them into the darkest corners, singeing the whiskers right off their noses.

I might not forgive everyone today, but sooner or later, I would. I was not going to let hate weigh down on me like a pack full of textbooks—no more pushing through life always angry and never knowing what my purpose was. I was more than that.

You certainly are, whispered a voice too deep to be Mel. I looked at her, then at the Angels on the altar. She nodded, confirming one of them was speaking to me.

What am I supposed to do? I thought at him.

A flash of light blinded me, and I wasn't in church anymore.

I STOOD IN the center of a star. Below me was a future where I was consumed by the darkness inside me. I scorched earth for Demons, leaving it a barren place where skeletal people scavenged for food and hid from monsters. I sat on a throne. My eyes had turned black and my hair was fire. Vertical scars outlined the arteries on my wrist. Rope marks were burned into my throat. A bullet-shaped scar marked my brow like José's Elf-stone marked his. He was chained beside my feet in a tattered silk robe and the Incubus was by my side.

In another reality, I was captured and broken as the world: unable to stop the apocalypse but unable to die with those I cared about.

And in yet another, Mel destroyed the world while I followed in her shadow.

The Angel showed me all the ways things might go wrong, but just when I was ready to give up hope, I saw one more vision, one in which I learned to control my rage instead of letting it control me. Like an ancient deity, I rained destruction on Demons in the form of lightning and faced the Incubus alone in the dark. In that vision, the world survived.

Chapter Nineteen

We recovered one of the missing girls, badly bruised and very pregnant. Neither she nor the child survived the birth. The priest says their deaths were a mercy; I can't help but wonder what would have happened if the child had survived and been raised by a loving family instead of a Demon. The child could have grown to be one of the most efficient hunters of this age, especially if it befriended the half Angel born to counter it.

—The hunting log of Jamison Evanstar, 1887

"Erin, it's time to go." José's hand was on my back, but his voice was far away.

Blinking, I shook my head. Pieces of the vision fell away like dust shook off a book opened for the first time in seventeen years. The faintly glowing altar came into focus, empty of both angels and humans. The church was deserted.

"I think I had a vision," I said, watching how the sun made red and blue spots appear on Mel's forehead.

"You think?" laughed Mel.

I stood up and stretched, begging the burn of stretching muscles to ease the anxiety lingering from the vision. "How long have I been sitting here?"

"Mass ended about twenty minutes ago. Mel told me not to disturb you until now," said José.

"I can't let them take me or turn me," I said to everyone and no one. My heart still raced while guilt and fear squirmed in my stomach like worms freshly skewered on a fishing hook.

"Who is them?" asked José.

"The Demons. The world will end if don't I electrocute them!"

"All of them?" asked Aunty Lucy.

"The vision wasn't that specific. I just saw a bunch of futures, and the only good one involved me throwing lightning bolts at a lot of Demons." I kept on describing the visions, how Mel or I could be used to trigger the apocalypse until I ran out of things to say. Everyone sat in the pews questioning me until Sister Marie finally suggested we move downstairs because, in spite of all the destruction I saw, I still had no clue who or what actually orchestrated it.

I followed Mel, Mike, and José down a winding staircase. Wood creaked and groaned until the steps finally ended in a dark room that reeked of moldy paper. Mel was the only source of light until she pulled a string and a fluorescent bulb buzzed to life.

As she walked farther into the room pulling strings, I saw the walls were lined with shelves. Each was overflowing with books covered in varying amounts of dust. Some were leather-bound while others were simply three-ring binders. Wide tables loomed in the center of the room. Each had mismatched lamps and computers in desperate need of an update.

"They've had plenty of updates," said Mel, responding to my thoughts out loud. "Mike is sentimental when it comes to old hardware. If you take a look at the screens, you'll see they're actually touchscreens. The guts have been pulled out of the old monitors and filled with hard drives."

"Are there other archives in bigger cities, or is this it?" I asked, realizing the room went on and on for at least triple the church's length.

"This is the New England archive. They're scattered across the country in places you wouldn't expect them. You won't find one in a major city." José stared at a collection of leather journals that were almost completely dustless.

I took his hand. "Do you come here often?"

"I do. Seamus thinks I'm wasting time I should be using to train physically, but I find words helpful. This section, the Journals of Jamison Evanstar, has a lot of information about Incubi. A big group of them got loose around here in the late 1800s."

"Until Jamison Evanstar used his virgin daughters as bait and caught the damned things in a Star Trap," growled Grandpa as he wheeled Aunty Lucy out of an elevator that looked like it belonged in a horror movie.

"Sounds kind of heartless to me." I wondered how the daughters fared in the trap. I hoped they were all well trained in the arts of violence and didn't end up as victims.

"Necessary things often are heartless." Pedro stepped into the room.

"Unfortunately, he's right." Grandpa stared at the floor, frowning as if he was embarrassed to admit heartlessness in front of me. After a few minutes, he looked up. "Let's get to work."

We spent the next two hours poring over old hunting logs. As I read the gruesome accounts, I got a better sense of why Grandpa had wanted to keep me away from hunting. By the time most hunters reached thirty, they all seemed to be hard, bitter people with more mental problems than me. How bad would I be in thirteen more years?

I was supposed to be focused on searching for times when a Fallen Angel, rogue Elf or Witch got up to no good by summoning and controlling Demons. Mike had programmed a spreadsheet to look for patterns as we entered information to it. He hoped organizing the data enabled us to predict what was behind the increase in Demonic activity and what that person or thing intended to do next.

Sitting still and staying focused on the words was a struggle. I had a dozen texts from Sam, sent during church, detailing a night of sneaking out to the woods to drink with a friend she never named, ending with one asking why I fell asleep, but I didn't have enough cell service to reply. Just when my thoughts slowed down and settled into the rhythm of reading, my senses heightened. I heard breathing, heartbeats, and the hum of lights. Then my Sight slipped open and I remembered that Mel glowed and the Estrellas had gems on their heads because unlike Grandpa and Sister Marie, they had no Elf blood at all, and therefore, they didn't have the Sight. Based on what I had read of the Evanstars, a lot of men like Grandpa had intermingled with Elves to strengthen their line of hunters; I didn't know how human I was or wasn't.

You can worry about that later. For now, focus on reading and entering data.

I tried not to think of why Mel told me to worry about it later instead of just answering my question. I tried to focus on closing my Sight and reading. I couldn't remember what part of the page I had been on, so I started from the top:

Oct. 13, 1962

This is the third night in a row that I've had to contend with a combination of Trolls, Spikes, and Crawlers. Everything in my body aches. I've got burns from ice and gouges from teeth. If this keeps up, I don't know how I'm going to manage my double life. Everyone at work thinks I'm on drugs or have a drinking problem because I come in looking and feeling crappy. Okay, I might have a bit of a problem, but it's only because I live a lie and see things that would make most of the desk jockeys at the firm crap their pants in an instant. I need alcohol and pills to even close my eyes at night.

Anyway, so while I was hunting tonight, Franky and I managed to capture one of the Crawlers. It's definitely working for something that scares it more than us because it wouldn't tell us shit. That means whatever is making these idiots stick together isn't human. The Pixies swear it's nothing from the Faerie realms, so that means we might have one of the Fallen on our hands. Pops said that happened back in The War. Bad crap went down then. Genocide. And with all the social unrest rocking the States right now, I wouldn't be surprised to see some kind of mass killing again. It would be easy for one of the Fallen to make it look like the humans did it on their own since so many of them hate each other.

I asked Pops how he and the other hunters discovered the Fallen back in The War. He said one of them figured it out by accident. How are we supposed to stop it if we don't even know where to start looking? There are more than enough bad guys in power these days. I've never felt so helpless or incompetent.

"This is useless," shouted Grandpa slamming a dusty tome closed. "Something is planning a demon invasion that could end the world as we know it, and we are sitting around in a library. We need to interrogate one of those bastards."

"You already tried that." Aunty Lucy rolled her eyes. "You didn't get much information out of it before you lost patience and banished it."

"We interrogated a Crawler. We need something more intelligent, like the Incubus. That nasty piece of hell-spawn actually has half a brain."

"Yeah and it outsmarts us every time we get close," said José, glaring up from a stack of yellowing typewriter paper. "We can't manage to banish it. How are we going to trap it?"

"But you did banish it." I stood up and began pacing the room to think clearer. The hunting logs were pretty disorganized. We could spend hours reading through them and never get anywhere.

"Only because it underestimated you. If you hadn't picked that moment to accidentally discover magic, then it would've killed me and captured you because I was completely unarmed," said José.

"Which was classic José stupid," muttered Dr. Estrella.

I paused my pacing and openly sneered at Dr. Estrella. If he raised a hand against José now, I'd beat him senseless and damn the consequences.

José stared at a shelf with his arms wrapped around his chest and his back to his father. His eyes were wide and wild; his lips curled into a nervous snarl. "Weapons aren't allowed at school and you know it. I had no clue Erin and Sam were going to drag me to the beach."

"Just because you get a night off doesn't mean the Demons are going to leave you alone," continued Dr. Estrella. "You could stand to be more resourceful. You should have—"

"Pedro, give the boy a break," interrupted Grandpa. He rose so he was standing nose to nose with Dr. Estrella.

I smiled, relieved I wasn't the only one who ever stood up for José.

"He did the best he could in the situation." Aunty Lucy wheeled over to Grandpa's side.

Outnumbered, Dr. Estrella changed the subject and soon his insult to José was forgotten in a tempest of theories on how to best investigate the rise in Demonic activity and get a more concrete idea of what their apocalyptic endgame entailed so we could stop it. The louder they spoke, the faster I paced. Soon, they were shouting just to be heard over each other. It was louder than the cafeteria at school, louder than a sports game; it was like a bunch of heavy metal bands trying to simultaneously play on the same stage, vying for the audience's' attention.

I couldn't understand a single thing they were saying. I covered my ears, but it wasn't enough to drown out the noise. My head throbbed. I wanted to scream, kick shelves, and throw books around the room. I took a deep breath, doing my best to resist the toddlerish impulse. I paced faster and faster until my heart rate elevated and I was drenched in sweat.

José and his dad were shouting in each other's faces. Their hands were clenched into fists. A purple vein bulged on Dr. Estrella's head. I paced closer to them, ready to intervene if things got violent.

Emotion rolled off them like heat from blacktop in the summer. It made me dizzy. It gave me an idea.

"All of you shut the hell up!" I shouted.

Everyone kept arguing right over me. I growled and shouted again. They ignored me again, so I picked up an old chair and screamed while I bashed it into pieces. That got their attention.

"Erin, what the hell is the matter with you?" shouted Grandpa.

I smiled, reveling in the silence for a minute before I spoke. "I wanted to tell you all something, but you were being idiots and arguing about things you can't change, when a smarter solution is staring you right in the face."

"And what solutions is this?" asked Aunty Lucy.

"Me. Incubi can feel emotion. The Incubus even told me he felt my rage while I was fighting it. If you want to capture it, all you have to do is use me as bait. Put me somewhere alone and angry. He will come."

"Absolutely not!" shouted José.

"It's actually a good idea," said Dr. Estrella with an impish grin.

"I can't risk it," said Grandpa. "If he got them, I'd never forgive myself. They're too new to hunting, too...valuable."

"They proved they can hold their own in a fight," said Aunty Lucy. "This might work."

"But the Demons didn't know Erin's strength before. They do now. They won't underestimate Erin a third time," argued José.

"I disagree," said Mel. "The Demons Erin and José fought were broken up and banished too quickly to report anything. Erin can almost beat me in a fight. They have no clue what Erin is capable of."

"I don't have a clue what I'm capable of," I added. "So they really can't."

"I don't like it," said Grandpa.

"I do," said Dr. Estrella. "Do you have a plan?"

I nodded. I hated agreeing with him, but he was the only one objective enough to back my plan. "I need to appear to be alone, angry and isolated in a place the Demons have limited access to: a peninsula that's connected to land by a small causeway. We can conceal Star Traps ahead of time. The trick will be convincing him I'm actually alone and vulnerable."

"I know how to make that work," said José. He was staring at the floor with his lips pursed and his jaw clenched. "But I'm not sure I have the stomach for it, even if it is faked."

Chapter Twenty

To create a Star Trap, close your eyes and slow your breathing. Empty your mind until you feel nothing but the world around you. Take energy from it while focusing on each line of the seven-pointed star. Send the energy into the lines, careful to mentally fuse the lines together where they meet. It is important to conceal these well, for any disturbance in the lines will ruin their ability to trap a Demon.
—The Demon Hunter Lexicon

The cold wind ripped through the front of my sweatshirt. I shivered, glad to be back near José. We sat on a park bench below Portland Head Light, watching the sky change color over a white-capped bay. My head rested on his chest. He tried to rub my back, but his hand tripped over the sword concealed beneath my sweatshirt. I'd been attacked by demons a few too many times this weekend to risk going out unarmed. He had weapons too, but they were in a backpack under the bench. I snuggled closer to him, both to hide from the cold wind and to savor whatever calm, peaceful moments I could before the hell I'd been dreaming broke lose.

"I love you," he whispered.

My muscles tensed as I took a deep breath. There it was again, that sentence he kept saying even though he shouldn't be. A sentence I wasn't sure I could say back. I cared enough to worry about how loving me might hurt him, but I wasn't sure if that was love, even when combined with a confusing attraction and solid friendship.

"It's almost dark," I said, pulling away from him. "We should leave."

"I don't want to." His arms tightened around me like quivering snakes, jangling my insides while they cut off the circulation to half my body. He buried his face in my hair while his whole body shook. "Can't we stay a little longer?"

"I promised Grandpa we'd be back at the archives before dark," I said through gritted teeth, unsure if José was panicked or just being stubborn.

"But we're late, my dad will be gone before we get back."

"Fine, but I need to get up and move," I said. My toes writhed in my shoes like sea worms in a box.

I sprang to my feet as he let go and walked to the edge of the rock. Salty wind clawed at my cheeks and cooled the hint of rage building in my gut. City lights and their reflections glistened to my left, illuminating the occasional splash of a mermaid tale. Out to sea, where the last colors of the sunset faded to dusky blue, the diesel engine of an old lobster boat disturbed the peace while the port and starboard lights lit up its smoke.

I texted Mel, telling her José didn't want to go back to the archives until his dad left.

She replied with an eye roll emoji followed by a promise to kick him out so we could get back soon. I turned around expecting to José to still be on the bench. I jumped when my nose almost crashed into his. He tilted his head and smiled while I caught my breath.

"What?" I asked when he kept staring.

"Can I kiss you?"

"OK." I cupped his jaw with my hand and pulled his face closer to mine. Our lips brushed lightly at first while José's hands rested on my back, to the left and right of my sword, so gently they tickled and made me crave pressure on my skin. I slid my hand from his cheek to his back and pressed him closer to me, hoping he'd hold me tighter in return. It worked.

While out lips spoke in a language I couldn't understand, his hands slid to my ribs and moved down my side, evoking a shudder—not the good kind—as they put pressure on the curve of my waist. Nausea rose in my throat and my hands itched to tug at the skin there.

He stopped kissing and pulled my hands away from the skin they wanted to rip and trapped them on my hips. "That bothered you."

"Obviously."

"Why?"

"I hate that part of my body. Touching it reminds it's there, that no matter what I cover my body with, that very feminine curve doesn't go away. I get nauseated when clothing touches it wrong, let alone your hands."

"Then I won't touch you there again." He let go of my hands and took a step back. "I'll stand still a minute. Touch me where I can touch you."

I blinked. "Are there any places you don't want me to touch?"

He shook his head. "Your hands can go wherever they please."

In the back of my mind, I knew we needed to get back, but Mel hadn't texted me yet to say if Pedro had left. José sensed something was making me uncomfortable but stopped right away. He was asking for boundaries, which I appreciated. As soon as we got back to the archives, we'd be surrounded by people until we were too tired to do anything but sleep. Who knew when we'd get this chance again?

I started with this face, brushing my fingers across his cheeks and jaw, rubbing his forehead with my thumbs. My palms crested his head. His breath hitched as I cupped his neck and throat before separating my hands and massaging his shoulders. His sweatshirt was soft, so my palms glided down his arms and rested on his hands. I stepped closer, so our bodies were a breath away from touching. Comfortable with the thick layer of fleecy fabric between my hands and his skin, I explored his back, avoiding his sides and anything on the front of his torso.

I paused, breathing hard with my hands on his hips. My whole body tingled. I looked into his eyes. His pupils were dilated, and I wasn't sure if the moisture around his eyes was from the wind or if these were the kind of happy tears I'd never truly experienced myself.

"Can we kiss again?" he whispered.

"OK." I opened my palms and slid them down to his ass.

"Are you sure?" he asked, voice breaking as he spoke.

"Yes."

As our lips collided, one of his hands squeezed on my ass and the other was planted between my shoulders, above to the side of my sword's hilt. His lips moved to my neck, sending secret messages to my body that drew it closer to his.

"Erin, please, please keep moving your hands to my front," he gasped. "Even if you don't want me to touch you there, please touch me."

I kept my hands right where they were.

His hands covered mine, slowly pulling them up towards his groin.

I yanked them away and stood up. "That's too far."

"Please," he said, pushing my hand into his rear pocket where he had a condom stored. "There is no one around, and no one is going to be around," he said. "Please. At least a blow job. I can teach you if you don't know how."

"No."

His hands shook as he squeezed my hands tighter and brought them around to the button at the top of his jeans. "Please touch me, Erin. I need to you do something."

I yanked my hand away, but he didn't let go.

"We can't do all that and just stop," he panted, trying to pull me close again.

"We can stop, and we will." The magnetic tingles fled from my body as I stepped away.

He threw his hands up and then stuck one in his pants.

"Don't do that in front of me." I crossed my arms.

"Then do it for me."

"No."

He took a few deep shaky breaths. "How long is it going to be this way?"

"As long as it needs to be. Kissing is fun, but I'm not ready to try anything else."

"What's the point of being lovers if we can't have sex? How is this different from friends?" He plopped down on the bench, running his hands through his hair.

"How is it not different? We've spent more time together, cuddled, kissed, and told each other things we used to keep secret. It's barely been two days, but nothing is the same," I said, aware that with each word, I got louder and louder.

"Now you're mad at me."

"Yes, and I have the right to be. You're pressuring me." My hands retreated to my neck, clawing at already raw skin as rage and frustration defeated me.

He stood, reaching for my hands. "I was asking."

"Pressuring, and it was a shitty thing to do." I took a step back and my nails ripped the scab off of the cut I'd made earlier. "If you want us to work, you need to get your head out of your dick."

"Stop yelling!"

"Then stop being an ass!"

"I'm not doing this," he whispered. "You hurt me every time we get close. And you harm yourself."

"What do you mean you're not doing this?" I backed away further and dug my nails in harder.

"I'm breaking up with you."

"But...I" My throat tightened too much to let more words out. I wanted to pin him down and scream that he couldn't just change his mind like that. I wanted to rip all my skin off so I could let my monsters out."

"We're friends, and we need to get back to the archives. I was stupid to think we could be anything more."

"You need to get back," I hissed. "It's not safe for you to be in a car with me right now."

"Erin, you can't –

"Leave," I yelled, "before I'm truly infuriated. Get the hell out of here!"

He backed away, slowly at first, then broke out into a run, leaving me alone in the dark with two honed blades. I glanced at the weathered bench we'd been sitting on earlier. His backpack was under it. He'd left me alone with two sharp swords, two loaded guns, and a dagger.

A demented smile strained my face and maniacal laughter bubbled out of my mouth. The smart thing to do was to call Mel. Instead, I scooped the backpack off of the ground and took the two guns out. They were black and heavy pieces of metal exactly the same as the guns at the shooting range Grandpa occasionally dragged me to. Grandpa could name any gun and rattle off its specs, but I hated the things. They made killing too quick. If I'd had a gun the night Ricky hurt me, he would've been dead long before Mel arrived.

A gust of wind tore through my hoodie. It was time.

I put the guns down where I could reach them easily and dialed Mel's number, but before I hit send, a hoard of Crawlers materialized out of nowhere. I dropped my phone, snatched the guns, and tried to focus on slowing my perception of time. Large teeth gleamed in the moonlight as jaws unhinged. Muscle rippled below thin white skin. With my perception of time slowed down, it seemed to take forever for their crooked feet to fall back to the ground with each step they took toward me. I lifted the gun and fired. My bullet sailed past one without coming close. I fired again. It passed an inch shy of a notched, moldy ear. I took a deep breath and steadied my aim. The next shot clipped one on the shoulder and the fourth made it explode into thousands of snowflake-sized pieces.

Its two companions paused ten feet away, snarling as they watched the other's remains float to the ground. They circled me in slow motion, diving and dodging each time I pulled the trigger. They were able to speed up their perception of time too, but couldn't sustain it as long as me. Or were they only faster because *my* perception was slipping back to normal?

I focused on breathing, willing time to slow again until the Crawlers were barely moving. I took aim again and squeezed the trigger. The gun clicked empty. Both Crawlers charged, but it was almost comical to watch. It was like they were in low gravity, soaring up into the air then floating back to the ground, feather-light even though they had to weigh over 200 pounds each. I unsheathed the katana. Gripping it with both hands, I danced forward and sliced the three Crawlers into a dozen chunks of steaming Demon meat.

"Is that all you have," I shouted at the dark ocean. I was just getting warmed up.

"The Crawlers were merely there to use up your bullets," said a deep voice that croaked like a bullfrog.

I spun with my katana out. It passed through where the Incubus's mid-section would've been if he hadn't vanished at the last second. He reappeared a few feet to the left with his black trench coat blowing open in the breeze, revealing a gleaming white body that looked chiseled out of marble. I tightened my grip on the katana and swung again, concentrating on how bad I wanted to cut him up into thousands of tiny pieces and scatter them across the universe, so he could never materialize again.

He vanished seconds before my blade made contact.

"That rage is so delicious," he said, appearing so close we were almost touching.

I took a step back, toward a specific section of grass, one Sister Marie and I had concealed a Star Trap in while setting the stage for our plan to defeat the incubus. He vanished and reappeared every time I swung at him, but once I got him in the trap, he'd be stuck in one place, fully solid and materialized.

"I know you want to fight," he continued, "but I'd rather do something more enjoyable. I could take that rage and use it to make something wonderful."

"I'm not doing anything with you," I snarled still inching closer to the trap. In all the stories Grandpa had told me, the Star Traps never failed to contain a Demon unless they were sabotaged. The tricky part was getting the Demon into it.

"I never said you had to be willing." He leered and advanced toward me.

"Who are you serving?" I shouted. "Who are you serving? Who—"

His laughter cut off my third repetition. It was so loud it filled my head, hurt my ears, and made it impossible to concentrate. It was like metal grating on metal but inside my skull. I covered my ears and took another step back so I was in the trap. I started my question again. "Who—

A rock, or something as hard as one, crashed into the back of my head. Darkness swirled on the edges of my vision and spots floated in front of my eyes. The Incubus's laughter morphed into strange syllables that formed words I hadn't heard before.

A cold claw grasped the back of my neck. I spun around, kicking as I went. My boot collided with the jaw of a Spike sending it tumbling to the ground. More charged me. I unsheathed a knife, with that in one hand and my sword in the other, I to parried the clubs they swung at me. They followed me into the Star Trap, and they followed me out of it. Shit.

"Those traps your people use are effective, but they have to be perfect. One tiny flaw and they don't work at all. Those wards Amelia set up to prevent interference were destroyed easily once I was informed of her methods."

"How did you know?" I asked, wondering if there was a traitor, or he was somehow spying on us.

"It was a bad plan, hilarious, really. That boy will stop at kissing forever if it is what you want. He hates himself for even pretending to pressure you. I would've feasted on that self-loathing if I wasn't required to retrieve you, not that your rage isn't scrumptious."

"You were watching?" I spun, blocked, and dodged as the Spikes tried to pummel me with their clubs.

"Oh yes. I only wish you'd heard the modifications Pedro suggested. For a minute, I thought the boy was going to shoot him."

"José should've shot him." Imagining what José's monster of a father suggested conjured a fresh burst of rage I used to cut a six-legged monster in half.

"If you want Pedro Estrella dead, I can arrange that. My earlier offer is still open."

"Go to hell!" I shouted before I realized how ridiculous it was.

The Incubus laughed again. My brain felt like it was being cut up in a meat grinder. A club hit my rib. Something cracked. Pain and rage turned my vision red. My knee gave out as another stick collided with it. I couldn't focus on fighting with his laughter in my head. I needed to shield, but I couldn't concentrate on that and fighting off the Spikes all at once.

Spinning wildly, I decapitated three demons in a row. "How did you know about the fake break up and the traps?"

"You should be more careful whom you trust," he said and vanished into a hoard of materializing Demons. There were hundreds of them. Spikes, Crawlers, Trolls and some thing's I didn't have names for. Some resembled deformed versions of insects: cockroaches the size of my Jeep and spiders the size of a horse. Others resembled dogs that woke up on the wrong side of a nuclear reactor with multiple heads, an odd number of eyes, and sharp, gleaming teeth.

"We want her alive," boomed the Incubus's disembodied voice.

"I'm not a her!" I shouted even though I knew it was useless. Misgendering me was another way for the incubus to conjure more of my "delicious" rage.

The Demons came at me all at once, but the brain-crushing laughter vanished. I swung my blades wild, happy if they connected with any flesh at all. I slowed my perception as much as I could, decapitating a Spike while my arm swung toward giant wasp, bisecting a Crawler mid-run and cutting the arms off a giant spider. I moved through the hoard at lightning speed, but I hardly made a dent.

Pressure built inside my skull until I thought it would explode. The Demons sped up. They came at me in waves, not caring if they wound up impaled. Their ichor sprayed on my face and their hands and tentacles closed around me. Nothing cut or bit me. They piled on. I kicked and hit wildly, desperate to break free, but there were just too many of them. My heart was beating so hard my chest was cramping up and the cold pressure of their hands was making it hard to get air into my lungs.

In the distance, an engine roared over the squishing and gnashing. I tried reaching out with my mind. All around me was bone-chilling cold, but just at the edge of my perception was something warm and bright. Help was here, but I didn't know if they could do much. Grandpa never told me any stories where this many Demons attacked at once. For all I knew, this was the beginning of the end and the hunters were driving to their deaths.

Within seconds, there were enough Demons on me to prevent me from moving. Every muscle cramped up as I screamed and tried to move against the hoard. My body was drenched in sweat even though it was freezing cold. If I didn't stop, I was as good as dead.

Worse than dead, I thought. *The Incubus was ordered to take me alive. Mel! Can you hear me? There are Demons everywhere!* I continued to reach out mentally, hoping that if I could communicate with Mel, she'd tell me what I needed to do to escape. I didn't find her, but I noticed something else: electricity coursing through the wires that ran underground and up through the lighthouse to its sensors and giant bulbs. Perhaps if I was able to harness that and figure out what would work against all these Demons, then I'd have a chance of getting away.

I had used electricity to make a laser gun when I fought the Demons in the parking garage, and before that, I had trapped it in an ice sword. Even if I freed my hands enough to control a blaster, more Demons might come and overwhelm me before I did any damage. I needed something bigger, something capable of taking out a lot of them all at once.

The hoard moved me. Panic swarmed my skin like fire ants. What if this was what I had been dreaming? What if they were going to drag me down into the cold ocean? They were not going to take me alive.

I closed my eyes and focused all my attention on the electricity humming through the ground and called it to me. It hurt like nothing I'd ever felt outside a dream. It burned my shoulders and arms where it entered. It scorched inside me, causing my limbs to shake violently, but the Demons touching me shook twice as hard and disintegrated into piles of ash. Screaming, I rose to my feet and shoved more energy out of me.

Lightning bolts flew out from the tips of my fingers, striking five Demons that writhed, smoked, and dissolved. More filled their place. I was screaming and convulsing, but I kept pulling more energy in and pushing it out. My body burned. Crackling yellow and white bolts flew out of me and danced across the hoard of Demons, destroying every icy monster they touched. I kept screaming, throwing more out until my body failed me. Utterly exhausted, I fell into a pile of something soft and cold. My eyes closed and an icy blackness consumed me.

Chapter Twenty-One

Niben, the youngest daughter of the Seelie Queen, was cursed to love only mortals and never find peace with a fellow Elf.

—From the Fae Chronicles, translator unknown. A copy present in every hunter archive

"What the hell just happened?" shouted a deep voice, garbled as if it came out of a broken telephone.

"They turned their self into a human Tesla coil," said an equally garbled voice.

"I won't be able to live with myself if they die after... after our fight" said a scratchy, crackling voice. Was that José?

"It wasn't even a real fight," said the second voice, a little louder and clearer.

"Erin?" José's hot hands frantically my touched my cheeks. Two fingers pressed on my neck, checking my twitchy pulse. "Erin, wake up. I love you." Big arms wrapped around my shaking body and pressed it against warmth. "Please wake up. Please be okay."

His voice cracked more with each word. It sounded broken, like bits of him were leaking out and dying each time I didn't respond. He kept talking, telling me how his dad wanted him to change the plan, but he refused. Tears poured out with his voice, soaking my limp, useless body. He sounded utterly hopeless and pathetic, and in that moment, I realized how broken he had been all along.

"Be careful with them," shouted Dr. Estrella, but José was inconsolable.

"Mel will fix them," said Mike. "Relax."

"How do you know Mel's even alive?" croaked José.

"I know," said Mike.

The stream of tears increased. I still couldn't move or see. I wondered if I was dying or if I was trapped like this, blind, paralyzed, and mute until I starved to death. Could Mel fix me? What if I had fried my synapses beyond repair?

"Mel's on her way. She'll heal you. You need to stay with me until she gets here. I love you." José rocked me back and forth, rubbing me like he was trying to revive a stillborn puppy.

"I said, quit crying," said Dr. Estrella.

José was ripped away from me, and my body fell limp to the pavement. I heard a thud and a gasp.

"Keep your hands off him," shouted Mike.

Dr. Estrella laughed.

There was another thud and a crunch.

"Don't tell me that was your first time punching someone without gloves," laughed Dr. Estrella. "I suppose your girlfriend will have to waste energy healing you now since you injured your hand trying to defend my waste of a son."

There was another thud, a rush of heat and a squealing shout. "Cut the bullshit now or I swear to God I will burn you from this earth."

I'd never been happier to hear Mel's voice.

I expected Dr. Estrella to be fearful or apologetic.

He laughed. "A mighty statement coming from someone like you."

Dr. Estrella kept talking, but Mel ignored him, talking to me instead. Their voices merged into a jumble of contrasting sounds. Fiery heat surged through my body, as if Mel was burning me from the earth, not him.

I know it hurts, whispered Mel in my head. *Your nervous system is all discombobulated. I'm trying to fix it, but it's going to hurt worse before it gets better.*

I melted into a ball of creational goop then reformed into a new body. I shook and convulsed as more energy surged through me, rebuilding connections that had been lost or burnt. Eventually, it stopped. I opened my eyes, finding myself looking up at my flickering cousin, panting on her hands and knees. I could make out the shapes of other people behind her, shadows hovering over a fine white powder that covered the earth.

"Thank you," I croaked. "When did it snow?"

"That's not snow," said Mike. "It's what happens when Demons meet electricity."

My voice was scratchy and weak, but it was functional. My fingers opened and closed, and I twitched my legs.

"Dear Amelia, you won't be smiting anyone for a while now," laughed Dr. Estrella.

My rage reared its head. I tried to sit up, but I flopped back to the ground like a useless fish. Dr. Estrella was standing a few feet away from us, flanked by a pair of creatures that would have looked human if it wasn't for their scaly legs and shark-teeth. Mike stood in the shadows behind him, clutching his wrist. José perched on the ground, absolutely still, prey trying to avoid a predator's attention.

I stared into Mel's swirling eyes and mentally replayed my conversation with the Incubus.

"Where's Grandpa?" I asked out loud.

"Right here, sunshine." He appeared out of nowhere with Niben beside him.

"Sunshine is too girly," I muttered.

"I'm glad you're okay." Grandpa's jaw relaxed and he smiled.

The Elf-woman looked unharmed, but Grandpa was bleeding, hobbling, and wheezing. Mel made eye contact with Niben, and a wall of stifling humidity surrounded us as she joined the mental loop.

After watching my memories, she snarled at Dr. Estrella. "What did you do?"

"What are you talking about?" he asked, biting his lip.

"You know what I'm talking about." Niben stepped closer to him while everyone watched, confused.

Grandpa crouched, well, more like fell down beside me. Mel leaned her head on his shoulder. I pushed myself upright and the world spun.

"You're not fully healed," whispered Mel. "Sit."

I obeyed and watched things play out, emotionally numb, more detached than I thought I should've been. I wondered if this was it was an after effect of the electricity. Could it have altered my brain chemistry like some magical versions of electroshock therapy? Or had I just seen too much to process in too short a time?

"Why did you want José to change the plan?" asked Niben.

"Because the initial one was stupid," said Pedro. "Plus, the less people knew, the smaller the chance that the enemy will find out.

Niben grinned. "Then why did the enemy know exactly what your plan was even though your son refused to carry it out? Why were the traps all sabotaged?"

"He couldn't have known. It's not like José had the balls to do it anyway."

"But the Incubus knew; he watched the whole thing go down and waited an hour to show himself." Niben grinned.

Pedro paled.

Mel closed her eyes as a single tear dripped down her cheek.

"What did they offer you?" asked Niben.

Pedro backed away.

Niben grabbed him. "What did they offer you?"

"Jalissa," he whispered. "He said he could bring her back."

José's eyes widened and looked up at his father. I couldn't tell if it was in wonder or disgust. Jalissa had been the name of José's mother, who had allegedly committed suicide when he was a baby.

"Who is he?" asked Niben

"I can't speak his name!"

"Tell me!"

"I can't. He'll kill me."

Niben laughed. "You're a dead man no matter what. It will be less painful if you tell me."

Pedro opened his mouth to speak, but no words came out. His body went limp. His pants got wet in the crotch and he collapsed.

The mermaids lunged toward Niben. She raised her hands and they stopped in their tracks, looked at each other, and then skulked back to the ocean.

"I should've seen it," whispered Mel as she collapsed in a heap of tears. Grandpa wrapped his arms around her and pulled her close, stroking her hair how he did to when she was little. "I could've saved him if I'd seen it."

"You can't save everyone," he whispered. "And he was less deserving of your kindness than most.'

Mel's only answer was more tears.

Niben rested a hand on Mel's shoulder. "Child, one much more powerful than you is behind this. Neither my people nor humans have the power to bring back the dead, and Pedro would not have turned on us for an empty promise. Even your father struggles to see through this plot."

Inside, I knew I should join them in trying to comfort Mel. It was what any decent cousin would've done. I stared at the body. Dr. Estrella's face was frozen in a grimace. His death had been quick, but the Demon he made a deal with ensured that he suffered for even considering speaking its name. He stank of piss and feces, nauseating confirmation that the man who broke José was dead.

I watched José too. A decent partner, a decent *human*, would've gone to him. I didn't do that either. I watched as he knelt over his father's corpse with a shifting array of emotions dancing across his eyes. He took his father's hand, lovingly, tenderly, kissed it, then stood up and stomped on his father's face.

"I forgive you," he croaked, "but I won't miss you."

Then he hobbled over to where I sat, feeling like a robot with a broken processor.

"Do you know what he wanted me to do to you?"

"Yeah, but I know you wouldn't. I trust you."

He sank down into the snowy ash, scooting close enough for our legs to touch "He's really dead. I have no more family unless you count the relatives in Spain I never talk to."

"You have me." I edged closer to him.

"Do I?" he asked as tears leaked from his eyes.

"Yes." It took all my energy and made the world spin, but I managed to hug him. His arms slipped around my back, shielding me from the cold night. The tears came slow at first, and then they morphed to violent sobs that shook us both.

Chapter Twenty-Two

Demons are all prisoners in Hell. Yes, there are ranks and hierarchies, but that doesn't change the fact that they are all trapped there, sort of. It's a shitty prison because they break out all the time. When they do escape, we send them right back.

—Arthur Bearclaw annotating a copy of the Demon Hunter Lexicon in the Portland archives

An hour later, I was home in my pajama pants snuggled up in bed with Bessie and José. Both of them refused to leave my side. The only time José had let go of me was when I went to the bathroom. I hadn't been able to stop Bessie from following me inside. If Mel had shared their fear of leaving me alone, I would've been worried I was in danger of dropping dead at any moment, but she was downstairs with Mike and Aunty Lucy, who were struggling to convince her she was not a complete failure. She sounded more upset than José, even though he was the one who lost a parent, not her.

After Dr. Estrella's confession and death, Niben and Grandpa had gone to dispose of the body, something they had apparently done before. They said any medical examiner would think he died of a stroke. They claimed if Dr. Estrella didn't have other suspicious injuries, they could've left him as he was. However, they didn't want to take any chances, so they were staging a car crash. It was exciting in a disturbing way, like a crime movie had been added to the weekend's insanity. I almost asked José how often he had to dispose of bodies, but one look at his clenched jaw and bloodshot eyes stopped me.

José's tears stopped, but I doubted his grief had. He had a lot to process and when he was ready to talk, I'd listen. For now, it seemed it was enough to just be close. I tried listening to his breathing and not to anything else, but my hearing seemed to be stuck at Elf level similar to how my Sight seemed to be stuck open, courtesy of whatever damage I did via my Tesla impersonation.

I wanted José to be my lullaby again, but I heard too much of the conversation below me: Mel was making her mother and fiancé listen as she went through every instance where Dr. Estrella did something remotely suspicious. They indulged her because it was keeping her from charging out into the night to hunt for more information. When they could get a word in, they argued there was no way she could have known. Dr. Estrella knew about her mind reading and would've been careful not to think certain things around her, arguing that he had even been extra kind to her, trying to avoid her suspicion.

"They saying anything good?" José's voice was raw and scratchy.

"Mel is blaming herself for everything."

"If anyone should've noticed something wrong with my dad, it was me. I lived with him, hunted with him, saw the worst of him... I think he really had been trying to kill me when he sent me after the Incubus alone. What I don't get was why he was still hunting. He could've just killed us all."

"I think they were using him as an informant, not an assassin. They wanted to learn what made everyone tick. The Incubus wants to turn me into a weapon his superiors can wield against humanity, not kill me. They can use you to get me to cooperate. They need us alive."

"But you electrocuted the Demons. It's over, right?"

I shook my head. "The Incubus left long before it happened. He's still out there, and until I get rid of him and the Fallen Angel he's working for, they can make their takeover happen. We're still potentially screwed."

"We're not screwed," said José. "We have hope."

I squeezed his hand. He fell back into silence, holding me as if he'd drown in a current of grief if he let go. I listened to Pixies chattering outside my window, to cars grumbling by, to Mel making Mike map out events of the past week, and to fingers clacking on a keyboard. My body was exhausted, but my mind was full of thoughts refusing to come into focus. Ideas were on the edge of being born, snatched away by one sound or another before I figured out what they were.

"Do you think you'll be up to going to school tomorrow?" José's voice was another attention nicking sound.

"I'm not sure I'll ever be up for school again." Opening my eyes, I rolled to face José.

"Why?" His face twisted to a frown.

I resisted the urge to glare. "My head will explode from all the noise."

He narrowed his eyes. "But other than that, do you feel strong enough to go there, walk around with me and sit through a few classes?"

"I guess, but what's the point of going to math if I'm going to also be hearing what's being spoken in three or four other classrooms around me and can't focus on any of it? Perhaps if I took ADHD meds, I'd be able to ignore the others, but can't. They're made for humans. I'm pretty sure the same genes that give me Sight make my brain incompatible with the meds I need."

"Talk to Niben when things calm down. Her people make their own medicines."

"For ADHD?" I asked, thinking how Niben referred to it as a "mortal disorder."

"I don't know. Elves get as sick as humans, but I'm not sure if they get the same things with different names, or are susceptible to a completely different range of stuff. It doesn't hurt to find out if it exists and what it will cost."

"But that's not going to happen tonight." Nothing about it would be simple. Since I wasn't fully Elf or human, they'd have to make some adjustments, maybe blend it with human medicine. The cost was another complication: Elves dealt in favors and goods, not money.

"No, but you can still come to school tomorrow even if you won't learn. Having you there will make it easier for me."

"José, who goes to the school the day after he lost a parent?"

He flinched. "I need to go. I need to be the popular, smart kid everyone likes for just one more day before they hear he's dead. After that, I'll be pitied. I'll be an orphan. I need to know how it feels to be free from him, be with you, and be popular all at the same time."

I wanted to tell him no, to tell him he was wrong, that we should spend the day in bed watching Star Wars and playing video games, regaining our strength for whatever hell was still to come. I opened my mouth to say as much. It hung open, letting air dry out the spittle as I watched José's pathetically hopeful puppy eyes. I tried to say no, but the word that came was "okay."

That one word transformed José's frown to a goofy grin. He leaned forward and kissed me lightly on the lips, then snuggled his head on my chest like a pillow. "There's only a few more months of senior year. If you can stick it out, then you'll be done. You can take college classes online, so you don't have to deal with all the noise, but I bet there is a way to fix your hearing, even if elves don't make ADHD meds. Niben will know how, for the right price. After all, she's managed to spend considerable stretches of time among humans."

"She doesn't have ADHD," I said.

"You don't know that," said José. He chattered on and on, making plans for prom and shopping for dresses. He talked about getting control of his trust fund and buying a little house we could start our lives in once I turned eighteen. Half of what he said seemed extremely impractical, but I couldn't bring myself to tell him. This was how he was coping with his loss, by making plans for a future that might never happen whether we stopped the apocalypse or not.

I indulged him by sharing the visions I had of our future but regretted it when he pulled up real estate listings on his phone, searching for houses with green bedrooms to see if I recognized any of them. It was one thing to know that one day in the future we were going to live together. It was another to go from friends to dating to housemates in a couple days.

Mel and Mike rescued me from further plans by quietly slipping into the room and sitting on the edge of the bed. Mel's eyes were bloodshot, which looked weird with all the swirling colors. Her scarred cheeks were red and puffy.

"What's up?" I asked, directing José's attention to them.

"Just checking on you" was what Mel said out loud. In my mind, she said: *We found a listening device downstairs and are checking the rest of the house to see if there are others. We're not removing them—don't want the enemy to know we found them.*

A listening device? Like a bug from a spy movie?

Technology cloaked in magic. Pieces of a cell phone transmitter attached to silver coins magically altered to avoid detection.

Then how did you find it?

I was replaying things over in my head. I knew I'd missed something and then worked myself into a state so I wasn't just reviewing everything that happened but everything in the present too and I felt something physically off in the room and found the source of it and had Mike analyze it. Then I asked the Pixies who had been here and it was a very small list: you, your mom, José, and Sam. And I remembered what you told me about the beach. How long was Sam alone with the Incubus for?

I'm not sure, I said as I replaced Mel's chaotic thoughts to make sure I didn't miss anything. Instead of smooth words and thought-provoking intrusions, Mel was spilling her worry and guilt all over my brain in the form of run-on sentences.

We need to check on her without raising the suspicion of whoever is spying. Its 9 p.m., so it's not too late for you to be up doing last-minute homework. Did you have any history homework?

I don't remember.

Call her and find out.

Mel handed me the landline; I called Sam.

"Hey Erin, what's up?" she answered, sounding completely normal.

"Umm, nothing," I said, trying to sound normal and failing.

"Uh huh. I heard you drove José to church on Sunday. You ready to spill details?"

"No." There weren't any details to share, at least, not the kind she was hoping for. "I forget, did we have history homework?"

Sam laughed. "Yes, but you have to tell me details first."

I scrambled to think of something to satisfy her. "Umm, we made out on the hood of my Jeep in a parking garage at the hospital, after we realized Grandpa was okay."

"Glad he's okay," said Sam. "I'm also glad you got some lip action. We have to read chapter twenty-five and answer the questions at the end. There's gonna be a quiz."

"Right. Thanks."

Tell her to email you something.

"Can you email me your answers and notes?" I blurted since it was the only thing I could think of. "I have a killer headache and don't think I can read much tonight."

"You okay? Usually it's the other way around."

"Yeah. But I should go. I have a lot to do."

Should we go check on her? I thought at Mel before I ended the call.

She shook her head. *We are all staying in for the night. Troops of Pixies are on their way, and once you reply to her email, Mike will have means of accessing her computer. The phone call gave us access to her phone. We'll watch her for the night, and I'll come to school with you in the morning to get a good look at her mind. We don't know for sure that she planted these. Pixies are good watchers, but they are not perfect. Pedro could have found a way to fool them.*

"There is something I need you to do now," said Mel out loud. Whatever it was, she mustn't have minded the enemy hearing.

"What do you need?" I looked over at Mike and José. *Did they hear all this?*

They heard me, but I couldn't focus on making them hear you. She sighed out loud. "I need you to get a good night's sleep, and whatever you do, try not to dream."

Make a circle holding hands, she said in my head. *I can't concentrate enough to make a mind meld without physical contact. And try not to think of much aside from what you want to communicate.*

"I'll try," I said, responding to both what she said out loud and in my head before taking a few deep breaths and pictured my mind as a quiet, empty place as we all joined hands like a group of teenagers at a séance or a prayer group.

Last week, you were able to control your dreams so they were all about José, thought Mel.

What did you dream about me? wondered José.

A lot of stuff. My cheeks turned beet red and my body tensed up. I imagined myself throwing a blanket over memories as they surfaced.

You are really bad at this mind stuff. Mel's giggling filled my head along with a wave of longing from José and amusement from Mike.

Stay focused, she continued. *I need you to fall asleep focused on a specific set of questions. Use the same method as last week, but instead of focusing on José, I need to you focus on the questions.*

What questions? I asked, trying to catch anxiety in a tea filter before it got to Mel.

Who is controlling the Demons? Who, other than Pedro and the Incubus, is working for that being? What are their objectives?

My stomach twisted up into knots. *We know the objectives. They want to take over the world.*

That is their general endgame, but how? To what extent?

Mel, I think they've had enough today. José pulled me closer to him, as if cuddling me somehow shielded me from the nightmares Mel was asking me to invite into my mind.

Mel shook her head. *For the most part, the trapped Demons didn't know anything new. The only additional information was that the Spikes were promised some kind of freedom from Hell. My father and the other angels have not been able or willing to give me any useful information. Our project with the archives hasn't gotten us any results.*

What about Sam? asked José as his fear tugged at our minds.

We don't know for certain. Mel sent soothing energy with her words, but it was tainted by sagging guilt and buzzing fear.

I'll do it. I thought before they argued any further. José's head was full of black holes and landmines while Mel's was guilt and worry. I wanted them both out of my head.

"Thank you," Mel said out loud, ending the mind meld.

She mentally reminded me of the questions, said goodnight, and left the room. I gave José a peck on the lips and then rolled over so my back was to him. He curled his body around mine and wrapped his arms around my waist. I squeezed his hands, taking comfort in the fact that he would be there when I woke from whatever terrors Mel's questions evoked.

I closed my eyes and focused on breathing in five-second intervals. I repeated a version of her questions over and over in my head until they were the only things on my mind. *Which being is controlling the Demons? Who is working for that being? What steps are they taking to conquer Earth? Why?*

WHEN SLEEP FINALLY came, moonlight illuminated an Elf's silvery hair. He dove behind a freshly carved gravestone as a black broadsword tried to decapitate him. He swung his legs at a black robe, but they passed through it. A golden-eyed female Elf with a mane of blonde hair stabbed the cloaked being with a glowing sword while the male got back on his feet.

The scene shifted.

Brick and fire surrounded me. Demons snatched people as they fled the flames. A Crawler bit a teenager's head off. Anyone who fell was trampled. I watched it unfold and I laughed.

I was pulled back to the graveyard. The stones were chipped and covered with moss. Mel and I stood side by side, facing the cloaked being. It laughed at us, called us fools and offered us the world if we bowed down and worshiped it all while mushroom clouds blossomed in the horizon.

Water rose to the thirteenth floor of the Prudential Building in Boston.

Soldiers died as green gas filled a bunker.

The leonine female Elf ran from the shadow, clutching a glowing child to her breast. As the sun rose, she collapsed on the doorstep of a red Victorian house. A woman in a 1940s floral-print bathrobe opened the door, picked up the child, and looked around, not seeing the Elf dying on her doorstep.

I hung from my hands in a damp cave. There was just enough light to see the Incubus standing in front of me with his lips twisted up in a sickly smile.

"Stop fighting the rage," it whispered. "Embrace the darkness inside you."

I spat. He laughed. His arms blurred, squeezing my naked body against his. I squirmed as my insides revolted against his touch. Color seeped into his cheeks until they were peachy. His black eyes became cool gray. His nose shrank and his jawline sharpened.

"Remember him?" it whispered. "Remember what your cousin didn't let you finish?"

Chapter Twenty-Three

I don't know how I would've survived high school without my brother. All the other students were ignorant idiots. I hated them. I envied them. I would have tortured them for their innocence if he hadn't been there to keep me sane.

—Lucy Evanstar's eulogy to Liam, a copy saved in the hunter archives in Portland

"It's not over," I said, flailing my way up to a sitting position, gasping for air. "He could still try to turn me. I saw the world burn and I laughed."

"He won't," said José, rubbing my back.

I looked around my room, trying to anchor myself in the present. My Kendo trophy was where it belonged on the dresser, and my vintage Star Wars poster still covered my closet door. A sparkly light glinted in my peripheral vision. Silver and blue Pixies peeked in the window. I took a few deep breaths, but they stung my throat.

"That's because you've been yelling and screaming all night." Mel illuminated my room, plopping on my bed. "José is going to need earplugs if he plans to keep sleeping in the same room as you."

José rolled his sleep-encrusted eyes at Mel. "It's your fault."

Ignoring José, Mel gave me a few minutes to get myself under control before she asked me about the dreams. I described them to her with as much detail as possible while she closed her eyes and listened with both her ears and her mind.

You didn't happen to look at the cloaked figure's eyes? she asked when I finished.

No.

Mel rubbed my head and told me I should go back to sleep.

Do you know what any of it means? I thought as she started to leave.

I need to think. We'll talk when the sun is up.

José wrapped his arms around me once Mel was gone. We lay awake for a few minutes while my mind flitted from one thought to the next.

"Are we really going to school?"

"Yes," yawned José with a sleepy smile. "And Will is going to let me borrow one of his uniforms so we don't need to go anywhere near my...near dad's...near...the house I lived in. I'm not ready to face that yet."

His smile faded. I squeezed him close to me, and soon he was snoring, but I couldn't fall back to sleep. My mind was clogged with fresh worries. If Will knew José had spent the night again, he was undoubtedly going to blab to all the guys and soon, the whole school would know I had "slept with José" this weekend, but not that we hadn't actually done what the phrase implied. Normally, the majority of the kids at school ignored me, but now that I was dating José, I was going to be the focus of their gossip and, possibly, teasing. At my old school, I had almost always responded to teasing with violence.

It wasn't just my doomed academic career at stake. José had deluded himself into believing that one more "normal" day would make losing his father tolerable, as long as I was there for most of it. Getting into a fight with Jenny or some of her ilk would certainly ruin that for him. He blamed himself for my previous near fight with her. I didn't want to add more guilt to the tempest of emotions he was already weathering.

I shuddered. My feet squirmed and my heart raced. I needed to either get up or think about something else, so I focused on deciphering my dreams.

The images I saw in my sleep were pieces of a puzzle. The disasters were results of a war and apocalypse the Demons were going to cause. The shadowy figure was the Fallen trying to initiate it. But why did the Incubus want me to kill Ricky? Did he think it would make me evil?

The scene that made even less sense was the one with the Elf and the baby. Who were they? And why did the shadow want the baby so bad? The red house looked familiar, but I couldn't quite place where I'd seen it. There were lots of Victorian houses in New England. It could be anywhere.

THE HOUSE PHONE rang half hour before my 6 a.m. alarm was set to go off. I got up, carefully extracting myself from José's arms. He mumbled and rolled over, but didn't wake. I hoped his dreams were providing him with a needed escape from reality.

I took the phone off its charger and answered as soon as I got out of the room. It was Mom, calling to let me know she was at the airport waiting for her flight. We made small talk for a few minutes, asking each other how the weekend went. I noticed her answers weren't any more specific than mine. She told me she wanted to take me out to dinner tonight to celebrate some "exciting news" but refused to tell me what it was over the phone. Frustrated, I hung up and proceeded to get ready for school.

JOSÉ, MEL, AND I were all showered and out of the house by 6:45 a.m. When I stepped into the damp foggy morning, the branches of the trees were full of colorful Pixies. At least twelve different variations of red, brown, purple, pink, and green were represented in their hair and wings. Some of the little creatures were wearing leaves and flower petals, while others were clad in candy bar wrappers. I looked down the street but didn't see nearly as many in anyone else's trees.

"They watch you in shifts." Mel put a hand on my back, steering me toward my car. "Are you going to be able to drive?"

"Yeah." I tore my gaze away from the Pixies. My car was covered with strange runes and symbols that glowed white hot and fiery orange. A similar pattern wrapped all the way around the house.

"Those are wards." Mel pushed me closer to the car.

José claimed the front on the grounds that it would look weird for me to pull up to the school with him in the back and the front empty. Mel agreed but didn't look thrilled to be stuck in the messy back seat. I regretted the arrangement as soon as I was on the road. Mel's replenished aura was glaring in my rearview mirror, making me see spots. I tilted it up like it was night, but that didn't help much. I made a mental note to make sure she sat in front from now on as long as I wasn't trying to sneak her somewhere.

Thankfully, the drive to school was a short one. Objects looked brighter and emitted auras of colored energy. I was pretty sure I saw farther than normal. However, I didn't see any more magical creatures until we got to school, where the grounds were full of Pixies and two-foot tall creatures wearing pointy hats.

Garden Gnomes, supplied Mel mentally.

I thanked her and pulled my jeep up next to Will's red VW Golf. He had been waiting there for us and got out of his car as I threw the Jeep into park. He pulled a black garment bag out from his backseat and waved José over. Before getting out, José closed his eyes. Each breath made his shoulders straighter and his hands steadier, a tide rejuvenating parched seaweed. I imagined that if I had Mel's ability to read minds, I'd hear him taking all the bad things that happened over the weekend and locking them up in a gym locker. He'd pull the good things out into the brighter parts of his mind and embellish them a little. He straightened his shoulders, slowly took his hand off of me, and got out of the Jeep.

I lingered in the car. They were both smiling with their chests puffed out. If I hadn't seen Dr. Estrella die, I would never have guessed José had just lost his father. When I got out myself, I made sure to leave Mel enough time to sneak out as I removed my backpack. I saw her, but she was supposedly invisible to everyone else at school, aside from Sister Marie and José. I took a deep breath, contorted my face to what I hoped was an amused smile and walked over to where Will's stupidity was already rubbing off on José.

"You know, there are these things called changing rooms." I crossed my arms and tried to look cool, but heat rose in my cheeks at the sight of José standing behind the open door of the Golf in nothing but his boxers and undershirt. Nervous monsters twitched in my stomach as I saw how careful he was being not to lift his arms too high or show any of the bruises hidden beneath his undershirt shirt. A flood of anger washed in but evaporated to something as dry and twisty as a desert snake when I remembered Dr. Estrella was dead and José's current way of coping was to pretend things were normal.

"I'm sure you saw a lot more this weekend." Will smirked and raised his eyebrows.

I glared. "I did not and if you tell people otherwise, I'll tell everyone on the soccer team about your Doctor Who shrine and your dress collection."

"Are you going to tell me you didn't give him those hickeys?" Will leered, pointing at two purple and red splotches peeking above the collar of José's shirt.

Both boys burst into laughter, which made it harder for José to change. He seemed to be enjoying the attention his bruise was getting him, and the laughter seemed genuine. I turned around without another word, locked the Jeep, and stomped off to the main entrance, leaving him in his pretend glory.

I walked past the buckling sidewalk and trees full of Pixies. They nodded as I went by. Worried about Sam, I resisted the urge to try talking to one of them and scanned the flock of students congregated around the doors for Sam's spiked hair.

So far, the groups consisted of José's cronies from the soccer team, Jenny Dunn, and the girls that followed her. They whispered, shouted, and laughed, but at who or what, I didn't know. I hoped it was at some joke swallowed in the babble of too many voices, but suspected I was the source of their snickering.

Seeing was easier to focus on. Everyone was in their uniforms: forest green blazers, matching pants or skirts, and white blouses. Most of the skirts were knee length, but Jenny's was barely covering her bum. The top three buttons of her blouse were undone, and her blazer was open in spite of the cold. Her high heels made sure everyone who looked at her noticed the exposed cleavage and barely covered rump. For a brief moment, her cold eyes locked with mine.

Her lips curved up into a terrifying smile that promised she was going to get revenge on me for stealing her boyfriend.

I swallowed, took a deep breath, and made sure Mel was behind me. She nodded her glowing head. *Ignore Jenny and focus on finding Sam. Figure out a way to make her think of the night at the beach. I can't go rummaging through all her memories.*

I know. While we were getting dressed, Mel told me that while she heard people's thoughts, she couldn't just go digging through the memories without damaging their minds. The easiest way to make her think about it was to directly ask her if she planted the bug. However, if Sam was innocent, and I accused her of such a thing, then she'd think I was crazy. If she were guilty, we'd let the Demons know we not only knew about the bug but the fact that they were using Sam.

I glanced over at Jenny again and saw her snarling at me. Mel rolled her swirling eyes and told me to focus. I kept looking, but there was no Sam—only Jenny and her clique staring at me as if I were breakfast.

She's not here yet, I thought at Mel.

The Pixies followed her here and saw her go in the building. She's inside.

It was unusual, but not impossible that Sam decided not to wait for me. I walked toward the building when I heard José's voice getting louder and louder. I paused, and his arm was on my waist, his hand clutching my hip.

"How are you holding up?" I leaned into his face like I was going to kiss him on the cheek.

"It's harder than expected." He kissed my temple.

"You want to go home?"

He squeezed harder. "What home?"

"Mine, I meant. I'm sorry."

"It's okay." He loosened his grip. "Maybe your mom will let me crash at your house for a few days when word gets out."

I nodded, and the ringing bell saved me from having to voice my concerns about being with him for days and days with no breaks. It might be okay. It might make me want to pull the hair out of my head.

I looked around one more time as I walked to homeroom, but didn't see Sam anywhere. Jenny strutted by José, trying to get him to look at her cleavage. José was too busy acting to notice her. Sister Marie winked as we walked past her and didn't swat his hand off my back like she had when he walked in with his arm around Jenny two weeks before. I glanced behind me in time to see her lecturing Jenny, who pouted, buttoned her blouse, and unrolled her skirt.

"I think Sister Marie approves of us." José's grinning game face returned while he watched me struggling to remember my locker combination in the gauntlet of hallway chatter.

I looked around while I dumped my Bio and Spanish books into my locker. Mel had followed us, and no one seemed to be paying too much attention to José and I. "Other than her, how many people know about hunting?"

"Most clergy know, but they do a good job keeping it a secret. Everyone else is oblivious unless they are part of it. We shouldn't even mention it here," he said with an oddly determined look on his face.

"Okay. No one is paying attention to what we're saying." I closed my locker and walked to homeroom, clenching my jaw so I wouldn't respond to what I could understand of the surrounding blabber.

"Just try to forget for now. Let me have my sanctuary." If the noise was a cheesecake, José's voice was a hot knife.

I nodded, stifling a retort about his mood swings and the lack of logic that argument held. How could he think of this place as an escape from the supernatural world when it was run by a half-Elven nun?

When we stepped into homeroom, everyone glanced at us between whispers, reminiscent of hundreds of rustling leaves. I wished I could make myself disappear. The funny thing was, I could've made myself invisible to them with the same method I'd used to make José's blueberries look like anatomical hearts. Unfortunately, people would ask strange questions if I just vanished right in front of their eyes. I resisted the urge to experiment and sank into a desk in the back of the room.

Chapter Twenty-Four

Last night, I convinced both my parents to come out to the movies with Lucy and me. We watched a science fiction film called Star Wars. *For a couple hours, it was as if we were a normal family. Mom came over after the film and Dad cooked us dinner. It was perfect, until Lucy fried the electrical panel in an attempt to make her own 'force lightning,' and started a fire in the basement. Mom was furious, but Dad and I got a good laugh out of it.*

> —The journal of Liam Evanstar, confined to the archives after his death

"Erin? Wake up. Homeroom is over." José alternated between rubbing my back and shaking me.

"I wasn't sleeping." I yawned. "Just almost sleeping."

I followed him into the hallway, cursing our rotating schedule as I tried to remember what class we had first on Mondays. I gave up and asked.

"Gym. Hopefully you and Mel can chat with Sam in the locker room." José held my hand, leading me toward the locker rooms. "Exercise without risk of death will feel good."

"Right." I yawned again. As we passed Sam's homeroom, where she normally caught up with me, I saw Mel, but no Sam.

Something's wrong, said Mel. *I'm going to look around the school. Stick to your normal schedule and see if she shows up. Call me if she does.*

With what? I thought, but Mel was already gone. I didn't know if she meant the fried phone I'd left at home or my mind. I supposed I could borrow José's phone, but not if we were in different locker rooms or classes.

Before I could I ask José if Mel spoke to him too, my ears were subject to the torture of Will and his buddies wolf whistling. They were vultures, anxious to devour details about José's three nights at my house. I decided to ignore their questions and rushed into the one place they wouldn't follow me—the hell known as the girl's locker room. I prayed I'd find Sam lurking in there with a tale of sneaking into school late.

SAM WAS NOT lurking in the locker room. What I found instead was far more terrifying than any of the Demons I'd faced over the weekend. Jenny Dunn and four of her friends were changing a few feet away from my locker.

Jenny was too thin. I saw each rib bone sticking out above her concave stomach. Her hipbones jutted out over a black, lacy thong. Even though she ran track and cross-country, there was no muscle on her skeletal legs. She took off her bra, and I realized the amount of padding in it surpassed the amount of boob she actually had. She looked like she lived in a famine-stricken country, not one where obesity was an epidemic.

"What are *you* staring at?" She put her hands on her gaunt hips.

"Nothing." I glanced at the floor and kept walking to my locker. I wanted to tell her she was too damned skinny and needed to go eat a chocolate bar, but I knew if someone had said that to me when I was that thin, I would've punched them in the face.

She laughed while I fumbled with my combination lock and gossiped to her nearly naked friends. "I don't know why he wanted to trade me for her. Look at how big her butt is. I bet she has chubby little handles on her hips."

A girl laughed. "Maybe he liked having something to grab on to when he, you know..."

I took a deep breath and counted to ten. If I reminded them I was non-binary, they and not she, it might be more ammo for them to bully me with. I grabbed my gym clothes and tried not to think of what I wanted to do to those girls.

"Hey Erin, you need help fitting your fat butt into your gym shorts?" shouted Jenny.

I closed my eyes breathing deeply while I fled toward the bathrooms. The only way to get that thin was to either not eat for a long time, or hardly eat at all. I knew because I had gotten down to ninety-one pounds during my sophomore year. I hadn't been trying to lose weight how I suspected Jenny was. I'd just been too depressed to think about food, especially with meds suppressing my appetite. The only reason my weight made me uncomfortable now was because it was in my breasts and hips, making it harder to match my appearance with how I felt inside.

"I think she's going to need help," giggled one of Jenny's friends. "Her ass is a mountain."

I stifled a growl. I knew I could beat them all up with my eyes closed. I pictured them flying around the locker room as I kicked their fake-tanned bodies; I imagined the sound they'd make crashing in the locker. They didn't stand a chance against me, but if I hurt them, I'd get expelled and that would upset José.

I walked while they gossiped about how big my butt was, how my stomach stuck out too far, and how I had too many freckles. Their voices got louder, accompanied by the clicking of heels on tile. I was almost to the safety of the bathroom stall when Jenny's boney fingers closed around my shoulder. "Erin, I was talking to you."

I kept moving forward. Jenny's acrylic nails bit into my shoulder, pulling me back.

"Don't touch me." I clenched my jaw and sped up. Jenny dug her nails in harder. Her friends got in front of me and pushed me back. Their hands were electric eels shooting writhing spawn into my skin. I growled, trying not to let them see me squirm.

"Did you growl for José? I know he's a little kinky."

I closed my eyes and tried to focus on breathing. Without my Sight distracting me, I could feel the girls: malicious balls of heat hovering around me. I let the hum of fluorescent lights distract me from their annoying heartbeats.

"Let's see how fat she really is," chortled one of the girls as she grabbed my neck. Another grabbed the collar of my shirt. The others grabbed my arms.

For a few seconds, I was back on the grass at Portland Head Light, being smothered by cold Demons. My heart raced as their icy hands grabbed me. I flailed and twisted to get free, but instead of being held down, my hands collided with a sharp jaw. My leg hit a warm stomach. There was a loud bang, a shower of spattering glass and electric heat danced in my limbs.

I froze and looked around. Jenny's friends had backed away, looking at each other like prey animals unsure whether to fight or flee. One had a cell phone out and the other told her to put it away. Jenny hadn't budged. Blood dripped out of her nose, pooling above her lip.

"You stupid bitch." She shoved me hard enough to send me stumbling into the stall. Lights flickered and exploded as

I struggled to get my balance. Unfazed, Jenny grabbed my white uniform shirt and yanked. Buttons clattered to the floor. Fabric cut into my neck. I counted to ten, but it didn't even take the edge off the rage. I couldn't let it win. Jenny's friends ran away, probably to report the exploding lights. I needed to stifle my monsters, to keep my cool until someone else saw what was going on and called a teacher or Sister Marie.

I reached out with my mind. Jenny reminded me of a dying cell phone. I reached past her. No one else was in the locker room. I couldn't find Mel.

Jenny kicked me in the stomach.

I stumbled back, balled my hands into fists and took a deep breath. I choked on smoke. Something was burning, and it was my fault.

"We have to get out of here." My eyes stung. My palm was wet with blood from my nails breaking my skin. I looked Jenny right in the eyes and grabbed her arm, "Come on; let's get out of here."

She shoved me again.

"You're going to get us killed," I hissed.

She slapped me. I heard another bang and pop. Orange flames consumed the ceiling and a bench below it.

"We have to leave now." I was done playing games. I threw Jenny over my shoulder and ran for the exit. The smoke thickened before I got out, but thankfully, as I came into clean, breathable air and blaring alarms, I ran right into Sister Marie. José was right behind her, game face gone. Sister Marie grabbed Jenny, set her on her feet, and dragged her away while José snatched my hand and pulled me to the exit. The whole school was outside, lined up in blocks while teachers took headcounts and Pixies watched, snacks in hand, as the fire department rushed into the building.

"Mel took your car to Sam's," whispered José. "The pixies that were watching her are confused, missing time. Something messed with their heads. Mel is trying to figure out what and how while Mike digs deeper into Sam's social media contacts. There was a guy she was talking to online that he can't find any real records of. At first, Mike wasn't suspicious because a lot of people lie online. But his name was Vincent. That's what she called Incubus on Friday."

"Demons use the internet?"

Before José answered, paramedics and shining lights surrounded me, and then I was being treated for smoke inhalation. Firefighters rushed into the building. Jenny was fighting the EMT trying to put a breathing mask on her. When he finally succeeded, the plastic and oxygen muffled the stream of insults she was still throwing. An extremely pale woman with Elf ears and black eyes clad in a police uniform walked toward us.

"Officer Karen," I muttered looking at the name badge.

"What was that?" asked the EMT.

"Nothing," I replied. He said something else, but it was lost to me. Sam was in danger, and it was my fault. I had practically ignored her for two days while the Incubus got inside her head. Now, it was likely that she was going to be bait to lure me into a trap, but Mel was out looking for her, not me. I hoped our grandparents were with her.

EVENTUALLY, THE EMTs deemed me unhurt and left me alone with Officer Karen. José broke away from the group of guys he was waiting with and joined us, ignoring the teacher who called after him.

"I'm half Demon," she whispered so quietly that only someone with supernatural hearing could hear. "But I'm on your side. In another life, I was a nun with Sister Marie. I joined the police force when I needed a break from religious life."

I gaped at her.

"It's true," said José, "but she's a hunter."

"I was trying to keep my distance, in case this was the same Incubus that made me and killed my mother, but now the hunters are too short-staffed and the stakes are too high. They need me. You understand?"

I glanced over at José, he nodded, and I nodded to Officer Karen.

"Now that that is all cleared up, I'm going to take a statement from you the same way I did from the other students. You can tell me the whole story, but I won't actually write down anything supernatural. Okay?"

"You can trust her," said Sister Marie, joining us on the bench. "But I want to hear this whole story too."

I told them everything that happened in the locker room.

Sister Marie closed her eyes near the end of my story, letting out a frustrated huff as I got to the end. "I'm sorry that happened."

"It shouldn't have happened at all," Officer Karen said to Sister Marie. "I doubt this was the first time Jenny bullied Erin."

Sister Marie opened her mouth to speak, closed it, and shook her head. "I'll discipline Jenny and her friends accordingly, but Erin, you need to learn to control your abilities no matter what the situation."

"Am I in trouble?" I half hoped Sister Marie was going to suspend or expel me so I wouldn't have to deal with trying and failing to cope with a combination of school and Elf hearing.

"Not yet." Relief and disappointment wrestled in my stomach while the monsters cast bets about whether or not I'd stay out of trouble.

Sister Marie looked down at her phone. "So you still haven't been able to turn your Sight off?"

"That's right," I said.

"Then I need to tell you something that might upset you. Mel wanted you to hear it from her, but she won't be back in time, and frankly, it's her own fault for not working up the guts to do it when you learned everything else."

I looked at José, but he just shrugged.

"Tell me," I said.

"Your mother isn't completely human."

"What?" said José and I at the same time. Apparently, he was as surprised and appalled by the secret as me.

"We're not sure what she is, exactly," continued Sister Marie, "but Mel thinks it's some combination of Elf, angel, and human. Your mother isn't aware of what she is. Your father tried to tell her, and it almost broke her, so he made her forget. Not even Lucy knows exactly what he did, but after he died, the parts of her that weren't human slowly shriveled and turned gray, but it didn't seem to affect her health. For those unaided by True Sight, it looked like normal aging. A few spots or wrinkles and a few gray hairs."

"So you're saying my mom is some hybrid, and that means that I'm not just a quarter Elf. I'm a mutt of Elf, human, and angel DNA." I gaped at the nun while my brain did a broken computer impersonation. I knew I should've felt some kind of deep shock or betrayal, but the emotion wasn't there. I was numb; my brain was full of Novocaine that wouldn't wear off.

José squeezed my hand. "Maybe it's why you pack such a punch."

"And why you're struggling with control now," added Sister Marie.

"I'm a diluted version of what Mel is, and she knew it all along and didn't tell me, even though I found out about everything else." I paused and looked at José. "And you didn't have any clue?"

He shook his head. "The Elf Stone uses a lot of energy, so I never use my Sight unless I have to. I've never seen your Mom with it on, and no one told me."

"Sister Marie, why did you just randomly tell me this now?" I asked, stepping from one foot to the other and looking around so I could keep my cool. I saw the answer before she spoke. Mom's car was in the line of parents coming to pick up underclassman.

Chapter Twenty-Five

After defeating the Fallen in Berlin, Phineas wandered. The Winter Elves are solitary creatures, so no one thought much of it until he missed his third consecutive Yule ball. A search was conducted, but no trace of him was found. Some hunters suspect he may have simply faded away from his exertions. Many of the Summer Elves believe the power he controlled to defeat the enemy consumed him and turned him into a monster. I believe he suffers the same emotional affliction many humans struggled with upon returning from the war. We're proud creatures, but we're not immune to illness, physical or mental.
—Niben, in a letter to Seamus Evanstar, 1956

The woman walking out of Mom's car was simultaneously familiar and alien. She wore my mother's clothes, but her jaw was too sharp, and her ears were too pointy. The tips of both her ears and jaw were covered with peeling gray flesh that reminded me of a snake ready to shed its skin. Her blonde hair was pulled back in a ponytail, but her brown roots were nonexistent. Dull flecks of light clung to her hair and shoulders. When her mouth moved, the voice that came out sounded like my mother's. "Erin, are you all right?"

The eyes that stared into mine looked so different. They were covered with translucent gray cataracts that rotated like hurricanes. Beneath them, I could barely make out dark feline pupils surrounded by swirling gold and green irises.

I understood why Mel thought she had Elf and angel DNA. The feline pupils were something almost every Elf and Elf-human hybrid had, with the exception of Grandpa. He was a quarter Elf, but even when I had my Sight open, his eyes looked human. Sister Marie and Aunty Lucy were half Elf, and they had the Elf eyes. When I had first seen my eyes with my Sight, they had looked Elven, not human. However, the swirling was not an Elf characteristic—it was an Angelic one.

"Erin?"

"Hi, Mom." I blinked, wishing I could turn off my Sight. I didn't know how to decode the spinning overwhelmed feeling taking over my body. I wanted the numb, broken-robot feeling to return.

"Hi, Mrs. Evanstar." José squeezed my hand so hard I thought it was going to burst. The glow of his Elf Stone told me his Sight was open now. He saw what I was.

"You both look like you've seen better days," she said with a distracted frown. She made eye contact with me. "You ready to go home?"

I nodded and opened my mouth to ask Mom if José could come over, but Officer Karen came back and asked to talk to him. Sister Marie asked to have a word with my mom, leaving José and me alone with Officer Karen.

"José, you're father's body has been found, and I'm supposed to bring you in to confirm his identity. We're going to go down to the morgue, then come back here and meet up with Marie, Mel, Seamus, and Niben."

"And what about me?" I squeezed José's hand.

"You are going to go home and not leave your house until one of us gives you permission. The Pixies are watching you. They'll tell us if you leave."

"Why?" I asked, crossing my arms.

"For your own safety."

I glared. "Mom's taking me out to dinner. I hope the Pixies don't try to stop me."

Mom returned. José threw his arms around me, drenching my hair with tears.

"WHAT WAS WRONG with him?" Mom asked as she put her car in drive. "One minute he looked hung over, the next he was crying all over you."

"Officer Karen just told him police found his father's body." I stared at the floor, wishing there were more things to distract me than the all-weather mats. "José hadn't seen him all weekend. They found him in a wrecked car."

"I'm sorry," said Mom, looking over her shoulder. I did the same. José was getting into Sister Karen's cruiser, not bothering to hide his misery. "It was only him and his dad, wasn't it?"

"Yeah. And the rest of his family is in Spain and Peru."

Mom bit her lip and put the car in drive. "He has friends he can stay with?"

I shook my head. "He's popular, but they're not real friends. He always acts around them and wouldn't feel comfortable staying with them."

"Has he turned eighteen yet?"

I nodded.

"So no one is going to be shipping him off to some distant relative."

I snorted. "No, he's going to be stuck dealing with an empty house, a will, and a whole bunch of crap that kids his age shouldn't even be thinking about."

"Were he and his dad close?"

"You want to know the real reason I let him sleep over

all weekend? His dad beat the crap out of him on Thursday night. Pedro was a drunk asshole who deserved what he got." It was the first time I had told anyone about the abuse, and it felt good. It didn't matter who knew now—Pedro Estrella was dead. Still, to be safe, I added, "Don't repeat that though. Not too many people know."

I expected Mom to ask how long I had known and then to lecture me on not saying something sooner and then scold me for swearing. I expected her to tell me not to speak ill of the dead. I didn't expect silence, followed by an offer to help in any way possible, even if it meant letting him use our guest bedroom until he got on his feet.

WHEN WE GOT home, Mom let me have some space, under the condition that I give her a detailed account of the weekend over dinner. She did want to know what happened with Grandpa, how José and I wound up as couple, and why Jenny was trying to provoke me into a fight when the fire started.

"I'm curious," she said as I started up the stairs. "What happened to your phone?"

I looked at the melted heap of plastic on the table. "It went through the wash on hot and the dryer on high."

Mom's face wrinkled then smoothed out. "We'll get you a new one after dinner. I think there is a new iPhone out."

I took the stairs three at a time, desperate to get away from the true version of my mother, even if she was offering me a new phone. I slammed my door behind me, then opened it, closed it again and decided to leave it open. I was angry, confused and afraid—all emotions that could lead to me cutting, which was less likely to happen if I had the door open.

I tried every trick I knew to keep myself distracted. I

went on Facebook and scrolled through posts about dating, weight loss, and kittens doing weird things. I had three messages from José:

IDing Dad's body would've been easier if you were with me.

It's over.

Back at St. Pat's. Going to archives. No phone service down there and Mike disconnected the WiFi. I love you.

I typed a dozen replies and deleted them before settling on: *I wish I could be there with you.* I scrolled José's timeline, watching words and images blur together into nothing. I wanted to know what I really was and how I had gone through the first seventeen years and nine months of my life thinking I was normal when I was so far from it.

I squirmed in my seat, scratching skin that felt more awkward and uncomfortable than ever before. I wanted to peel it off and find out what or whom I was inside. Was I Erin, the awkwardly angry human trying to make something of their self? Was I the Elf-human hybrid who was destined to hunt and destroy Demons? The failed suicide attempt oppressing a Demon-ruled, post-apocalyptic earth? Or was I something else entirely?

My fingernails bit through the skin on my forearm and drew a slow trickle of blood. Bright red pooled on my skin. It formed a bead then crept toward my hand. The feeling of it oozing out of me was satisfying, in the same way feeling José's fingers brushing my skin was. It made me feel alive, but more importantly, it made me feel human.

A wet nose sniffed my arm. Bessie barked and proceeded to clean the self-inflicted wound with her tongue. She leaped up on my bed and stared at me with big brown, reprimanding eyes.

I had a problem, but I was indulging it when I should be

fighting.

"Is everything all right?" shouted Mom from downstairs.

I said yes, but nothing was all right.

Mom's feet creaked up the stairs. I grabbed a sweatshirt and threw it on, hiding the cuts just in time to see Mom's strangely familiar face peering in my room.

"What was Bessie barking at?" She took a few steps inside, scrutinizing me.

"She wanted to come in." I stared at the storm clouds covering Mom's eyes, wondering what the hell they were. Magical cataracts? Part of whatever my dad did to her?

"Let me know if you need anything." She started to leave.

I watched her hand grab the knob and start pulling it shut. Guilt and fear choked me. I was supposed to tell her if I cut. Just because I had to hide one thing didn't mean I should throw away all the progress I'd made toward building a better relationship with her, but if I told her and she told my doctor, I could very well end up on a new antidepressant, which I suspected would suppress my Sight as much as the other meds had. I couldn't go back on either drug again, no matter how badly I needed them. I'd worry about my mental health when I knew I had a future. If I was going to die anyway, or be tortured until I became a monster, what was the point?

Mom paused with the door half closed. "Erin, are you sure you're okay?"

"Yes. Glad you made it back from your trip."

"I'll be in my room, unpacking." Mom let go of the door but didn't close it.

Guilt chewed my stomach while I listened to her pad down the hall. I dug one of Bessie's toys out of the mess that was my floor and tried playing tug. It wasn't enough of a distraction to stop the tears from dripping out of my eyes. I wiped them and went back to the computer where I dove through pictures that documented the lies I had been living.

When I got to photos from my freshmen and sophomore year and saw how thin I'd been, my thoughts finally drifted away from my mother. I resembled a skeleton in my black cargo pants and blood-red tank top. My hands wandered to my stomach, much bigger now than it was in the photo. Part of me wished I could look as stick-like as the kid on the screen so I could pass for either gender, but I never wanted to feel like that person again.

I kept going back to older pictures. Mom hadn't let me have my own Facebook account until I got to high school, so I ventured onto Mel's page. In my middle school era photos, my skin was warmer. There was more meat on my bones. Most images showed me smiling on the beach or in a tree. There were even a few images of me with a scrawny prepubescent José. Mel's pictures didn't go earlier than when I was in the 5th grade, but my thirst for old images was far from quenched.

The pull-down attic stairs were hidden in a closet at the end of the hallway. They squawked like angry gulls and shed sneeze-evoking dust. Everything in the attic was covered in the same thick dirt as the stairs.

I hunted for the boxes labeled "photo albums," eventually diving into one with "early 2000s" scribbled on its top. I took the albums out, arranged them on the floor and stared until my eyes settled on a scrapbook labeled "Erin's First Year."

I was a normal baby in the pictures: rosy cheeks, dark green eyes, and rounded ears. I came to the conclusion that contrary to what people say on ghost hunter shows, cameras could not actually see things that were invisible to the human eye. Both of my parents looked completely human in every single picture. I didn't see anything strange until the photos of my baptism. At first, I thought it was just the glare of the flash, but then I noticed a pattern—the glare was only present in images that the four-year-old Mel was in and the pictures Nana (Mom's mother) was in.

I flipped through more albums. There were more pictures of Mel than Nana, but every printed image that one of them was in had either a blurry glow or a glare around their heads. It seemed their angel aura was the only supernatural thing the camera was capable of capturing. Even Niben, who was 100% Elf, appeared human. It made sense. If Nana was like Mel, then Mom was a quarter angel with a little bit of Elf, which meant that I actually was a disproportionate mix of human, Elf, and Angel.

I stayed in the attic until Mom came up to tell me Mel was on the phone. I took it cautiously, still afraid of Mom and mad at Mel for hiding the truth from me even after I learned the other secrets Grandpa forced her to keep from me.

"Hi."

"Erin, how are you doing?"

"Okay."

"I wanted to let you know José, Grandpa, Sister Marie, a few others, and I are heading out to look for Sam. Between stuff we found in her computer, and then in the archives, we think she is going to meet the Incubus in an old, secluded cemetery to participate in some kind of ritual."

In one of the dreams, when I saw a cemetery, I was fighting beside Mel.

"Can I come?" I looked up from the photos and realized Mom was still in the attic, watching me.

"No. You need to make sure you are home before dark. After what you did last night, every Demon left on Earth is going to be looking for you. Plus, you haven't finished healing from electrocuting yourself, and you're not completely in control. It's safer for everyone if you stay home."

I wanted to argue, but I couldn't with Mom sitting right next to me. Maybe it was better if I didn't go. We were trying to change the future, so if it was the same graveyard I dreamed about, then not being there theoretically set us on a different path.

"José wants to talk to you," continued Mel.

"Okay." Dragonfly wings summoned a wind to beat the angry monsters away. José's voice flowed out of the receiver. He said my name. He told me he loved me. He asked me if I was okay. The sound of it made me want to be close to him so I could feel his heat and hear his heartbeat. I needed to make sure he was okay and stayed that way.

"Erin, are you there?"

"Yeah." My voice crackled. "How are you?"

"I miss you. I wanted to hear your voice before we left for the hunt. What are you doing?"

"Looking at pictures with Mom."

"What kind of pictures?" asked José.

"Old ones. You're in some of them." I wanted to relay Mom's offer to let him crash at the house, but Mom thought I was talking to Mel, and it would be too hard to explain why José and Mel were sharing a phone.

"I've got to get going. I love you."

"You too. Call me later, okay, when you can talk longer."

"Okay," he said and ended the call before I could say goodbye.

I looked at Mom, who was staring at me with a frown plastered to her decaying face. "What?"

She closed her eyes and took a deep breath. "I was talking to Mel for a few minutes before I brought the phone up. She was worried about you. She told me you tried to cut this weekend, and José had to wrestle a knife away from you."

Every muscle in my body tightened up. It got hard to breathe. It was bad enough she hadn't told me about Mom. It was worse that she had told mom something I wanted her to keep a secret. I hadn't asked Mel not to tell my Mom, but I shouldn't have needed to. She knew what the consequences were, and she went and blabbed just like she did every time I trusted her with a secret Mom wouldn't approve of. I understood why she did it a few years ago, but now she was just creating another obstacle for me, making it harder for me to help save the world.

"Erin, is that true?"

I nodded. My jaw was clenched too tight to speak.

Mom sighed. "Honey, what made you do it?"

I closed my eyes and forced my mouth to move. "I hurt him."

The floorboards groaned. Mom's bony fingers closed around my shoulder. "What do you mean?"

"José kissed me and I panicked and hurt him. I didn't ask him to stop; I shoved him across the room. The next time I squeezed his neck so hard I drew blood. And the worst thing is that he was so forgiving. I abused a boy that I love, a boy who was already being abused by his asshole dad."

Mom pulled me into a hug. "Honey, it was a panic attack. He's the first boy you've dated since Ricky. Does he know?"

"I told him after." I wondered if enough time had passed to tell Mom how far that night had gone. She knew Ricky tried to make do things. She knew there was a fight. She didn't know Mel was the only reason Ricky survived to graduate from high school.

I snuggled up to her. With my eyes closed, everything felt normal. I pretended Mom and I were both human—no Demons lurking in the dark—and she was a normal mother, comforting a normal teenager who was having normal relationship problems.

Chapter Twenty-Six

Fallen: Beings that were once Angels but lost their Grace when they followed Lucifer. They became bitter, twisted, evil creatures determined to destroy humanity. They created Demons to do their bidding but often hatch their own apocalyptic plots. They are the true enemies of both the hunters and humanity.
　　—The Demon Hunter Lexicon

Mom and I were in an old ship that had been converted to a restaurant. Dark wood tables filled what was once the ocean liner's ballroom. Ours was next to a brass-rimmed porthole looking over Casco Bay and a handful of little islands. I had just spent the past half hour telling Mom as much truth as I could about the weekend. There was no point in lying about the little breakdown I had since Mel had spilled the beans. The most important thing for me to do now was convince her that it was a one-time thing, triggered by the combined stress of Grandpa's stroke and having a new boyfriend get hands-y in the same day. "I guess I'm not that good at coping with stress. This is the first time anything big has happened since before we moved."

Mom frowned. "One slip is all it takes to get hooked again."

"I know." I kept telling myself the scratch on my arm was an accident. I hadn't known how hard I was scratching, but no matter how much I lied to myself, I couldn't hide the truth. I wanted to cut. It felt good when my nails finally broke my skin.

Mom and I ate in silence. Lettuce smothered my monsters so they couldn't move while the pieces of half-digested crab reformed and attacked with pincers. The twisted gnawing feeling faded from my stomach and my head felt more focused and awake.

Mom was the first one to break the silence. "I had something I wanted to tell you, but I'm not sure now is the best time."

I swallowed a mouthful of spinach. "What is it?"

She stared at me.

"Mom, you can't say that and not tell me," I continued, wanting to end the silence and start a conversation that wasn't focused on me.

"All right," she sighed. "I've been seeing someone."

"Dating a man?" I smiled for a moment, thinking back to all the nice clothes she had packed to go to a conference. Then the smile faded because whoever this man was would never know the woman he was dating wasn't completely human.

"I'm dating a...woman," she said hesitantly. "Are you okay with that?"

"Of course! I'm happy for you." I forced my lips back into a smile and asked Mom for details about her girlfriend. I learned she was a University of Rhode Island Psychology professor Mom met at a conference. So far, most of their relationship had been conducted through phone calls, Skype, and email. The only time they saw each other in person was at conferences, but they wanted to change that. If it was okay with me, Mom was going to go stay with her one weekend every month and invite her to our house for one weekend.

"If you can have sleepovers with your girlfriend, I get to have sleepovers with José."

Mom laughed. "I already said yes to that."

I smirked. "Then we have a deal."

THE HARBOR GLOWED with evening sun when we left the restaurant. Mermaids sunned themselves on rocks while cormorants dried their wings on mooring balls and old pylons. I hoped the mermaids had already had their dinners because I didn't want to see another of my favorite birds get eaten.

Romantic small talk kept my mind off more serious things for a while, but the low sun drew my thoughts back to the supernatural. Mel had told me to make sure I was home before dark because she thought more Demons would come after me. Sister Marie and Officer Karen hadn't wanted me to go out at all. I knew staying out was risky, but the city was calling me. I had a feeling I needed to be out, even if everyone felt it wasn't safe. If dreams could be real prophecies, then why not hunches?

They were looking for Sam and the Incubus, but what if the key to saving the world was out here somewhere. Maybe I had to trust my instincts. Maybe this was something I was meant to do alone.

I paused halfway to the car. We had at least an hour before it got completely dark, but I didn't expect to be home before that. I had the kind of queasy déjà vu that suggested one of my dreams was going to happen soon, but I didn't recognize anything from it. In one story Grandpa told me, my dad had wandered around dozens of neighborhoods with abandoned houses trying to feel which one he dreamed because, in the dream, he had just seen one room. I didn't have nearly as much experience with my dreams but knew I was close to something important and needed to wander around to figure out what it was.

"Can we walk around a little?" Exploring my hunch would delay my return to nervously pacing around my room. An injury at the hands of a Demon wouldn't get me put back on meds, but cutting might.

"Of course." Mom smiled.

WE WALKED. I rambled about silly things: bad pizza and test scores. Eventually, Mom talked more about herself. I did my best to listen, but a lot of her words were lost to the sound of traffic, squawking gulls and other people's conversations.

We passed the ferry terminal where I had first fought the Incubus, back before I knew what it was, and then wound our way down the bike path I had been planning to walk with Sam but never did. Mom stopped talking when she realized I was paying more attention to the scenery than her. I kept an eye on the old train cars outside the museum, half expecting a group of Crawlers to rush out at me. Nothing attacked, but I did notice a flock of Pixies glaring at me from the wires.

Silence filled the walk while I tried to figure out if there was a way to learn more about what Mom was without sounding delusional or disturbing the illusion she lived in. Mom believed both her mother was schizophrenic and her sister, my Aunt Rita, had a similar diagnosis. Nana had been in a facility for as long as I could remember because she was paranoid and appeared completely detached from reality. Aunt Rita, on the other hand, managed to have a "normal" life running an Inn in Shelburne, MA.

I glanced at Mom. "How is Nana doing?"

Mom blinked at me a few times before answering. "Worse than usual. Why?"

"I've just been thinking...she's getting old, and we only see her a few times a year. How is she worse?"

Mom slowed, running dainty fingers through her blonde hair, showering the ground with glittering dandruff. "She's been refusing all her meds and Rita threatened to sue the facility if they forced her to take them. Last time I talked to her, she was completely lost in her own world."

We meandered to the water's edge. "What type of stuff did she say?"

"Do you really want me to tell you?" Mom squinted, struggling to read between my words.

"Yes."

She shook her head. "Nana is obsessed with Demons. It's part of her paranoia. She thinks they're following her, trying to abduct her. She's been fixated on you, too. She asked to talk to you last week, but I told her I wouldn't let her unless she went back on her meds. I didn't want her upsetting you, especially since you just came off yours."

My brain froze. I walked so I could process her words. Demons were real. What Nana wanted to tell me might actually be important, even if it was twisted by paranoia. "Demons? What did she say about me?"

Mom followed me back to the path. "It's pretty disturbing."

"Tell me. I like disturbing."

"Erin, this isn't a movie. It's real life."

"I want to know what she said."

Mom frowned. "She claimed there were Demons following you. She said they wanted to take you away and make you have their babies. They wanted to torture you until you 'went over to the dark side' and helped them end the world. It's ridiculous. You don't need to hear that stuff."

To me, it wasn't ridiculous. It was my weekend. For a second, I wondered if she meant she was misdiagnosed, but paranoid schizophrenia was more than hallucinations. Just because Demons were real didn't mean the medical professionals were wrong so much as it meant they were missing a key piece of information they needed to treat her. Still, if she was part Angel and had dreams anything like mine, it was possible she knew something I didn't. "So does she hallucinate this stuff all the time or does she dream it?"

Mom stopped walking. "Erin, are you okay?"

I froze, realizing I had asked one question too many. "I'm fine."

She stared into my eyes with the same look she had when she came into the attic to tell me Mel had blabbed. For a few seconds, the gray clouds thinned. Behind them were brown and gold irises slowly swirling around black feline pupils. "Erin, are you sure? I can't remember the last time you asked me questions about her."

I could almost feel Mom's mind getting closer to mine as she struggled to figure out what I wasn't telling her. I put my shields up, just in case she actually could somehow read my mind.

"Erin?" Mom waved her hand in front of my face.

I didn't break eye contact as my brain rushed to come up with a reason she'd believe. "Grandpa's stroke scared me. He could've died. Almost losing him only made me appreciate him more and start thinking about my other living grandparent."

Mom's shoulders dropped. "For a minute, I thought you were going to tell me you were hearing voices or something. It wouldn't be unusual with our family history."

"Mom, I promise you, I'm not hallucinating," I winked at the Pixies hovering a few feet above, who were obviously hearing the whole conversation. "Next time she calls, you should let me talk to her. She might be sick, but she is my grandmother."

Mom frowned, but she didn't say no. "I'm guessing you don't want me to cancel our April visit?"

I definitely didn't want her to cancel it. I wanted to know exactly what else Nana knew of the Demons and the apocalypse. However, I also couldn't ask Mom more questions without raising her suspicion, so I let the conversation drift to less important subjects like college majors and the weather while we strolled through the shops and cafés. I let my shields down so they wouldn't drain my energy and tried to act as if everything was normal.

Chapter Twenty-Seven

Demons rarely exhibit human-like emotions, but there have been rare cases where an Incubus has fallen in 'love' with one of its victims or a Troll has grown attached to a child it kept as livestock.

—Gertrude Bearclaw, 1922, annotating her copy of the the Demon Hunter Lexicon

"We should get home," said Mom as we stepped out of the phone store. "I'm tired from the conference, and you must be exhausted from the weekend you had."

The sky was deep denim with fragments of dusky purple clinging to cirrus clouds. I didn't dare delay my return home anymore. I might enjoy defending myself if I got attacked, but I didn't know how it would affect Mom. I watched her stormy eyes, wondering if actually seeing something supernatural might undo the magic binding her sight shut, or if she'd look right at something that could kill her and not see it. I shuddered.

"I'm going to call José on my way back to the car." I power walked toward the street. "I'll let him know I have a new phone and see if he wants us to pick him up anywhere."

I started dialing his number but paused when I heard a muffled scream and a sharp slap. I paused. "Did you hear that?"

Mom looked around. I concentrated on my hearing. My heart and Mom's thundered in my ears. Further away, someone whimpered. Someone else huffed and grunted. The next scream was like knives in my ears. Before Mom could stop me, I ran in the direction of the sounds. I heard her stomping behind me as I bolted through an empty parking lot and into an alley between a closed bank and office building. I saw the source of the noise as soon as I rounded the corner. Mom dialed three numbers on her phone.

The Incubus, in its long black trench coat, had a blonde girl pinned to a wall. It had one hand over her mouth while the other pinned her wrists to the bricks. I growled as the monster inside me reared its head. Mom called my name, but I ignored her. I had one goal: end the Demon.

I took my next breath as slowly as I could. My heart rate dropped. The Demon's movements slowed. Its head turned. Before his black hole eyes were on me, my body collided with the mass of cold, ripping it off of the shaking girl. It felt like wrestling an iceberg as we tumbled to the cobblestones. I raised my fist to slam into his face, but his cold hand caught mine. In one swift movement, he pushed me off and sent me flying through the air. My back smashed into the bank's brick wall.

I couldn't breathe. The Incubus blurred to its feet. I rolled just in time to avoid his fist. Even with my perceptions slowed, he was moving fast. I leaped to my feet, swung at his face and missed. I readied another punch, he moved to block, and I kicked him in the statuesque groin. He doubled over. I shoved my knee into his icy face, grabbed his head, and smashed it into the wall. Deep laughter echoed in my head, making me sway. *You're a feisty little one.*

I grinned. If I got the upper hand in the fight, maybe I could get some answers. We knew he was working for one of the Fallen, but I hoped Mel or Niben could tell us more about what it wanted if they knew which one it was.

"Whom do you work for?" I backed away while I told my mental Bessie-beast to close the blast doors and power up the shields. That was barely enough time for him to recover and punch me in the stomach. I bent forward, gasping for air as his fist hooked sideways into my temple. I stumbled into a puddle. "Whom do you work for?"

He stared at me with his black hole eyes and laughed. I pulled energy from the water. The molecules slowed down. As I raised my right hand to block his next blow, ice filled my left.

"Whom do you work for?" I asked for the third time, stepping back to catch my breath. I raised my fists in a defensive position, willing the ice blade to be clear and invisible.

"Even I dare not speak his name. Your little friends are arrogant to think they can defeat him, especially in such a carefully laid trap."

Bessie-beast growled and I felt a wave of exhaustion hit me as the Demon attacked my mind. I closed my eyes. I was sitting in a spaceship's cockpit beside the brown and gold bear-dog. Shapeless shadows pummeled the invisible deflector shields. Fire came next, but it couldn't penetrate the energy field. A control panel beeped, informing me the shields were down to 50% power.

The attack stopped.

"How do I fit into your plans?"

I opened my eyes. The Demon's shoulders were slumped in exhaustion.

"How do I fit into your plans?" I did a roundhouse kick worthy of a Chuck Norris joke. Cold seeped through my sneakers as my foot hit the Incubus's jaw.

"How do I fit into your plans?" While he stumbled, I lunged with my ice knife, aiming for what I assumed would be his heart.

"You're the key and the counterweight, capable of unlocking hidden power and tipping the balance in our favor." He tried to dodge. The knife sank into his shoulder. He steamed and sizzled but didn't explode how the Crawler did.

The Incubus laughed. "You will help us take over the world and save humanity from itself. It will burn and be reborn."

I watched his black blood while I caught my breath and weighed my options.

"Reborn how? For who?" I tried to reach out in search of electricity, but I couldn't feel anything past my shields.

"Let your shields down and I will show you." He smiled, swiping my mental shield with a shadowy tentacle.

It had to be a trap. If I let them down, the Incubus could get inside my head and control me. That happened to a few hunters in Grandpa's stories. The Demons hadn't only been able to read the people's minds but to control them. In one story, a hunter nearly killed his own son before my dad freed his mind by banishing the Demon. Lowering my shields could let the Incubus force me to be a vessel for its spawn.

His fist flew toward my face. I got my hand up just in time to block. We traded blows, dancing a jig of punches and kicks. He was stronger and faster than any human, but so was Mel, and I had been training with her for most of my life. Confidence strengthened me. I hit him more than he hit me. I kicked him into the wall, hard enough to crack the bricks. He hissed and muttered strange words, conjuring an obsidian blade.

I stepped back, fashioning an ice katana as he swung. I parried his next stab with no seconds to spare. I swung at his neck. His parry took a chip out of my blade.

"Where is Sam?" I blocked a stab at my midsection.

"Safe," he growled while sweeping his sword at my legs. "Safe from this world and the idiots who populate it."

My head swam with confusion. I hadn't expected him to answer the first time asked, and I certainly hadn't expected him to sound protective. That moment of disorientation was enough for him to get the upper hand. I misjudged his next move allowing his blade to slice into my hip. "Surrender now, swear fealty to me, and I promise you I will spare your mother."

The blood rushing out of my hip was almost as euphoric as it was painful. It made me calm, giddy, and confident. Drunk on pain, I smiled, swung my blade, and watched black blood ooze out of the smile-shaped cut I'd made in its stomach. The Demon looked down as the tight skin on its forehead moved like it was raising its eyebrows, except it didn't have any eyebrows. I swung my blade at his neck, intending to decapitate him. He blocked without looking, then simultaneously stabbed my shoulder and kicked me in the stomach. His sword burned through muscle; his foot knocked the wind out of me. I crumpled to ground swiping at his feet while I struggled to breathe.

"I'm done playing. You have one more chance. Surrender willingly or watch your mother die." He kicked, but his foot never made contact.

Mom tackled him hard enough that he stumbled but didn't fall. She punched him in the face screaming. "Leave my child alone!"

He laughed and threw her off of him. There was a sick cracking sound when she hit the wall. She crumpled into a motionless heap, smearing the brick with blood.

Time slowed further. I rushed over to Mom and shook her. She didn't respond, but I heard her heart beating as she sucked rough breaths into her lungs.

"Look what you did," snickered the Incubus.

Fresh waves of rage rushed through me, erasing my pain and my ability to think rationally. I dropped my shields, swiftly sending my mind out in search of electricity. It buzzed just on the other side of the brick. I called it to me, but it couldn't seem to get past the brick. I searched for moisture, sending it into old cracks and fissures. Soon, the searing energy coursed through me. I screamed, stood up, and forced the energy out of me like I had at the lighthouse.

Bolts shot out of my fingertips and consumed the Incubus.

"Erin stop!" shouted a familiar voice.

I ignored it.

"Stop, stop, you're killing him!" she shouted again.

I kept throwing voltage at the Incubus, watching him try to control the energy as bits of his body disintegrated into snowy ash.

I couldn't remember the proper words to banish it, so I focused on making it go away as I poured more bolts into it. It lit up, hissed, screamed like a teakettle then exploded into a million ashy shards. I sent electricity chasing after each piece of Demon, screaming for them to go to different parts of different worlds.

I was still screaming when two loud bangs interrupted me. I let go of the power and collapsed to my knees, exhausted and shaking. A pale woman stood deep in the alley with her hands clenched around a gun. Two bullets slowly sailed away from her on two different trajectories. I followed the path they took towards the chests of the police officers. I looked back at the woman and realized she was a girl. Shadows hid the details of her face, but I recognized the silver pentacle and spiky hair. It was Sam.

Her lips moved, but the sounds were so slow I couldn't figure out what words they were supposed to be.

Two more bangs echoed through the alley. Bullets floated out of the cop's guns toward Sam. Two more bangs. Bullets from her gun were heading straight for the blonde girl who was huddled on the ground. I didn't want anyone to die in this alley, regardless of who they were and what they had done.

I felt like I was Mario, watching the bullets sail through the air. I wondered if jumping on them would make fall to the ground like the big Bullet Bills that came out of the cannons. It was so ridiculous that I laughed in spite of the pain I was in. My perception of time was slowed to the point where I could move faster than bullets, and all I could think about was a video game.

With a growl, I forced myself to my feet. I mustered the strength to run to Sam and tackle her out of the path of the police's bullets. My head throbbed. My legs wobbled. I threw myself across the alley in the other direction, grabbing Mom by the hair and dragging her out of the line of fire. The cops were next. I pushed each one down with one hand as I ran between them.

I turned to the right where the girl was cured up. Cold blue eyes stared blankly at the bullet inched closer to her face. I stumbled, realizing it was Jenny Dunn. I hesitated as her cruel words played out in my head. The bullet got closer. I tugged her arm, but she didn't budge. With one final push, I threw my body on top of hers.

Pain ripped through me, but it didn't last. It faded to blissful release as blood flowed out of me. Shadows blurred my vision.

Jenny croaked a weak "thank you."

Sam shouted. I could just see her charging toward me through the shadows. She shook me. "Erin, you idiot. She was following you with this gun. She wanted to kill you.

Vincent was hungry, so I told him to take her. You were supposed to live, you were supposed to join us."

"He's a monster. Jenny's just a girl," I said, trying to blink the shadows away.

"It's not his fault," pleaded Sam. A man in blue tried to grab her, but she pushed him back. "I met him online. We've been talking for months. I didn't know what he was at first, not until the beach. I was furious, but he talked sense into me. He—"

"You have the right to remain silent," said the officer grabbing Sam again. She struggled against him, pleading, saying he didn't know what he was doing, but he cuffed her anyways and hauled her out my failing sight.

Gloved hands touched me, but I couldn't see whom they belonged to. Blackness swallowed me. Two girls who tried to hurt me, Jenny and Sam, were both alive and safe. I was happy with that. I forgave them for their hate and betrayal. I deserved Jenny's wrath. Sam had been fooled. I tried to sit up and tell the officers that Sam had been defending me, but my body disobeyed.

I was as light as a jellyfish, suspended in dark water hearing nothing but the beat of my own heart echoing inside my skull. I wondered if I was dying. In my last moments, could I leave my body to find José and tell him I loved him? Apologize to Mom for lying? Thank Mel for all she did when I was depressed? Tell her what I'd learned so she'd have a better shot at defeating the Fallen? I couldn't die without doing those things. I tried to swim upward, hoping to break the surface of the dark water, but the current kept pulling me down.

The harder I swam, the harder the undertow pulled. When I stopped fighting, it gently rocked me, pulling me further into the depths. Somewhere inside me, I knew if I gave in, then I would die. I did not have the same assurance about winding up in the good version of the afterlife. I had caused too much pain and hadn't had enough time to make amends for it.

I swam as hard as I could, desperate to get out of the current and live. Eventually, swimming got easier. I wasn't fighting the current anymore but riding it up and up. I saw a light. In all the movies, the light was where people went when they moved on. I stopped swimming, but I kept hurling forward. I didn't want to move on, even if it meant going to Heaven.

I wanted to live.

Chapter Twenty-Eight

Dear Erin,

Love can make a girl do crazy things, especially if it is the kind of love that comes on strong and fast. Today I shot you, my best friend. You took a bullet meant for another person, one who I was trying to save you from. It turns out that in spite of the darkness Vincent sensed in your soul, you are selfless.

Vincent and I were supposed to take you alive. I was supposed to pretend I was his hostage. He didn't think you would risk hurting me if it came to that, but for the most of the fight, you both were moving so fast I couldn't see. Then you destroyed him. I was furious. I tried to shoot you in the leg, so I could take you to the Master and beg him to restore Vincent, but you were too quick and I was too slow.

The police arrested me. Mom's lawyer says I'll make bail. It doesn't matter though. Vincent is gone. The other Demons will come for me, and they do not look kindly on failure. I'm sorry I hurt you. I was only trying to make the world a better place. I hope you understand.

Your Friend,

Sam

I tried to open my eyes, but the light was too bright. I supposed I should've been expecting that. If Angels, churches, and Holy Communion glowed, then Heaven would too. I guess I was more surprised by the fact that I was there and not the other place. I forced my lids open again and could barely make out a few human-like shapes in the blinding light. I tried to call out to them, but no sound came. Instead, I gagged on the plastic tube forcing air into my lungs. I became aware of sound next. An ear-splitting beep was keeping pace with my heart.

"I don't need a break." José's voice was hoarse. He needed a good night's sleep and a steaming cup of green tea with honey.

"Darling, you've been here for three days," said a soft female voice. It sounded familiar, but I couldn't place it.

"I can't leave them."

"The doctors said they might never wake up. The longer they're out, the lower their chances are."

"You can't stay here forever," said the woman. "You should at least eat."

José sniffled. "I'm not hungry."

"I'll get you some soup."

Heels clacked, gradually getting softer. When the sound disappeared, José's warm hand closed around my cold one. His hot lips brushed my cheek, and my body woke up. This definitely wasn't heaven. Perhaps it wasn't hell either, but it sure hurt like it. There were holes in me where there shouldn't be, and it felt as if cold objects still sped through me, tearing through veins, muscles, and organs. I only managed to squeeze José's hand before I fell back into the soothing black current.

THE NEXT TIME I woke, there were hands all over me. I recognized José's thick fingers; the others felt boney and female. Voices prayed the Our Father in harmony. I held my eyes open long enough to see José, Sister Marie, Aunty Lucy, and someone I hadn't seen since Christmas, my mom's sister, Rita. They were holding hands, praying over me with their eyes closed. My lids slammed shut before theirs opened, but I stayed a while, listening to them talk to me.

They shared their favorite memories with me, told jokes and talked about the news. Police searched for the vandals who dented a truck's hood and drained the battery. Sam was arrested for shooting me and at the police. Jenny Dunn was physically okay, but the rumor was she hadn't left her room since she'd returned home from the hospital.

When the others left, José's words became softer, more intimate. He told me how much he loved me and how much I meant to him. He thought I was the most beautiful creature in existence since the first day he remembered seeing me when he was four and I was three. He never forgot me and always looked for an excuse to see me when I went down the cape with Mel. He hit the jackpot when he was thirteen and I spent the whole summer there. When we both wound up in Portland, he thought he could finally be with me, but I was too depressed to want him, and it became his mission to make me smile. I listened as long as I could, wishing I could talk back to him.

A LOUD SNORE jolted me to consciousness. My eyes fluttered open long enough to see Grandpa cover José with a blanket then slowly back out the door. He stood up straight, not putting any weight on his cane, and his face was smoother, like he'd gotten Botox treatment in a Hollywood hospital, but it was probably from Niben's magic. In the hall, a flash of red and green caught my eye. Niben winked at me and whispered three words: *Sleep and heal.*

PRICKLY HAIR MADE my neck itch. José had toppled over in his chair and was sleeping with his unshaven face buried in my neck. I felt stronger this time and managed to move my arm with minimal effort.

José jumped upright when my hand brushed his arm. "Erin?"

I opened my eyes and looked right into his. They were bloodshot, caked with dried tears, and surrounded by a black and blue raccoon mask.

"I love you." He smiled then pushed the button to call the nurse. He leaned down and kissed my forehead and then turned around and told her I was awake with more enthusiasm than a child tearing into presents on Christmas morning.

THE HOSPITAL STAFF told me it was a miracle that I woke up and recovered so quickly. While I had been in my coma, my stab and gunshot wounds had healed faster than the doctor thought possible.

"You must have an angel watching over you," said a nurse whose badge said her name was Gina. She checked my pulse and blood oxygen levels and wrote notes on her chart. "The doctors didn't think you would wake up."

I frowned, wondering why I had been out so long. I had a half-angel watching over me, and I didn't remember seeing her in any of my brief moments of consciousness.

"Sorry, I didn't mean to offend you if you're not a believer. I try to not say things like that, but they come out regardless."

"I believe. You just made me think of something else."

As soon as I had a moment alone with José, I asked him if Mel had healed. He told me she got hurt and was staying at Grandpa's, too weak to even go home.

I also worried about Mom. José couldn't seem to tell me much about her, aside from the fact that she had been in intensive care all week. He knew she was stable but didn't know exactly what was wrong. He promised my Aunt Rita could explain next time she came to see me. That was all I got to hear before the doctors came back to poke and prod me and do all kinds of annoying tests.

AUNT RITA CAME in around the same time the hospital brought my supper. José was helping me eat when Bessie nearly knocked him and my food over so she could lick my face. She was wearing a red vest that claimed she was a service dog and warned people not to pet her. Technically, Bessie was a support pet, not a service dog, so I assumed the vest belonged to Aunt Rita's psychiatric service dog, Jules, who must be enjoying a day off.

"Bess, if you behave that way, they'll know you're a fraud," said Aunt Rita, holding a snapped leash. "Jules won't appreciate you giving service dogs a bad name."

Bessie looked over at Aunt Rita, barked, and sat down beside my bed like a proper service dog. I petted her while I stared at my estranged aunt. Her honey hair was a poof of long untamed curls and frizz. She wore a long skirt of patchwork pink, purple, blue, and green below a black cardigan.

"Have you seen my mom?"

Aunt Rita nodded but didn't answer.

"How is she?" I adjusted my bed so I could sit up more. "No one will tell me anything."

Aunt Rita frowned. "They finally got the swelling to go down in her head. She is breathing on her own and opens her eyes, but is otherwise unresponsive. I'm sorry."

Tears filled my eyes and my already sore throat burned. "Will she get better?"

"I don't know." Aunt Rita sat on the edge of the bed and put her hand on my leg. "The doctors said she could improve, but they doubt she'll ever be the same as she was. However, those same doctors thought you wouldn't wake up at all. You had stopped breathing for so long they thought for sure your brain was damaged beyond repair, but so far, you seem fine."

I cried. José rolled my tray away and wrapped his arms around me. I buried my head in his shoulder and soaked him with my tears until Bessie nuzzled her head in between us and licked them away.

"Mel might be able to help her in a few weeks." José wiped Bessie's drool away.

I looked back and forth between Aunt Rita and José.

"I know about her," said Aunt Rita. "I was a bit of a mess when I got in here. I have a hard time in hospitals and thought I was going to have an episode when your Grandparents walked up to me and promised me it was all real. I thought Niben was another hallucination, but then José here started talking to her."

"Does that mean you don't have schizophrenia?" I asked.

Aunt Rita cocked her head. "No. It means *some* of the things I thought were symptoms are not. I don't plan to stop taking my meds anytime soon."

I wiped at the snot on my face, trying to decide what to ask next. I had a ton of questions but settled on something easy. "How long have you been here?"

"I've been in town six days, staying at your mom's house. They called me when you and she were brought in, but it took me a day to get myself out here."

"And where are my grandparents now?"

"I'm right here, Sunshine," said Grandpa, walking into the room. "I was on my way as soon as Mel told me you were awake. José was supposed to call, but he forgot."

"Sorry," muttered José. "I got a little overwhelmed."

"It's okay. You've done well taking care of Erin." Grandpa ran a hand through José's hair, messing it up in a surprisingly affectionate way before he bent down and kissed my forehead.

"How and where are the other hunters? And what actually happened at that cemetery?" I asked the two of them.

"Sister Marie has a broken ankle, but it wasn't enough to keep her out of work."

"Okay. What about everyone else?"

"Sister Karin got some minor burns and bruising."

"And Mel?" I wiped a few fresh tears away and glared at José. "Someone changes the subject every time I ask."

"We walked into a trap, and she saved us all," said Grandpa with a sigh. "Demons corralled us in the graveyard's center. There was a bomb buried in a crypt. She and Mike were trying to defuse it when it went off. She shielded him from the energy and absorbed enough of it so we didn't get cooked, but she got third-degree burns all over. Instead of healing herself, she used the excess energy to disintegrate most of the Demons. She's getting better, but it's a slow process. She's been sleeping nearly twenty hours a day. Mel may be the strongest of us all, but she is not invincible."

I scratched my head expecting to find my hair a tangled mess, but my fingers found smooth, knot-free locks. "They knew you were coming. The Incubus used Sam to lure you there, right?"

José took over scratching my head. "Right."

"Is Sam still in jail?" I asked, struggling to focus through the simple pleasure of his touch.

"She made bail, and word is she is in some private hospital waiting for trial. She just keeps going on about Vincent being gone and the world being doomed. At least, that's what the Pixies we sent to spy on her told us," said José.

"Is he really gone?"

"As gone as a Demon can be," said Grandpa. "The way you took him down impressed Mel's father. She said it was one of the most efficient banishing he's seen in a few centuries. It will be thousands of years before that thing puts itself back together."

"What about the Fallen it was working for?"

Grandpa shook his head. "I don't know. Mel thinks we just delayed its plan, bought ourselves time to regroup and investigate. How are you feeling?"

"I don't know. I'm sore, nauseated, drugged to the point that I can't open my Sight, confused, worried, and relieved all at the same time."

"Things will work out." Grandpa leaned down and kissed my forehead. "You've got me, you've got a boy who's crazy about you, a couple nutty aunts who love you, the best dog a person could ask for, and Mel."

LATER IN THE evening, a physical therapist and social worker had me walk down to my mom's room. With the painkillers holding my Sight closed, Mom looked the same way she had looked for most of my life, except for the fact that she was sleeping peacefully in her hospital johnny with tubes in her arms and nose and a bandage wrapped around her head. I sat with her for a while, apologized for all the crap I gave her over the years, and told her I loved her before they brought me back to my own room.

By that time, Grandpa and Aunt Rita had gone home. José was still with me. The hospital staff had gotten used to him being present and were on a first name basis with him. They brought him snacks, checked his bruises, and helped him change a bandage that was covering a nasty gash on his back all between the rounds they made to my room.

I held his hand as the night went on. I was afraid to sleep—afraid of slipping back into the darkness that had held me captive for a week. I lay awake long after he dozed in the chair that had been his bed all week, but eventually, sleep did come and so did the dreams.

I WALKED DOWN the aisle in St. Pats with my arm linked with Grandpa's. Ahead of me, José nervously waited beside Mike and Will. Mel stood in the maid of honor's place. Sam and Jenny Dunn stood next to her.

Sam and I were by the ocean laughing. She had a toddler on her hip that kept trying to grab the Pixies buzzing around my head.

A woman with frizzy gray hair rocked back and forth in bed. One shriveled hand clung to the plastic rail. The other held a picture frame. Her lips quivered as she looked at the image of a blonde woman standing beside a redheaded teenager.

"Erin," whispered the woman. "This is only the beginning."

The room exploded with blinding light. Gray hair became platinum blonde. Her wrinkled skin became smooth. Her ears were pointed knives and her eyes swirled like sky and cirrus clouds. Thorny brown vines snaked around her wrist, tying her to the bed. Her light attacked them, but they didn't burn or loosen. "Free me before the solstice. I can help you stop the Fallen."

The light faded. Nana was an old woman again rocking back and forth in her bed.

The scene shifted. I stood in space with Mel, surrounded by stars but somehow breathing and not exploding from the lack of air pressure.

"Stop being so literal. This is my dream now, not one of your premonitions," she said before crushing me with a hug. "How are you?"

"Confused."

"I know." She smiled. "I was asking to be polite. To answer the many questions in your head, we are outside of time seeing it the way I understand it. Instead of getting dragged down a current of your visions, here, we can see many potential futures all at once."

She waved her hand, showed me how to touch the currents, examine them, and see what happened when a pebble was thrown in. It was far from exact, but by the time we were done, I had an idea how we might be able to stop the apocalypse.

"Why didn't you do this before?"

She wrapped her arm around me. "I've tried to bring you here dozens of times, but it never worked before. Dying changed you. I'm not sure how, but no one returns unchanged."

"Returns from where?" I asked, but Mel was gone. The stars faded to the hospital room.

"ERIN, WHO ARE you talking to?" asked José.

"Mel," I yawned. "She is being all cryptic."

José smiled. "I love you."

"I love you too," I sat up and kissed him.

His soft lips parted and his hands dug into my hair. I didn't know for sure what was going to happen to Mom or the world, but I knew that no matter what happened, José was going to stick with me through it all. Although, after my outer space dream sequence with Mel, I was pretty sure we stood a chance at canceling the apocalypse our shadowy enemy had set in motion.

Epilogue

PINE NEEDLES TICKLED my legs as they flew up from under my sneakers. Each gulp of cold air made my aching ribs hurt more, but I ignored the pain and ran harder. Today, I was going to win. Mel started out ahead of me, but she was tiring quickly. Her labored breathing grew louder as I closed the distance between us.

I took a few deep breaths letting my Sight and other senses open wider. I was surrounded by energy—buzzing colors connected to the not quite awake trees. Mel's white light was fainter than it should have been. Every exposed piece of skin was still covered with pink, rippled burn scars. She claimed that in a few more weeks, there would be nothing left except for flawless skin, but I had a hard time believing her.

Do you want to bet on it?

No, but I am going to win this race.

Laughing, she picked up her pace. I grimaced and took a few slow breaths letting my perception slow down a little. Soon, I closed the small gap between us. I gained as much momentum as I could downhill. I sailed past her when we got to the bottom and pulled ahead as we went up the other side.

She growled, struggling to catch up. Her breathing and stomping feet kept getting quieter. A few minutes later, I broke through the trees onto a wider path and sprinted down the road to the oval lot my jeep was parked in. José was sitting in the back with the tailgate open and a textbook on his lap. I didn't stop running until my hand touched the car. I turned around, leaned my back against the cold metal, and watched Mel jog the final stretch.

"Nine minutes and twenty-one seconds," said José. "How far did you go?"

"Three miles." I sucked cold air into my lungs.

"You're not supposed to just stop, especially when you go that fast." Mel panted Mel as she caught up. "You need to walk so you cool down first."

"You say that every time we run." I stood back up and walked around the car.

"And you never listen." Mel joined me.

"Should you even be running today?"

Mel shrugged, but her sly smile told me all I needed to know. She was being impatient and should have been focusing on healing her skin, not wasting energy racing me.

You need to start training. Plus, I don't want to get out of shape while I heal.

I shook my head and finished my cool down. After my third lap around the parking lot, José handed us each of us a bottle of water. The cold liquid chilled my throat, and then I walked around until my heart rate dropped to a more human pace.

WE ALL HAD dinner at Grandpa's. José grilled steaks under Grandpa's watchful eye while Mel and I smothered carrots in maple syrup and altered a Mac and Cheese recipe so it had more bacon than anything else. A group of Pixies sat on the blades of the ceiling fan while we cooked, munching on a bag of chocolate chips and speaking in rapid-fire chirps and whistles. One time, in mid-conversation, Mel randomly burst out laughing at something they said.

"Can you actually understand them, or are you reading their minds?"

It took Mel a few minutes to stop laughing and answer. "Mind reading. Their language is extremely complex and doesn't translate well to English, but their minds are so vivid. The things they think are just hilarious."

Mel burst out into another fit of giggles while I stirred the carrots and gazed through the window. Grandpa sat in a lawn chair, watching José flip the steaks. I couldn't see José's face, but his shoulders rose and fell in laughter.

The door squeaked and the floorboards creaked. Grandpa's voice boomed over Mel's laugher. "The steaks are done, how are your sides coming?"

I gave the carrots a stir. The water, syrup, and butter had reduced to a thin glaze. The timer on the oven said the cheesy bacon with some macaroni needed three more minutes. "They're almost done...not that Mel's been much help."

Laughing, José put the steaks down on the table and then slid his arms around my waist. "Anything I can do?"

"Don't distract me." I leaned my head against his shoulder, more interested in cuddling than cooking.

"Erin might fall asleep if you keep holding them." Mel got between the stove and us, turned the carrots off and took the casserole dish out of the oven, even though the timer hadn't gone off yet.

It's done enough, and I'm starving.

A few minutes later, we were all sitting around the table. José and Grandpa kept eyeing the sides Mel and I had made, but she refused to share on the grounds that they contained too much fat and sugar for humans. Apparently, she and I had faster metabolisms and needed to eat a high-fat diet, but Grandpa and José were better off with salads.

Grandpa cleared his throat. "So, José and I were talking outside."

Mel smirked, reading his mind.

"He said you were planning to go back to school on Monday to try to get back into your normal routine," continued Grandpa. "It's a good half-hour commute from here, but only a few minutes from your mother's house."

My fork froze halfway to my mouth. When I was having fun, it was easy to forget the real reason we were all staying at Grandpa's. He had legal custody of me until Mom woke up or I turned eighteen. Mel was spending three-quarters of her days in a healing trance and was using the unique energies that flowed around Grandpa's house to expedite the process. José's father was dead, and while José technically owned a house now, he couldn't stand to spend more than ten minutes in it.

Reality hit me like a swarm of wasps—thousands of them buzzing around inside my stomach and chest. The vibrations of their wings made me feel like I was going to explode. Their stingers poked tissue and intestines, filling them with burning venom. My head spun and my palms got sticky. I could try to get back into my usual routine of school and homework, but nothing would be normal about it. I'd be alone with Bessie. I'd see the Pixies watching me and have to go out hunting if any Demons came in the area. Nothing would ever be normal again.

"Erin? What do you think?" asked José, leaning in close to my face.

"Of what?"

He cocked his head. "You and me staying at your house for the week, then coming back up here Friday night."

Some of the wasps escaped through my open mouth.

José's smile turned down into a frown. "If you're not comfortable with it, just say so. I know we haven't been going out long, and we're young, but I don't want to be away from you, and no one wants you to stay alone. Seamus has to go away for a few days to organize some of the other hunters in the region, but I can stay here with Mel and Aunty Lucy can go with you, or we can put more Pixies on guard or—"

"José," I interrupted his nervous rant. "I want to spend the week with you. I'm just shocked *Grandpa* is okay with it."

"It was his idea," said Mel between giggles. "A little bird may have told him about your wedding dreams. He figured if you two are going to wind up hitched, then he's not going to keep you from each other now."

"I think it's more like a little Angel told him," I said, smiling at Mel.

"Half Angel," she winked. "I don't have wings, so don't compare me to a bird."

I glared. "But you're the one who made the comparison in the first place."

"It's actually kind of a sore spot for her," chuckled José. "She's burdened with the ability to read minds, but doesn't get to soar through the skies."

We spent the rest of our meal bantering. Soon, the laughter smothered my anxiety. I was with my family tonight, and that was all that really mattered. I'd face my house tomorrow, and school the day after. When Mel got better, she'd heal Mom's brain. According to my dreams, there was even hope for Sam to be redeemed. Things would never be normal again, but I didn't need them to be. Normal meant feeling lost, frustrated, and alone, but in this new, strange version of my life, I had a soulmate who loved me, and I had a purpose. I had a world to save. I wasn't sure if I was more hero or anti-hero, but they were seldom "normal."

Acknowledgements

Power Surge and its characters have been part of my life for over a decade, so there are a lot of people to thank for helping me bring this book to life. I'm acknowledging them more or less chronologically. However, some may seem out of order since some people helped with the project in different stages.

Thank you to:

Anyone who taught a college-level creative writing class I was in because I probably worked on this story, or a story set in the same world, while I was in their class.

Friends like Abby, Danny, and David, who listened to me ramble out this book years before I had the focus or skill to complete it. Even if many of the characters you helped me create were cut in revision, you helped me figure out a lot about the book's universe.

Artemis, who read pieces of my early draft when I decided to return to it years after I started. Who knows what would have happened if she hadn't pointed out all the irrelevant parts. Later, when little remained of the first draft, Artemis read the whole thing and provided very helpful feedback.

Adam, who went through chapter by chapter, pointed out the logical flaws, marked the places where the characters didn't react, and teased me about my "comma ands".

Melissa, one of my first beta readers, who encouraged me to keep writing, and to figure out what was missing from the book.

My mom, for asking me to read the book out loud to her while sitting on the beach. I caught a lot of grammar problems this way. Throughout my life, you always supported me and encouraged me to take the stories out of my head and put them on the page. You've always believed I could do anything, even when I was ranting about how scary the publishing industry can be.

P.D. Sanders, my second beta reader and the first who didn't know me in person. Sanders gave me helpful feedback and the confidence to use online classes and social media to find more readers for future projects.

The people in the International Writing Program's How Writers Write Fiction MOOC who read and critiqued excerpts.

My critique group, Joe, Terry, Clare, and Marcella. You all read many iterations of my opening chapters and always pushed me to keep writing and revising. Outside the group, Clare carved time out of her busy schedule as a mom and full-time teacher to read and critique the whole book.

My editor, Rae, who helped me shape *Power Surge* into something I'm excited for people to read.

Thank you to everyone who played a part in the journey of this book from helping me dream it up when I was in college and later, after I had finished a different book, helping me take a chaotic, incomplete draft and transform it into a book I'm proud of.

About the Author

Sara lives, writes, and plays on a lake in Massachusetts with a cat, Goose, who "edits" their work by deleting entire pages and a scruffy puppy, Tavi, who makes sure they get lots of fresh air. Sara teaches and tutors writing at a community college. They've published over fifty short stories and poems in markets like *Broadswords and Blasters, Vulture Bones, Alternative Truths,* and *Drabbledark. Power Surge* is their first novel.

Facebook: www.facebook.com/saracodair1

Twitter: @shatteredsmooth

Website: www.saracodair.com

Other books by this author

Half Breeds
"Snow Fox" within *Once Upon a Rainbow, Volume Two*

Also Available from NineStar Press

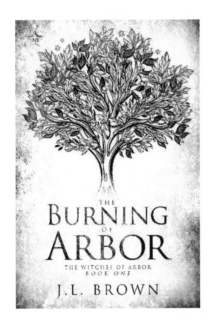

Connect with NineStar Press

Website: NineStarPress.com

Facebook: NineStarPress

Facebook Reader Group: NineStarNiche

Twitter: @ninestarpress

Tumblr: NineStarPress